BEYOND INNOCENCE

kit rocha

Beyond Innocence

Edited by Sasha Knight

ISBN-13: 978-1514761878
ISBN-10: 1514761874

This one is for the dreamers.

.

beyond innocence

1

T WO PILLS STOOD between Lili and damnation. She tried not to look at them as she applied her eye-liner, her hand steady from years of practice. The rest of her was shaking, but the line was perfect—smooth black kohl along her lower lash line. She could smudge it into a smoky shadow, but that might be too subtle for the night's festivities.

Her gaze dipped to the two white tablets lined up beside the empty bottle. Just two. She'd come to Sector Four with so few possessions to her name—a gun, a nightgown, and a fur coat. But that coat had deep pockets, and she'd filled them with high-end drugs before she fled her home. At the edge of the desk, seven empty bottles traced the desperation of her last few months, her attempts to cope.

After tonight, she'd have to do it on her own.

She jerked her gaze back to the mirror. No, subtle

wouldn't cut it. These O'Kane women were bold. Brazen. Survival meant adaptation. She had learned to play wife when her life depended on it. Now she would learn to play something else.

Whore.

She could hear her dead husband snarling the word at her, taunting her with the most degrading insult he could imagine. Nothing was so crass and despised in Sector Five as a woman who denied a man her body until money exchanged hands. Except perhaps a woman who denied a man her body altogether.

Making that mistake had almost gotten Lili killed.

Forcing back the memory, she thickened the line beneath her eye. She wasn't bold or brazen, but she wasn't meek and submissive, either, no matter how successfully she'd played that role. The makeup was her mask. If she applied enough of it, she could disappear into someone else.

The pills would make it easier. Lex hadn't wanted to let her keep them, but Lili had begged. She'd been numb enough to survive the shame of that. Hell, she'd been so numb there had been no shame. She'd lost her family and her life—she hadn't been ready to give up her peace of mind.

So Lex let her keep the pills, but she made it clear there would be no more. And Lili had tried to make them last. She rationed them out, saving them for when her own reserves of icy numbness just weren't enough.

Two pills left, and not even the strongest ones. She'd sacrificed the last of those to endure the most recent fight night, insulating herself from the raw violence and terrifying lust. Every horrifying warning her mother had ever whispered about sex paled in the face of brutal reality—a man, bloody from battle, slamming a woman against the side of the cage to sate his urges in front of the entire sector.

beyond innocence

It was uncivilized. It was *barbaric*. But the women of this sector faked enjoyment with a finesse that made Lili look like a clumsy novice. Either that, or they were like the dead-eyed girls who'd clung to her father's men—so broken and hopeless they'd convinced themselves they *wanted* to be pawed at and violated, because wanting the inevitable made it easier to bear.

The liner pencil slipped from her grasp, and Lili realized she was trembling. Curling her hands into fists, she shoved back from her vanity and stalked to the bathroom. No fancy tub or pristine counters piled high with fluffy towels here. Her shower was tiny, the tiles newly laid and crooked. The bulb over her head was bare. The walls were unrelieved cement.

But she had a sink, and a glass on the edge of it. Lili filled it with water and returned to the bedroom. In the mirror, her reflection stared back at her, a stranger in garish makeup and leather, with too much skin on display.

She had the too-short skirt. The too-tall shoes. The dark lipstick and lined eyes, the corset that all but demanded men stare at breasts she'd never even shown to her husband. But she didn't have the ink, and she would never have the attitude.

Without those things, she'd never be an O'Kane. Just a confused girl playing dress-up.

Closing her eyes, Lili swept up the pills. They were bitter on her tongue, and she washed them down with the entire glass of water. The drugs were good, some of the best Sector Five had to offer, and especially popular inside Eden. She'd overheard her father's bodyguards laughing about it once.

I guess it makes that high-strung Eden pussy more agreeable.

Well, where's the fun in that?

Agreeable. A word that covered a multitude of sins, figurative and literal. The well-bred ladies of Eden took

5

the drugs to numb themselves to the ways their husbands violated their bodies.

Lili needed to be numb to watch the O'Kanes violate each other.

She set the glass aside and checked her reflection one last time, while she still cared enough to make it perfect. Her hair was a disheveled mess of curls, the front held back from her face by twin braids that circled the crown of her head. Her fingers itched to smooth everything into place, more out of habit than desire. *Tidy* fit this place about as well as *restrained* did.

Somehow, she had to learn to be neither.

The rooms she'd been given were on the third floor of the building where most of the O'Kanes slept. Every time she turned around someone was up here, hammering or painting or hooking up plumbing in another new room. They were expanding, adding blood to their ranks as Dallas's power grew.

That was why Dallas wanted them all at his weekly parties—so that the new faces would know him, and he would know them. It had seemed harmless enough until Lili appeared obediently at the first one only to discover how intimately the O'Kanes defined *know*.

Fighting a shudder, she straightened her back and lifted her chin. The drugs hadn't kicked in yet, but she imagined she could feel the comforting distance wrapping around her as she descended to the second floor. The party room sat at the end of a long hallway, but the door was open, and she could see flashes of skin.

That was the danger of being late. They'd already started taking their clothes off—at least the ones who'd worn any to begin with.

Just before she reached the end of the hall, Trix walked out of the room with a cigarette in one hand. The redhead was usually as pristine as Lili had always been, embracing the fashion of Sector Five instead of rejecting it.

Not tonight. Instead of a perfectly tailored dress and crinoline, Trix had a man's shirt slipping off one shoulder and falling to mid-thigh. Her hair was a tousled mess—not the artful tumble Lili had labored over, but the kind of disheveled that only came from being tangled around a man's fist.

In spite of that, the woman was smiling. So Lili did the only thing she could—she smiled back. "Trix."

"Lili." The woman's smile didn't fade, but her expression took on a guarded quality. "Having a good night?"

They didn't trust her. The harder Lili tried to blend in, the more she felt the distance between them. And with her most of all, because Lili knew her father had hurt Trix. Her father had hurt every woman who touched his life.

Trix and Lili were the only two who'd survived the association.

Her smile hadn't worked, so Lili let it drift away and settled for being politely impassive. "I am, thank you."

Trix lifted one eyebrow as she brushed past her. "Don't do anything I wouldn't do."

Faint warning. The things Trix did on stage at the O'Kanes' bar shocked Lili enough, but when Trix's lover won his match at the last fight night, the two of them had—

No, the drugs weren't strong enough to protect her from that memory. And they weren't strong enough to insulate her when she crossed the threshold into Dallas O'Kane's private den of sin.

The sounds were the most visceral part. There was so much skin, but she could unfocus her eyes, stare at nothing in particular. But that didn't protect her from the sounds, and they were still so alien, even after all these weeks.

Laughter. Moans. The slap of flesh against flesh, of bodies coming together with a force that made her cringe

7

inside. Voices rose and fell in and around the cries of pleasure, as if they were gossiping over tea instead of...

Lili didn't even have a word for it.

A couple was kissing just inside the door, the man's hand barely hidden beneath the woman's sheer skirt. Lili jerked her gaze away and scanned the edge of the wall, desperately looking for a safe corner.

There were so many men. More than there were women, so many more. A few of them tried to catch her gaze, but Lili stubbornly refused, though she knew she'd have to give in to one of them eventually. A woman on her own in the sectors didn't last, and Dallas O'Kane hadn't been able to hide his disappointment at learning how little she knew about the inner workings of Sector Five. His tolerance would wear thin soon enough, and if she didn't have a man willing to claim her...

She'd trained to be a wife, but Sector Four didn't seem to have those. She didn't know *what* they had—mistresses was the nicest word she could come up with. It was better than the alternative. At least a mistress might have *some* duties outside of the bedroom.

But if she had to be a whore, she'd do that, too. She'd do whatever it took.

A flash of white in the shadows drew her gaze, and Lili's heart shot into her throat.

Amazing how homesick a well-tailored dress shirt could leave her. She didn't miss much about her life in Sector Five, but she had understood the rules there. The man on the couch in the corner was perfect in a way that felt familiar. Not just well-dressed, but refined. His crisp white shirt and impeccably fitted slacks stood out among the leather and denim popular with the O'Kanes, but he didn't appear to care.

In that, she envied him.

She didn't make the decision to drift toward him, not

on a conscious level. It simply happened, like it was inevitable. Like he was a magnet, and she was steel instead of ice, tugged toward the only person in the room who was like her.

It was an illusion. It had to be, if he was here at an O'Kane party. Putting on a nice shirt didn't make a man safe and boring any more than putting on a leather skirt made her wild. But she still stopped next to the couch and did her best to smile. "May I sit?"

He looked up at her, his gaze lingering for only a moment on her breasts. "Please."

The drugs weren't working. They couldn't be, because her cheeks warmed as she did her best to sit without flashing the room. Even with her knees together and her ankles crossed, the skirt barely covered her underwear. She was showing more skin than she was hiding, but she hadn't really felt exposed until he looked at her.

He shifted his glass—whiskey, from the looks of it—and held out his hand. "I'm Jared."

He didn't give a family name, so maybe she didn't have to, either. It wasn't as if she had one she was eager to claim. "I'm Lili," she said instead, slipping her hand into his. So intimate, his skin brushing hers, his fingers wrapping around her hand. These people touched all the time, and Lili wasn't sure she'd ever grow used to it.

"I know who you are."

She studied his expression, searching for signs of disapproval or distaste, but his mask was even better than her own. "Is that a problem? Who I am?"

In response, he flashed her his naked wrists, clearly visible beneath the rolled-up sleeves of his shirt. "It doesn't matter what I think."

So he wasn't an O'Kane, either. Just a man secure enough in his place with them that he made no effort to fade into the background. Not a man to cross. "It matters to me."

Jared shrugged. "I never knew your father—or your husband. Except by reputation."

If he was lying, he was flawless. His lack of concern was as perfect as his face—and oh, how perfect that was. So many of the men here were rough-hewn, rugged, and worn. Jared was a sculpture carved by a master, all strong lines and beauty.

Maybe that was why he didn't intimidate her in the same way as the O'Kanes. He didn't seem entirely real. "I wish I'd only known them by reputation."

A sympathetic smile tilted his lips. "Of that, I'm sure."

She gestured to his wrist. "Why are you here? Are you thinking of joining Dallas's men?"

That made his smile widen. "Me? I'm here for the view."

He looked to the side, and her gaze followed his before she could stop herself. And then the warmth wasn't just in her cheeks, but creeping down her throat and bubbling up from inside her.

She knew Rachel. The blonde bartender had been friendly from the beginning, making overtures to Lili even after her inability to reciprocate had driven away some of the other women. There was something comforting about her, especially when she was dressed in overalls and smudged with engine grease. She wasn't familiar, but her differences were tantalizing, a hint that women might have more choices than cooking and sewing. Rachel fixed cars and brewed beer. She wore whatever she wanted.

She wasn't wearing anything at all right now. Naked and apparently unconcerned with the fact, she knelt in front of the two men sprawled on a couch, pleasuring one with her mouth and the other with her hand.

Lili groped for the safety of chilly numbness, but those two sad little tablets weren't strong enough for this. If it had only been fear, she could have managed—fear was vital, the basis for survival. But the sick, confusing way her body heated, the way it prickled and ached, like a limb waking up...

She averted her gaze and tried to unfocus her eyes again, but there was no safe place to look. Not even at Jared, because when she turned back to him, the perfection of his face didn't evoke polite appreciation.

He made her tingle and ache, too.

"This must be odd for you." His voice was lazy and low, casual as he lit a cigarette. "Even after a few months. It isn't much like Sector Five, is it?"

"I don't know," she admitted, flinching when her voice wavered. "I didn't see much of Sector Five. But no, it's not like my life was."

"And you doubt it all." It wasn't a question.

To doubt it, she'd have to have a point of reference. Something she could comprehend to begin with. "I don't understand it."

"Fair enough." He drained his whiskey. "Out of curiosity, what do you see?"

He *was* asking now, so she forced herself to look at Rachel again. The taller man—Cruz—had his hand in her hair, trapping her so that she had no choice but to let him take whatever gratification he wanted from her mouth. But she was still working at the other man, too, as if having the responsibility for one man's satisfaction wasn't enough.

Lili closed her eyes, but that accomplished nothing because of the *sounds*. The trio was close enough for her to hear the men's groans of pleasure, and Rachel's moans of—

Satisfaction? It should have been impossible, but she was as loud as the men, and so sincere it rattled Lili's confidence. "I don't know," she told Jared without opening her eyes. "I told you, I don't understand."

The leather cushions creaked. When Jared spoke, his voice was only inches from her ear. "She has them both begging," he rumbled. "Completely at her mercy. That's what *I* see."

The tingling in Lili's body intensified. Goose bumps rose on her skin, and she rubbed her hands over her arms. This was the danger of all those years of numbness—being raw, vulnerable to feelings she'd never experienced, much less learned to manage.

And Rachel was still moaning. "What I'm seeing isn't the confusing part," Lili whispered. "She sounds..."

"Like she's getting off on it?"

The words were incoherent, obviously slang for something else her life in Five hadn't prepared her to understand. "Does that mean she's enjoying it?"

Jared huffed out a soft laugh. "You enjoy a fine drink, good company, or a particularly beautiful desert sunset, Lili. Something like that? It tears you apart, then puts you back together again. It's pleasure, love. Real pleasure. It's not something you merely *enjoy.*"

The ice protecting her nerves was melting. The ice beneath her feet was cracking. One more whisper and it would shatter, plunging Lili into the depths of sin.

And she wanted it.

2

THE GIRL WAS flailing.

Jared could see it in her eyes, behind the drug haze softening the sharp blue, as he watched her from his new position across the room. He'd decided to give her some distance, just in case he was the cause of her raging nerves, but it didn't seem to help. She kept glancing around, then staring down at her lap, as if she didn't know where to look. Perhaps she wasn't sure whether it would be acceptable to let her gaze linger too long in one spot.

Of course, they *were* in the inner sanctum of the O'Kane empire. Everything was acceptable, provided someone got off on it.

He pulled a second cigarette from his case and had just popped it between his lips when a battered lighter, already struck, appeared in front of his face.

"Evening, Jared." Finn—Trix's man and new

O'Kane—offered the lighter, stretching out one scarred, inked arm.

Jared arched an eyebrow as he lit his cigarette, then nodded his thanks as the man flipped the silver lid shut, snuffing the flame. "How's it going, Finn?"

"Not bad." He shoved the lighter into his pocket and nodded toward Lili. "She talked to you, huh?"

She was still sitting there, barely moving. Not even shifting or fidgeting the way a person usually would, but immobile, static. As if simply being here was a test she had to pass.

She didn't belong. Not because she wouldn't be accepted, but because she wasn't comfortable with the rampant, naked affection curling through the room, and Jared couldn't blame her for that. It took some getting used to, even if you were as accustomed to sex as he was.

And she wasn't, not even close. He could read it in every innocent line of her lush body, through the brash clothes she wore like armor, or a costume. Little Miss Lili was damn near untouched.

Finn was watching him, waiting, so Jared cleared his throat. "I spoke with her a little. I think I remind her of home."

"Yeah?" Finn leaned back against the wall, but he didn't look relaxed. "Wouldn't think that'd be a plus, all things considered."

"Maybe not, but familiar's familiar." And even bad reminders could be comforting when you were out of your element and drowning. "It'll pass. It always does."

"What? Needing something familiar?"

He shrugged. "Thinking that maybe I'm the answer to her problems."

Finn stared at Lili for another endless moment before swinging his gaze to Jared. "Happens a lot, huh?"

"Every other day." A flash of white caught his eye as the music changed, and he looked up in time to see Jeni—

in her favorite platinum-blonde wig—dragging Lex out onto the makeshift dance area in the middle of the room. Heads turned. People always stared at Lex, especially when she decided to be wicked, and now Lili was staring too, her cheeks flushed and her eyes wide.

The women weren't dancing. They were grinding against each other, their arms in a tangle, legs entwined, their mouths only inches apart. And inches away from something else, judging from the look on Jeni's face.

He knew that look. She'd thrown it his way more than once over the last couple of years. An invitation to sin, sure, but something more, too—an invitation to explore the sweetest depths of her submission and pleasure.

In her shadowed corner, Lili shifted and crossed one leg over the other. Her skirt rode damn near all the way up her smooth thigh, but she didn't seem to realize. She dug her fingers into the leather couch until it dimpled under her grip and *watched*. As if she wanted to look away but couldn't, because she was teetering on the edge of some painful revelation.

"Lex'll be the one who fucks up her ordered little world," Finn murmured as the woman in question slid one hand beneath the fluttery hem of Jeni's tiny black dress. "If Lili was less sheltered, she'd probably figure they're climbing on each other because the guys like it. So maybe that'll make the truth easier on her, not knowing shit about what assholes like."

She might still assume they were putting on a show. She'd been in Sector Four long enough to understand the concept. But Jared was more interested in what she'd do when she realized all of it—every slow caress, every lingering touch, every kiss and sigh—was for their own pleasure.

Lex pushed the top of Jeni's halter aside, baring one breast, and pinched her nipple so tight that Jeni's head rocked back. She moaned, a tortured, satisfied sound that twisted in Jared's gut, and he took another long draw from his cigarette.

What would she do?

"Shit's about to change, you know. With Lili." Finn dug out his own cigarette and held it in one hand without lighting it. "She came here with her pockets stuffed full of all the drugs popular with Eden's high-strung wives. She must be out of the good stuff, or she wouldn't be turning pink over there."

"I'm surprised Dallas let her keep that shit in the first place." The only person who got away with being high around the O'Kane compound was Dylan Jordan, and that was only because the man's medical skills made him indispensable.

Finn shrugged. "Her family was dead, and Dallas had just trotted her past the other sector leaders and made her tell them all the ways her husband was a crazy motherfucker. She begged. So I told him and Lex I'd keep an eye on her while she came down."

An act of mercy, then, in a world that lacked it all too often. "I can't tell if Dallas is getting softer or smarter."

One look at the man answered the question. Dallas was standing at the edge of the room, talking to Jasper, but his gaze was on one thing, one person, and it wasn't soft. Not nearly.

By the time Lex released Jeni's nipple, the pale flesh was pink, savaged. The brunette bent her head and soothed it with her tongue, licking in slow, languorous circles that left Jeni clutching at her hair. Begging without saying a word.

Lex dragged her down to the cushions on the floor, one hand already between her thighs. Jeni arched, writhing as Lex's teeth scraped her nipple and the line of her jaw before fastening on her lower lip.

Jared chanced another glance at Lili. She was still watching—riveted, barely breathing. He could almost hear her heart pounding as she drank in the scene before her, and it kicked his own into a faster rhythm.

The question sprang to his lips, every syllable counted out by the visible pulse throbbing in the hollow of Lili's throat. "Will she make it without the drugs?"

"I don't know." Finn finally dug out his lighter, and Jared could tell he was buying time as he lit his cigarette and exhaled slowly. "I was there, you know. The night her father gave her to Logan Beckett. She was fifteen, and she started doping herself out of her skull the next week."

And escape got to be a habit, just like anything else. She'd never know if she could stand on her own, if she could walk into an O'Kane party without cringing, until she had to. Until she *tried.*

Jeni grew louder, her moans melting into cries. She bucked, clutching at Lex's arms as they rocked together. Faster and faster, until Jeni stiffened and threw her head back. Nothing showy—no screams or squeals, just a long, shuddering orgasm that didn't end until Lex pulled her hand away and trailed her wet, glistening fingers down Jeni's leg.

Lili exhaled unsteadily.

Jeni made a sound that was part laugh, part growl and rolled Lex over onto her back. She straddled her hips, her light skin contrasting wildly against the supple black leather the other woman wore, and pinned her wrists to the cushions.

A provocation—but not to Lex. Dallas broke away from Jas with a grin and stalked over to sink a hand into Jeni's hair. He hauled her upright with practiced ease, dragging her head back and leaning down to whisper something that had her trembling all over again.

Lili went rigid, and her nails dug into the couch until they threatened to pierce the leather.

"She still needs someone to keep an eye on her," Finn said quietly. "Maybe more, now. But I can't do this part.

All I am to her is some scary bastard who was there for all the worst fucking moments of her life."

Jared watched the blush that had bloomed in Lili's cheeks creep down her bare throat to her chest. "I'm the wrong person to ask, Finn. She can't even watch Lex and Jeni screw around without wanting to cover her eyes. What makes you think she'll want a whore looking out for her?"

"Not asking you to fuck her," Finn retorted. "But like you said—you're familiar. Maybe something familiar will make the first few weeks without the drugs go a little easier."

Dallas had Jeni bent over again, her ass in the air. She had pushed Lex's shirt up, and the woman arched and keened as Jeni lavished attention on her breasts. As a reward, Dallas shoved Jeni's dress higher and worked his fingers into her pussy.

It was a shameless display of lust and pleasure, and Jeni was falling into it like a starving woman. And she *was* starving, of course she was. Selling sex could make you rich, especially when you were as dedicated to your craft as Jeni had always been, but it couldn't get you the kind of raw affection the O'Kanes traded about like it was nothing.

Like it was *easy*.

Jared sighed and faced Finn. "I'll think about it. But I'm not one of you. O'Kane might prefer that I stay the hell away."

"She's not one of us, either." Finn's lips turned up on the word *us*, as if he couldn't help but smile every damn time he said it. "I don't think Dallas will care, not if it keeps her from unraveling."

He wasn't a caretaker. That had always been Gia's thing. Hell, even Ace was better at it than he was. Jared's specialty was the fantasy, a grand, sweeping passion that ended when the sun came up.

beyond innocence

That was easy. Caring for people was hard. And letting them rely on you? That was damn near unthinkable.

"I'll keep it in mind," he murmured. "That's the best I
can do."

"Fair enough." Finn leaned over to crush out his cigarette in a nearby ashtray. "If you know someone who's got
a piano, it'd be easy. You could park her in front of it, and
she wouldn't notice if you were there."

"I have one." A slick, polished baby grand in the middle of his living room.

"No shit." Finn quirked an eyebrow. "You play it?"

"It's not for looks." Watching his fingers dance nimbly
across the keys usually gave women ideas about what else
he could do with his hands, even if they weren't musically
inclined.

Finn's hands were big and scarred, his joints popping
as he flexed them. "Better you than me. If you could let
her borrow it…" He trailed off, flexing his fingers again
before letting his hands fall to his sides. "I'd owe you one."

If it was worth a favor, then it meant something to the
man, but damned if Jared could figure out what. Lili had
lost her flat expression and now wore one of confusion. Her
chest heaved with every breath, her breasts threatening
to burst free of her corset.

She was flailing, but she wasn't in danger. Finally,
Jared just asked. "What does it matter? The girl is Dallas's
responsibility, not yours."

"Now, maybe." Finn glanced across the room—not at
Lex and Dallas and their display of filthy, beautiful passion, but at the opposite corner, where Trix stood chatting
with Nessa, clad only in Finn's shirt. "I spent a lot of years
watching bad shit happen to Lili. Used to think you
couldn't go back, but it turns out it's never too late to start
giving a damn."

An inarguable motivation—and an equally unassaila-
ble reason. "All right. But you owe me, and I *will* collect."

19

"Wouldn't have it any other way."

The worst thing about a king was his tendency to keep you waiting.

Jared spun a pen on the scarred surface of Dallas's desk. When it slowed and finally wobbled to a stop, he reached for his whiskey and drained it before checking his watch.

Four in the morning. Plenty of time for a man to exhaust two women—if the women in question weren't as voracious as Lex and Jeni.

It took two more spins of the pen—and another double whiskey—before the door clicked open and the king made his appearance. Dallas O'Kane had palpable presence, even barefoot in threadbare jeans and a rumpled T-shirt.

One of his eyebrows swept up as he caught sight of Jared in his chair, but he didn't say anything. He didn't apologize either, just slid his fingers through his tousled hair and grinned. "Lex said I should invite you back with me. I think I'll take pity on Jeni, though. She was passed the fuck out."

"Smug bastard." Jared retrieved the tiny plastic data card from his pocket and slid it across the desk. "It'd serve you right if I took your woman up on that generous offer."

"You call her *my* woman and she might revoke it. I'm the only one who gets away with that." Dallas sank into one of the wooden chairs and dropped his hand to cover the data card. "Give me the highlights."

"Peterson thinks you're up to something. The man doesn't have the balls to bring it up officially, but he's been chatting up the other Council members at every party and weekend barbecue. So far, no one's biting."

"Dumb fucker." Dallas shoved a stack of papers aside

beyond innocence

and surfaced with a battered cigarette case. "If I wanted to grab Five, I would have done it in the first place, not waited a few months for all the assholes over there to dig in."

Most everyone in Eden knew and understood that, too, which was why Peterson's witch hunt had failed to gain any momentum. "There's a fairly new member on the Council. Young, idealistic, still wants to do right. Could be worth watching."

"Yeah? What's your read on him? They gonna beat it out of him?"

They could—given enough time. Every man had his breaking point, even one as earnest as Nikolas Markovic. "I think that depends."

"On?"

"Whether you get to him first."

Dallas grinned around his cigarette and struck his lighter. He inhaled slowly, tilted his head back, and blew smoke toward the ceiling. "Well, then. How quick can we get to him?"

"There is no *we*," Jared reminded him blandly. "You're not forgetting that, are you?"

"Bullshit. You're not wearing my ink, but you're risking as much or more than any damn one of us, and without the best parts. Someday *this...*" he jammed his finger down on the data card, "...will be over with, and people will know you're an O'Kane. Doesn't make you less of one now."

Sometimes, it didn't seem real. He'd always thought giving in to Dallas's recruiting speeches would come with ink, way too much alcohol, and enough brotherhood to choke an elephant. Instead, Jared's sign-up package had included secrecy and business as usual—except for the spying.

But he'd asked for it, and he couldn't deny he was well-suited to the task. The bar code he'd bought and paid for allowed him easy entry to the city, and his reputation and money took care of the rest. He was a fixture in Eden society, as familiar to its wealthy citizens as their own faces. No one questioned his presence, even when they resented it.

And no one realized he was listening.

"I can get to Markovic," Jared assured his leader. "But it'll take time. The man isn't fond of corruption, and let's be honest with ourselves. I spend my days swimming in it."

"Yeah, you do." Dallas reached for the whiskey and twisted to grab a second glass. He poured it nearly full before refilling Jared's, as well. "You holding up okay? Spending that much time ass-deep in hypocrites can't be a picnic."

Jared indulged himself in a wry laugh. "Your concern is heartwarming, O'Kane, but I've been doing this for a long time. I'm quite accustomed to hypocrisy."

"That wasn't supposed to reassure me, was it?"

"No." He knew better than to make excuses for his lifestyle, for his work. Once you scratched past the surface of endless money and women, it wasn't exactly the stuff dreams were made of. "Why do you think I work for you now?"

"Yeah, well…" Dallas abandoned his cigarette, slowly crushing out the tip before dropping it to the ashtray. "If you need a break, you tell me. I'm half a second from pulling you out anyway. If we didn't need the intel so damn bad—"

"But you do." And, really, what was his discomfort weighed against the potential welfare of dozens, even hundreds, of people?

"But I do. For now." Sighing, Dallas swept the ashtray aside. He leaned forward, his elbows thumping on the desk, and gave Jared a serious look. "I want to bring Bren and Cruz in on this. You need more people watching your back. People with connections inside Eden."

"*No.*" The denial was reflex, backed up by his hammering heart, and it took him a moment to pin down his sudden fear. "Not Cruz. If something happened and it blew back on him, it would kill Ace. I can't risk that."

Dallas didn't waver. "And if something happens to *you,* Ace will kill *me.* If Cruz doesn't get to me first. If you don't think he's already worrying about you..."

"I can handle it."

For a tense moment, he didn't think O'Kane would relent. But he did, sitting back in his chair as he picked up his whiskey. "All right. Bren, for now."

"Acceptable." His freedom to move about Eden society would only last as long as his association with the O'Kanes was vague, fluid. If anyone inside the city found out he'd allied himself with Dallas...

His spying days would be over. And so would his life.

3

COOKING HAD ALWAYS been Lili's favorite of her duties. It was soothing. It was complicated. It required attention and focus, but if she followed the rules, she was usually rewarded with success.

Food wasn't always predictable, but it was manageable. She could control it.

And it made an amazing bribe. Especially here.

It hadn't taken Lili very long to realize that almost no one in the O'Kane compound enjoyed cooking. Some of them *could* cook. Lili had encountered Six baking biscuits or simple bread, always farm fare. More rarely, she found Mad creating dishes that could have come from one of her treasured pre-Flare cookbooks, the one that featured rustic Latin cuisines.

She'd left behind everything when she walked away from Sector Five, but the cookbooks were one of the things

she missed most. Pulling up recipes on the tablet Noelle
had provided her didn't feel the same. It was all so sterile,
crisp. Unblemished. Foolish of her, she knew, to miss the
imperfections, the curling edge of a cover that had fallen
victim to a pot boiling over or the sauce recipe stained from
the spatter of a dropped spoon.

Everything had to be put to rights before her husband
returned home. The kitchen spotless, her clothes immaculate, her presentation flawless. But the battle-worn pages
had been as comforting as old friends, reminding her that
the perfection was a lie, a game she had to keep practicing.

Or maybe it was good she'd left them behind. Maybe
it was a lesson best forgotten, because she was starting to
believe the O'Kane women weren't lying. Not about sex,
not about loving it, not about *anything*.

Lex *could* lie. Lili had no doubts on that count. She
recognized the level of control in the other woman, the
ability to school her features and hold her tongue. But for
the first time last night, she'd watched Lex, watched her
touch another woman, kiss another woman, do things to
her that made Lili's entire body throb...

And she'd tried to remember Lex's last lie. Unpalata-
ble truths fell from the woman's lips often, raw reality
delivered without hesitation or flinching. Lili had seen her
do the same to men and women alike, fearless in her honesty.

Maybe every moan and every smile was a lie. Maybe
the other woman's shuddering and begging and pleading
had been lies, too.

But *why?*

It always seemed like fear must be the answer. She
convinced herself of it again and again, every time she
crawled back to her rooms, overwhelmed and *feeling*, feeling all the things she'd spent a lifetime not knowing were
possible.

She'd felt so much last night. Because she didn't think

even fear could motivate anyone to lie that convincingly. Not forever.

Lili had crawled out of bed this morning, still aching, still feeling, and had faced a neat row of empty bottles. A silent line marking the end of everything she'd known about life. If she was going to survive in this new, terrifying reality where her skin was too tight and women might be more than nothing, she needed to understand.

She needed a friend.

So she went to the kitchen. She found ingredients. Some of Six's leftover bread and two types of rich cheese to grill, and everything she needed for brownies gooey enough to win over the most reluctant sweet tooth. Then she took her culinary bribes in search of Rachel.

She found the blonde in the garage, smudged with grease and frowning down at a long, handled contraption that almost looked like a cookie press. "Hi," she said absently, barely glancing up.

"Hi," Lili echoed, already uncertain. *Nerves* were another thing she could barely remember. The flutter in her chest as her heart beat too quickly, even over something as foolish as this. "I made lunch, and I had extra. I thought..." Trailing off, she held out the plate.

"Oh hey, that sounds good." Rachel waved the metal cylinder in the air. "Some chucklehead didn't clean it out, and now it's clogged. How am I supposed to grease my fittings with a clogged gun?"

A rhetorical question, undoubtedly, but the correct response was so ingrained, it was a reflex. "I'm sorry. Can I help clean it?"

"Thanks, but nah. It'll wait." Rachel laid the grease gun aside and walked to a small sink beside the workbench, where a tub of sludgy soap awaited her. It didn't lather as she rubbed it over her hands and arms, but it did cut through the grime amazingly well. "Tatiana makes it for me," she explained as she dried off. "Have you met Tatiana?"

The name was familiar, but so many of the faces blurred together. She'd met so many people in those early days, the hazy ones full of grief and pain and all the drugs she could take.

But she knew how to temporize. How to evade. "I think so. At one of the fights?"

Rachel levered herself up to sit on the workbench and smiled gently. "I wasn't sure if you'd remember."

Her muscles started to tense, and Lili didn't even know *why.* It wasn't as if she'd ever developed any pride. That would have been suicidal, at best, and impossible besides. But maybe this was why people needed it—to protect against the awful, empty humiliation of having a weakness laid bare.

Everyone knows. It was horrifying, really. But it left her with no reason to lie. "I'm not sure I do, I suppose."

"You've been pretty out of it." The words were matter-of-fact, and Rachel tilted her head. "Not today, though."

"No, not today." Lili was still gripping the plate, so she forced her fingers to relax and set it down on the bench next to Rachel. "I remember enough, though. I remember that you've been...kind to me."

She picked up half of the grilled cheese with a tiny shrug. "When I first came here, everyone made it really easy for me. And it was still hard as hell, and I hadn't lost anyone, either. So."

Lost. The word was like Lili's world on drugs—numb and soft and disconnected from reality. She hadn't *lost* anyone. Her family had been stolen from her as punishment, and if she let herself think about it too closely, the guilt would burn her up from the inside.

She grasped for something else. Anything else. "You aren't from this sector?"

"I grew up in Eden."

28

beyond innocence

For the first time, Lili couldn't even school her features. She felt her mouth start to drop open and snapped her teeth back together, but it was too late. Eden. The woman who danced on stage at the O'Kanes' bar, the woman who wandered naked through parties, trailing *two* dangerous, possessive men behind her, the woman who was staring at her now with a smear of grease on her nose, perfectly at home in a place that usually belonged to men...

She was from Eden. Perfect, pristine, holy *Eden.* "Oh."

That made Rachel laugh. "Don't worry. I was never from the proper part of the city. You could say I've always been a bit of a street rat."

Lili covered her hesitation by breaking off the edge of a brownie. The taste was dizzying, the sweetness of the honey playing off the sharp, bitter edge of cocoa in a way her nutritionally balanced sweeteners never could. The leaders of Five had access to plenty of the food manufactured in the factories of Sector Eight and on the farms beyond the borders, but so much of it was processed past the point of recognition. It tasted fine. It worked perfectly.

It just wasn't real.

She wanted to reach for the rest of the brownie, but denying herself was another habit. She'd made the mistake of tasting too much while cooking early in her marriage, and had been educated thoroughly on the consequences of developing unnecessary curves.

"How long have you been here?" she asked instead, tucking her arms over her chest to remove temptation.

"A few years now. I make beer, fix stuff, tend bar. Dance." Rachel took a bite of her sandwich and chewed before closing her eyes with a soft noise of appreciation. "This is good."

It was more approval than Logan had ever shown her. And it felt...nice. Warm, gentle. Not overwhelming, but satisfying. "I had a lot of time at home. Cooking was enjoyable, though finding good ingredients could be difficult."

Rachel leaned closer and lowered her voice. "Drop a bug in Dallas's ear about what you could do with the right setup, and he'll make sure you have it."

She imagined the empty kitchens. How few people ate there, and how many ended up buying food from the marketplace instead. There were so many people here that feeding half of them could quickly become a full-time job.

But it was one she was capable of. One that wouldn't require finding a man and letting him...

She smashed the memories back down. Dallas's hand in the woman's hair last night. Logan's hand in *her* hair. Pain, fear, *confusion*—

Even if the O'Kane women weren't lying, Lili would be. And maybe the men here wouldn't like manufactured sweeteners when they could have honey.

"I—I might like that." She found strength in the possibility. Hope. "If you think people would enjoy having me cook."

"Better than me doing it. I burn everything. Dallas thinks I do it on purpose to fuck with him—" She stopped, and a vague shadow of guilt fell over her face. "Okay, sometimes I do. But not as much as he assumes."

So many ground-shaking revelations in so few words. That Rachel dared burn food on purpose to irritate a sector leader. That he knew it. That she got away with it. That she wasn't cringing at the consequences.

Lili could have told her about the time she'd burned her hand and dinner, too. How Logan had dragged her to the sink, shoved her hand beneath the tap, and washed away the med-gel. How calm he'd been as he told her he was doing this for her own good, so the pain would teach her to take better care of his most treasured possession.

She still had a scar across the heel of her palm. An

imperfection. A reminder.

Lili might be sheltered, but she wasn't stupid. And she didn't want to see pity in Rachel's eyes. "Does he deserve it? When you burn the food, I mean?"

"On purpose?" Rachel snorted. "Always. He's been better since he and Lex figured out their shit and hooked up, but he still has his caveman moments."

"Lex is..." Lili gave in and smiled. "I've never met anyone like her."

"She looks out for us. If you have any problems, you can go to her, you know."

The smile had been easy enough. Keeping it from slipping was harder. "Oh, compared to where I'm from, I have no problems at all."

"Okay." Rachel laid down the rest of her sandwich and wiped her hands on the towel she'd used to dry them. "You can come to me, too."

Once upon a time, Lili had known how to joke. She'd been funny enough to make her younger brothers and sisters dissolve into hysterical giggles. Not much of a challenge, maybe—children who'd never been more than a half mile from their home didn't exactly have sophisticated tastes in humor—but she remembered that sometimes. Laughing. Wanting to make other people laugh.

I know, that's what the brownies were for.

It wasn't funny when it was so tragically true. "I am, a little. Right now."

"Oh yeah?" Rachel tucked her wild, messy hair behind her ears. "What's up?"

"It's not that I have a problem," she said quickly. "I just... Well, I'm not out of it."

"And you need something to do."

She hadn't thought of it that way, but it resonated. Even numb and icy, she'd never been good at simple *existence*. She'd distracted herself from the silent loneliness of her house with endless mundane tasks, because at least that made her feel useful. "I'm not really accustomed to just sitting."

Rachel regarded her thoughtfully for a moment. "You don't have to work. But, if you want to, Lex is the person to see."

People had said that to her before. *Dallas* had said that to her during the tense ride back from Sector Two, after she'd stood before the other sector leaders and let them paw through every indignity of the past five years of her life. *An obvious pattern of cruelty*, one of them had declared as she left the room.

As if it was a surprise.

"Everyone else works," she said softly. "I should have to, too. Shouldn't I?"

"Probably," Rachel agreed. "But I don't think anyone would blame you if you needed some time."

"I can't be the only person who came here from a bad place."

"Of course not." She toyed with the crust of her sandwich without picking it up. "You're kind of a special case, though. You already know that. You gave Dallas something he needed, and that buys you breathing room."

Yes. She'd paid with pain, and then cheated, drugged herself so she wouldn't have to feel it. "Did it help? What I did?"

"Oh, hell yeah." Rachel reached out and grasped her hand, squeezing for only a moment before letting go. "But it must have been difficult, and Dallas and Lex understand that."

Dallas and Lex care. That was what she was really saying, and she believed it. All the little signs of self-control, the ones Lili recognized in Lex—Rachel had none of them. Just earnestness and openness. Faith. She wasn't saying it, but everything she said screamed it.

"I don't know if I need a job," Lili said, forcing the

words past her sudden nerves. What she was about to ask for was foreign and strange, but the word itself made her slowly melting heart ache with longing. "I think I need a friend."

A wide grin curved Rachel's lips. "Yeah?" It was so bright, that smile. It tugged at all the cold and lonely places inside Lili. It made her want to smile back—for real, this time—and she hadn't done that in so long. "I'm lost. I don't know the rules. And if I start guessing..." She'd offend people. She already had, and she'd do it again. Worse, probably.

"*Oh.*" She slapped her forehead. "Of course. You need someone to help you figure out Sector Four. Holy shit, I'm an idiot."

Rachel still sounded friendly, but caution was a habit Lili might not ever break. "Did I say the wrong thing already?"

"Not at all. I'm just laughing at myself." The woman's cheeks turned pink. "I've been busy lately. *Too* busy, apparently."

With the men, Ace and Cruz. The artist and the soldier. She'd witnessed Cruz's capacity for violence in the cage, but Ace was the one who made Lili's pulse race with panic. Instincts she barely understood screamed that he was dangerous, even in the face of Rachel's blushing, dreamy smile.

Lili didn't know how to ask why anyone would want *two* of them. It might be the truth, but it wasn't exactly polite. "How long have you been together?"

"A few months." She lifted one hand to the ink that encircled her throat—pretty swirls that Lili had always assumed were meant to look like lace or ribbon. Here, up close, she could pick out the letters. The *names.*

She'd seen the tattoos before, the ones the O'Kanes wore on their wrists, on their shoulders and arms and bare chests and hips. They decorated their bodies with the same attention to detail that Lili had always used with her makeup—but makeup washed away if you made the wrong choice. Rachel had etched their names on her skin. Forever. It made the heavy ring on Lili's left hand feel like the empty promise it was. She hadn't bothered to take it off yet, but she *could.* Thank God.

Rachel's voice cut in to her thoughts. "If you need help selling it..."

Lili realized she was staring at the diamond. It had always been too big. The first month she'd had it, she'd knocked it into a dozen things, scratching walls, cupboards, her own skin. It had seemed fitting, though. It was beautiful and icy cold and only for show.

Just like she needed to be.

The world seemed to constrict for a moment. It was hard to breathe, like the air around her had gotten heavier. Her heart racing, Lili twisted at the ring, dragging it off her finger. When it clattered to the workbench, she managed her first deep breath. "Please. I don't want it anymore."

Rachel picked it up, testing its weight with a few bounces of her hand. Then she held it up to the harsh, bare lights and whistled. "Might take a while, but you could get a ton for it. Then it'll be gone forever, and you'll have money." She winked at Lili. "Kill two birds with one stone."

It was such an outrageous pun that laughter bubbled up in Lili's chest, but it caught in her throat. Or maybe she caught it, because she *had* to. If she let the laughter free, she might not stop, and God only knew what would follow behind it. Rage and tears and five years' worth of sorrow and terror.

Too soon. It was too soon to put so much on a friendship that had been built on a few kind words and a sandwich. She smiled instead, and it felt sadder but safer.

"Then I'll owe you more brownies. Or cake? Cookies?"
But Rachel only grinned. "Eh, what are friends for?"

 hawk

F INN HAD ONCE told him that the cars were the
only thing about Sector Four that made sense to him
at first. But Finn had grown out of that—trial by fire and
true love made for a lot of motivation for growth.

Cars were still the only thing about Sector Four that
made sense to Hawk.

Though Jasper McCray was a close second. Dallas's
second-in-command had offered to help Hawk fix up his
car, since it had nearly been wrecked during Trix's rescue
and their wild dash across Sector Five. The car was his
baby, the first one he'd restored on his own, every part
traded for, every modification carefully planned.

And the bastards from Five had riddled her with bul-
lets.

"How long have you had her?" Jasper asked as he replaced a worn sanding pad with a fresh one.

"Altogether? Close to seven years." Hawk ran his hand over another spot he'd just sanded smooth. Filling in the bullet holes had taken weeks' worth of stolen moments, proof of just how badly he'd abused his poor car. "She's only been running for two, though. Some of the parts were hard to find, even scavenging all the way out to the ocean."

"Too bad you weren't here. Ford can find anything. Mia, too."

"You guys do have all the good shit." He grinned. "Our garage wasn't bad. Shipp put a lot of work into getting us supplies, but it was still nothing like this."

"Dallas has a lot of money," Jas confirmed. "And a lot of pull. That's why you're here, right?"

It was nothing but the truth. Put like that, though, it almost felt like an accusation. It wasn't—if Jas McCray wanted to accuse him of something, he didn't have to dance around it. But it hit too close to the uncomfortable feelings that kept him out in the garage, obsessing over his car, when he could—*should*—have been bonding with his new brothers and finding his place.

"I'm here because Dallas is looking forward," he said after a silence just long enough to be awkward. "I can't ignore the shit that's coming anymore."

Jasper eyed him for a moment before nodding. "Fair enough."

It didn't feel like *enough*, so Hawk fell back on humor, on the joke that held more truth than he liked. "Plus, it's my only chance of meeting any women who aren't my half-sisters or stepmothers."

"You haven't been doing so hot with that," Jasper pointed out. "You know, since the only woman I've seen you checking out happens to be Dallas and Lex's girl."

Oh, *shit*.

Hawk froze and realized a moment later how fucking guilty it made him look. He resumed his sanding and fought to keep his voice casual. "Who, Jeni?"

Jasper chuckled. "Yeah, Jeni."

The first time he'd seen her, she'd been on stage in the Broken Circle, dolled up in edgy makeup, a wig, and not a lot else. He'd seen strippers in the slums surrounding the warehouses of Six. He'd seen them in other sectors, too, usually bored or tired, ready to roll you in a back alley for a few credits.

He'd never seen anything like Jeni. Hot. Passionate. Uninhibited and unashamed, screaming her way to an orgasm that didn't sound even a little fake to the delight of a crowd who had, apparently, been trained to give a shit whether it was fake or not.

The giving-a-shit might have been the weirdest fucking part. But Hawk couldn't exactly blame them. He'd developed a pretty inappropriate fascination with her not-at-all-fake orgasms.

And then he'd realized who she was—and who she was sleeping with. "What's the deal with that, anyway? I thought Lex and Dallas were…" He gestured to Jas's arm, where Noelle's name filled his forearm. "Y'all's kind of married."

"They're together. Always." The other man shrugged. "Doesn't mean they can't care about someone else. For a night, for a year. Forever, if that's how it ends up."

Forever. The word twisted in his gut, so Hawk did what he always did—ignored the fuck out of it. The only thing that was allowed to matter was the ledger in his head, the one he'd been slowly filling with favors performed and help given. He'd need to call in those favors someday, maybe sooner than he wanted.

Now was not the time to wonder how far in the red he'd sink if Dallas caught him eyeing the wrong woman.

He was about to sand a hole through the metal, so he eased off. "If she's their girl, seems like it doesn't matter. I'll be more careful where I look."

39

"Even if she's been looking at you, too?"

Now Jas had to be fucking with him—or trying to fuck him up. "Doesn't make her less the boss's girl," he said, holding up his wrist. "O'Kane for life, right?"

"I'm just saying, you never know what could happen." Jasper locked the sanding plate in place and grinned. "You might find yourself invited along to the next private after-party."

Not likely. He was struggling to strike up a rapport with the men, but at least that was happening, if slowly. The women, though...

He wasn't an idiot. He had a couple dozen sisters, and that glint of mischief in feminine eyes rarely ended well for any men in the vicinity. And they *all* had it here, all the damn time. They whispered about him and grinned at him, and he was pretty sure half of them might be thinking him and beds and naked skin and not-at-all-fake orgasms.

And it didn't do him a damn bit of good, because every time he closed his eyes, he saw—

"I'm not thinking about that," he said firmly. "We need to have the gardens done in time to plant. We're one bad harvest away from the world ending. Again."

"We work hard, but we play hard, too." Jasper held up his own wrist. "You're falling down on that last part, Hawk. And if I've noticed, so has Dallas. Don't be surprised if he asks you what's up."

It was a message. Hell, coming from Dallas's right hand, it was damn near a warning. Not that he had to get to fucking, but that he'd better have a better reason than wanting someone he couldn't have. "Got it."

"You should come over and hang out with me and Noelle tonight." Jasper held up both hands. "Nothing like that. But she wants to get to know you."

Somewhere out there, his entire family was scraping by on a farm that owed a larger and larger percentage of its yield to Eden each year. There was hardly enough to survive on as it was—only Shipp's smuggling kept food on the table these days, and that was barely getting it done now.

Sooner or later, the lives and livelihood of everyone he'd known and loved might depend on his place with the O'Kanes, on what sorts of assurances he could have waiting for them when the time came to abandon the farm. He needed alliances, not girlfriends. He needed favors owed and markers he could call in, not friendly dinners and cuddles.

Unless he'd been going about it all wrong, and dinners and cuddles were how you became one of them. How you became so much a part of the gang that it wasn't about markers and favors, but having each other's backs.

And the worst he had to lose was one night. "I'd love to."

NOELLE CUNNINGHAM DIDN'T act like a council-man's daughter.

Lili had never met Edwin Cunningham. Her father had not-so-cordially loathed Noelle's, and had partnered with his rival with a glee he'd never bothered to hide. But she'd met men *like* Edwin—rich and powerful, cultured and condescending. On the very, very rare occasions they'd brought their wives and daughters with them, the grand ladies of Eden had stared past Lili and her mother as if they were beneath their notice.

Sector trash. That was what she'd been to them. A grasping, greedy girl reaching above her station. Lili had still been capable of rage in those worst moments—not for herself, but for her mother, who suffered enough indignities for being Mac Fleming's wife.

Noelle was nothing like them, and it wasn't just the

change of wardrobe and the vibrant tattoos. She was warm, soft, smiling widely from the moment Lili opened the door at her knock. "Hey, Lex needs to see you in the bar."

It didn't exactly sound like an invitation. Lili was dressed decently enough in a skirt and sleeveless blouse, but she wasn't *dressed*. Her hair still hung loose around her shoulders, and her makeup sat untouched on her dresser. Without both, she felt naked. "Is everything all right?"

"It's fine." Noelle waved a hand at Lili's shoes. "But you need to put those on and come. Lex is perplexed, and trust me, she doesn't like being perplexed."

Still friendly, still so *warm*, but there was a hint of command there, too. Casual confidence, and it was as intriguing as seeing Rachel at home in the garage. There was no way Edwin Cunningham's daughter had been raised to believe she could command people's obedience.

So Lili put on her shoes.

Noelle linked their arms together as soon as she closed the door, all but dragging Lili down three flights of stairs and out into the bright spring morning before speaking again. "I heard you like to cook. And that you're good at it."

The compliment rubbed some of the edges off her nerves. "Well, I do enjoy it. And I've learned some tricks."

"Don't be modest." Noelle grinned at her. "Yes, modesty is ladylike, but it also pisses Dallas off. He likes to know what sorts of resources he has at his disposal."

It was an odd way to look at it. Cooking had always been expected of her, and anything less than talent equaled failure. It might still be an obligation here, but perhaps a valued one. "I'll remember that."

"Good. You're going to be okay." Noelle pulled Lili into a hug so abrupt it was already over before she could unlock

her muscles. Noelle seemed unbothered by her lack of response and was already dragging open the back door to the
bar. "Go straight through the kitchen. Lex is in the main
room."

Still stunned, Lili followed her directions, navigating
the cramped kitchens and pushing through the swinging
doors on the other side.

Lex stood beside a huge wooden crate, her arms
crossed over her chest and one eyebrow upraised. "Deliv-
ery for you, Lili."

Lili stopped next to the bar and stared.

The crate was *huge*, almost as tall as Lex. "I...don't
know what to say. I wasn't expecting anything."

A short, sharp laugh escaped Lex. "Think we should
shoot it a couple of times, just to be safe?"

It might not be the worst idea.

Still wary, Lili ran her fingertips along the edge of the
crate. The wood looked recycled, old and worn down until
it was almost smooth. There were holes where nails had
been driven before and pulled free, but that told her nothing. In the sectors, wood was always reused. "The person
who delivered it didn't say anything?"

"Sure, he did. *Package for Miss Lili Fleming.*" Lex
stepped up on the bottom rung of a stool, reached over the
bar, and came up with a crowbar clutched in one hand.
"You want to do the honors?"

It was an order, not an offer. Lili gingerly took the
crowbar and, praying she wouldn't accidentally damage
something, began prying off the front of the crate. The
nails gave way easily, and Lex helped steady the heavy
plywood as Lili lifted it away to reveal the last thing she'd
expected.

"Huh." Lex stared at the scarred, ancient wood inside
the packing crate. "It's a fucking piano."

It was. A beautiful upright with enough height to produce a full, rich tone. And old—not just pre-Flare, but

something that would have been antique even then. The wood was scratched and battered, and someone else might have assumed that made it less valuable.

But the outside wasn't the important part.

Lili set the crowbar aside and lifted the fallboard. The keys were aged, not just discolored but smoothed into silky softness. But when she found middle C, the note came clear and perfect. "A very well-maintained piano."

Lex leaned against the side of the crate. "Yours? Something an old friend from Five sent over?"

Her piano had been brand new, flawless and beautiful—not because anyone valued her pleasure in it, but because it wouldn't do for anyone to think Mac Fleming and Logan Beckett couldn't afford the best. "No, I've never seen this one before."

"Ah." The woman shoved her hands into the back pockets of her jeans and rocked on her heels. "Well, I only know one person who could pull this off, Miss Lili Fleming. I believe you've made his very refined acquaintance."

She almost said *who*, but there was only one person it could be. "Jared?"

"The one and only."

"But I barely talked to him." He'd been polite. Enchanting. Surreally beautiful and pleasant enough that she'd ached a little at the loss of him when he took his leave. But then Lex had started...touching and kissing, and Lili had been fervently, humiliatingly *glad* to be free of the temptation of his presence.

If he'd stayed, she would have made a fool of herself.

"Barely talked?" Lex shook her head. "Somehow, honey, I don't think that matters, not with a man like him."

She couldn't resist touching the keys again. She wanted to settle in, remember how her fingers moved, how it felt when she knew a piece so deeply she didn't have to think. "I don't even know what sort of man he is."

"Complicated," Lex answered simply, then took a step back. "I'll round up a few of the guys and see if we can get this moved for you. In the meantime..." She turned on her heel and started walking toward the back exit. "I hear he likes cookies."

Lex vanished, leaving Lili alone with the gift.

Gift.

She settled her thumb on middle C again and played the first scale she'd ever learned. C Major was simple enough, but she'd been young, her fingers clumsy and too short to make it easy. She'd practiced for hours every day on that first piano, one that hadn't been so different from this. Scarred and old but well-loved.

On her fifteenth birthday, her father had gifted her with a pristine grand piano. She'd never seen anything like it, had never imagined anything so perfect could be meant for *her.*

Because it hadn't been.

Gifts were a trap. Sometimes they were brownies in exchange for friendship. And sometimes they were beautiful pianos, in exchange for...

That was the question, wasn't it?

Already regretting it, Lili eased her fingers from the keys. Whatever the price was, it was too high. She had nothing to offer that could be worth this. Offering *everything* wouldn't be worth this, even if she could bring herself to do it.

She would start with cookies. And she'd find a way to break it to Jared that whatever he was looking for, he wouldn't find it in her.

No one ever did.

It wasn't unusual for Ace to show up unannounced.

Over the years, he'd appeared at Jared's door at all hours of the day and night, sometimes dragging a man or a woman—or both—along with him. He'd never brought baked goods before.

"Did you do it, man?" Ace demanded, sprawling on the couch without relinquishing the plate of cookies. "Lex thinks it was you, but I told her she's nuts. And that went over great."

"I imagine so." He could only be referring to the piano, but Jared hadn't climbed this high by making assumptions. "You'll have to be more specific, though. Did I do what?"

"Come on." Ace rolled his eyes. "Did you give that girl a goddamn piano?"

"Oh, that." He shrugged. "Sure. Finn mentioned she'd like to have one, and I can well afford it, so I figured why not?"

Ace stared at him.

He stared back. "Is there a problem?"

"Fuck, you tell me." He lifted the plate. "She was about to toddle her terrified ass over here with fresh cookies. Should I have let her?"

"No. Hell, no." The point of the instrument was simple. He could fulfill Finn's request with a minimum of personal effort—or contact. Even if he wanted to look out for Lili in a more hands-on capacity, this was the worst possible time to do it. "Finn asked me to help her, but this is all I can manage."

"Finn asked…" Ace trailed off with a sigh and dropped his head back against the couch. "He got his guilt all over you, huh?"

"He seems to have plenty of it." Jared reached for a bottle—one of Nessa's best, an exquisite single-malt—and poured out two healthy measures.

"Yeah, well, Lili was pretty messed up. I was there when she showed up on the compound." Ace accepted the

glass but didn't drink. "Did anyone tell you what she did?"
"I didn't ask."
"Nah, you just bought her a piano."
Jared pinned him with a quelling look. "It didn't cost me much." Far less, in fact, than investing his concern in a lost girl from Sector Five.
Ace relented by raising his glass. "I guess to you, *much* is pretty damn relative."
"Very." If Ace could relent, so could he, just a little. "I feel bad for her, of course I do. But I don't have the time or the energy to save someone, Ace. That's what you O'Kanes are for."
"Honestly, I don't think she'd appreciate saving." Ace swirled the liquor in the glass and squinted at it before taking a sip. "Goddamn, you got Nessa to sell you one of her experimental batches? She won't even let me have one."
Dallas had given it to him—part gift and part pay-ment—when he'd joined up. "I'm a persuasive man."
"You better not be persuading in her pants," Ace re-torted with a not-entirely-mock growl. "She's a kid."
Jared didn't resent the suspicion. It always came down to sex. That was his life, his livelihood, and Ace knew that better than anyone. "I've been good, brother."
Ace took another sip before poking at the plate of cook-ies. "Do you remember how Gia was in the beginning? Not right after Eladio found her, but once he'd gotten her cleaned up and in control of herself."
Still a bit feral, but she'd managed to lock it down. Hard, because she'd believed she had to be that way in or-der to survive. "I remember."
"That's what Lili reminds me of. Damned if I even know why, because that girl should be a sheltered little sector princess..." He trailed off and glanced up at Jared. "She shot a guard in the face and walked out of Five. In a virginal nightgown and a fucking fur coat covered in

blood."

"So she knows how to survive. Wants to." O'Kane could work with that, the same way Eladio had with Gia in those early years.

"She knows how to stay alive. Fuck, that's all she knows."

"It's the first step. The most important one." Everything else could take years. Decades. Hell, sometimes he wasn't entirely sure he'd ever made it past that point himself.

"I guess, man." Ace tilted his head toward the plate. "You should try the cookies. Rachel says she really can cook, *and* she likes it. That'd be new. If you ask Six to cook for you, there's a fifty-fifty shot she'll stab you."

"Maybe later." He drained his glass and squinted at his oldest friend. He'd been keeping his distance for fear of having Ace discover his clandestine activities, but he worried that distance might seem more personal. "How have you been?"

"Good." Ace rested a hand over his side. Jared had seen the scar there—smaller than it should have been, thanks to regeneration technology, but the wound that had almost killed Ace had been too serious to erase entirely. "Emma's gonna fix up my ink in a couple weeks. Well, do what she can anyway. I don't even feel a twinge anymore."

"What about your marks?" Rachel's were visible to the world, curving lines of ink framing her throat in obvious symbolism. "Have you and Cruz had yours done yet?"

Ace finished his drink and rose with a grin. "Oh, yeah," he drawled, dragging his shirt over his head. "Emma fucking nailed it."

He turned, revealing the newly inked expanse of his back. He'd always guarded that skin jealously, refusing to have needles touch it until the perfect image presented itself.

beyond innocence

And it had. Two angels—one sweet, and one clad in a warrior's garb—covered each side of his back. They were both grasping on to a poor, fallen soul between them, lifting him out of the flames that covered the small of Ace's back.

A spark of jealousy raced through Jared, quick and hot and extinguished in a heartbeat by his sincere appreciation for his friend's newfound bliss. "I'm happy for you. They're beautiful."

"Yeah. They are." Ace dropped back to the couch without putting on his shirt. "Cruz wanted me to invite you over to catch up, but Rae's taken a shine to Lili. Will that get awkward? I mean, even if it's just a piano to you..."

If she got ideas about some grand romance, he'd handle it. But, somehow, he didn't think the wide-eyed girl from Dallas's party was eager to throw herself at him. "It'll be fine. Thanks for thinking of me."

"So you'll come over?"

"Name the time." Jared refilled his glass and lifted an eyebrow at Ace. "Another?"

"Hell, yeah. Nessa never shares." Ace leaned over and held out his glass. "You think maybe we could crash in on Gia? I'm not going alone—she's been fucking pissy since Dallas stole Jeni."

"On his stage *and* in his bed," Jared agreed. "Which one upsets our darling Gia more?"

"Like I ever know for sure. I *think* she wanted Jeni for the business." Ace shrugged. "She's in a mood, though. Has been since Tatiana's shop burned down."

"Come on, she can't blame Dallas for that."

"It's not about blame. Tatiana ended up an O'Kane. At this rate, Jeni will, too."

Jared schooled his features and gestured toward Ace's wrists with the bottle. "You wear the man's ink. You're uniquely positioned to explain to Gia how that's not a bad thing."

51

kit rocha

"Oh, trust me, I've tried." Ace rubbed one thumb over his O'Kane cuff, tracing the ink almost absently. "Maybe it's harder for her, after the kinds of clients she had to take, especially in the beginning. I don't know if she can let a man own her, even if it's just symbolic."

"And she doesn't have to. But she can't begrudge others following their own path, even when she doesn't understand it." It was one of the first things Eladio had taught them, back when they were all still kids he'd plucked out of the gutter. *Escúchame—come on. Sit down and listen. Sometimes, people won't like what you do. Do it anyway. It's better to be happy and hated than miserable.*

Ace's frown only deepened. *Brooding artist* was a common enough look on him, but it seemed worse tonight. "Sometimes..." He trailed off, shifted upright to rest his elbows on his knees, and finally met Jared's eyes. "I feel like I left you guys behind."

At one point, Jared might have agreed. But he'd been more heartsick than anything, saddened by the harsh realization that Ace didn't love him, not like that, and he never would. "You belong exactly where you are, Ace. And no one was happier than Gia when you hooked up with O'Kane's crew."

"Yeah?" Ace half-smiled. "Figures, I guess. Is there anyone she doesn't want to save?"

"No. She's that much like Eladio."

"And as likely to admit it." Ace lowered his voice. "I won't push. Just tell me you're still thinking about it. Joining up, or even just getting out. None of us can do it forever."

The irony was enough to choke a man. For a moment, Jared considered telling Ace the truth—but the risks far outweighed his friend's peace of mind. "As a matter of fact, I have been thinking about retiring. It's time."

Ace's sudden smile was radiant. Jared had gotten over

beyond innocence

his foolish infatuation a long time ago, but that open, brilliant grin still hit him square in the chest. "Well, thank
fucking God."

"None of us can do it forever," he agreed quietly. "And
I have enough money now to do whatever I please. Go
wherever I please."

"Buy pianos for whoever you please."

"That, too." He flashed Ace an arch look. "Should I
take it back?"

"Nah. At this point, we'd just have to get her another."
Ace lifted his drink with a wry grin. "Turns out? Girl can
play."

"Then do me a favor, would you?" Jared set the bottle
on the coffee table with a *thunk.* "Stop busting my balls."

"Nope. Someone's gotta." Ace sprawled back and
picked up the plate of cookies. "You gonna eat these?"

He shouldn't. He'd have to spend hours in the gym
working them off, but they smelled—and looked—damn
good. Nothing like the ones the bakery carts in the market
burned to a crisp, but golden and still soft around the
edges.

He leaned forward and took one from the plate. Only
a hint of warmth remained as he turned the cookie over in
his hand. "Did I ever tell you my aunt used to bake?"

"Did she?" Ace seemed to take it as permission and
picked up two cookies. "Was that her job?"

"Mmm. She worked for a baker who'd set up shop near
the border between this sector and Three, back before the
marketplace was established. She made bread—hand-
shaped peasant loaves the baker charged way too much
for." Jared broke off a bit of the cookie. "When she could,
she'd sneak enough ingredients to whip up a pie or some
brownies. She even made a cake once."

"My mother never had money for sugar and all that
crap. She blew it all on art supplies for me." Ace shoved
half a cookie in his mouth and groaned. "Fuck yeah, this

is the good shit. Not like that time Eladio tried to bake for us."

"He was terrible at it." But he'd tried, and that effort had meant more to a young child than anyone would ever know. "Refined sugar, real butter—is there anything O'Kane can't get his hands on?"

"You?" Ace joked.

The truth would shock, even anger him, so Jared only smiled. "One thing in the world? Not a bad track record for your fearless leader."

"Who knows? Maybe Lili and her cookies will get you yet."

Jared groaned and dropped the cookie back on the plate before absently licking a smudge of chocolate from his thumb. "If the rest of Dallas's courting hasn't worked, what makes you think big eyes and desserts will?"

"Hey, maybe they won't." Ace straightened and dragged his shirt back on. "You busy tonight? We could give Gia the cookies, if you don't want them. You know she can't resist sweet things."

In more ways than one. Jared capped the bottle and rose. "Deal. We'll bring the liquor, too. Do some catching up."

Him and Ace and Gia, just like old times. No matter how guilty Ace felt about moving on and leaving them behind, he never had, not in the ways that mattered. He was always there for them, the one constant in their lives.

There was comfort in that, in having someone who'd seen you at your worst and still wanted the best for you. Lili didn't have that, but if she stuck with the O'Kanes, maybe someday she would.

LILI'S QUARTERS WERE generous, to be sure, but she didn't have room for a piano.

So she made room.

Deciding what to sacrifice wasn't easy. The bed had to stay, obviously. So did the freestanding wardrobe that held her meager but growing collection of outfits appropriate for Sector Four.

It came down to the vanity or the table. The place where she hid with her meals, reading and eating in solitude, or the place where she put on her makeup—her *armor*—and gathered the courage to face the world.

Not really a choice at all, in the end. The table went, and the piano took its place, all but filling one cement wall. Noelle vanished while the men were moving it into place and reappeared as they were leaving, dragging a dusty but elegant stool that was almost the perfect height.

"I was never any good at it," she confided as she filled Lili's tablet with sheet music she'd somehow hacked from the network inside Eden. "If you want hard copies of any of these, Ace has a chemical printer. Rachel can show you." And that was that, as far as the O'Kanes were concerned. If any of them found it odd that Jared had gifted her with something so extravagant, they gave no indication. And Lili couldn't tell if that was soothing or even more alarming.

The rules of Sector Four were varied and incomprehensible. Maybe a gift like this had a meaning, one they all assumed she knew. Maybe accepting it had a meaning, too. She should have rejected the gift, should have insisted Lex put it someplace public, somewhere everyone could use it, so it wouldn't be *her* piano. *Her* bargain.

She should have, but she hadn't. The piano had seduced her from the very first note.

And playing it was heaven. She stayed up late, remembering how to move her fingers. Not gracefully, not at first. She hadn't played in the months she'd been in Sector Four, or for some time before that. Not after she'd gotten her hands on the newest drugs, the most exclusive ones that delivered the sweetest, numbest oblivion.

Her husband had been pleased to have her so uncaringly obedient—but less pleased that the fog made it harder for her to find the right notes or care when she didn't. He'd stopped demanding that she play for his guests, and it hadn't felt like a loss. They'd tarnished something that had been hers.

Now, one missed note at a time, she could take it back.

By the second day, she'd almost forgotten the piano came with an unknown price. She bathed and dressed with every intention of venturing out of her room to find Rachel, but the keys beckoned and she gave in. Just one piece, but one turned into two, and one hour into four.

She could *feel* the music again. The thrill of success

beyond innocence

when her fingers raced ahead of her mind, when she felt poised on the edge of a mistake because she was going so fast, but thinking didn't matter anymore. Just her in-stincts, her memory. Her heart.

She made it through a simple sonata without a single error, and was still basking in the satisfaction when a knock at the door dragged her back into her body, into her cement-walled room in Sector Four.

Back into her trap.

She knew before she opened the door. Somehow she *knew*, if only because instinct and experience had taught her that two days was as much respite as anyone could hope for, and already too generous for most. But even with all of that—

God, he was perfect.

She of all people knew what a lie perfection could be, but his didn't feel shallow the way hers always had. Jared was flawless, from his carefully disheveled hair and chis-eled features straight down to his tailored clothes and polished shoes—though how anyone kept their shoes *pol-ished* in Sector Four was a mystery.

Or just plain magic, because he didn't seem entirely real. That had made him comforting, with drugs to soften the edges of her fear. Now, he made it hard to breathe.

Then he smiled. "Miss Lili."

"Mr...." She tilted her head. "I'm sorry, I don't know your last name."

He only nodded. "Everyone calls me Jared. May I?"

She stepped back and pulled the door wider, forget-ting until he'd crossed the threshold that she'd gotten rid of the chairs that went with the table. "I'm sorry, there's not really any place to sit."

"I don't mind standing."

Which meant she must, as well. She started to close the door, but thought better of it at the last moment. That could be another signal she didn't understand—or, worse,

57

kit rocha

an invitation she couldn't afford to issue. Leaving the door ajar, she turned and summoned a smile. "I hope Ace conveyed my gratitude for the gift. It's a beautiful instrument."

"Yeah." The corner of his mouth quirked as he leaned against the wall beside her vanity. "He brought me the cookies."

Her cheeks heated. "It's hardly adequate repayment, I know—"

"They were good. You're very talented."

He was flattering her. Simply being polite, that was all. But even perfunctory compliments fed some sad, lonely place inside her she hadn't known was there until now. "Thank you."

"It's true," he argued gently. "And I would know. My aunt was a baker by trade."

"But they're still just cookies." She gestured to the piano and made herself say the words. "This is... It's too much."

"Relax, Lili." His smile widened, and he rubbed his jaw with one graceful hand. "I didn't build it."

No, he'd just spent a significant amount of money on it. Maybe he had so much that he wouldn't notice the loss, but people rarely acquired that much wealth by spending it on whimsical gifts for strangers.

Why? It hovered on the tip of her tongue, but it wasn't the polite, civilized question, and he seemed like a polite, civilized man. More so standing in her bare concrete room surrounded by so much wildness.

"Thank you, just the same," she said instead. "And if you ever need anything..."

He nodded, then tilted his head as he studied her. "It's a whole different world, isn't it? Not just Sector Four, but here. On the compound."

Laughter rose, and she couldn't hold it back this time. "It's a different universe."

beyond innocence

"Which begs the question, I suppose." He hesitated.
"Do you *want* to be here?"
Such an odd question. So few people had the luxury of caring about the answer. It was better not to ask it, not to even think it. "I'm grateful to be here."
"Of course you are. But I didn't ask if you were grateful."
Lili shrugged helplessly. "There's nowhere else I'd rather be. Eden might be more familiar, but—"
"But it might not be as hospitable," he finished. "I understand." He drew his finger along the scarred wood edging her vanity mirror. Once upon a time, it had been a beautiful piece—rich wood, elegant design, solid construction. But it hadn't weathered quite as well as her piano, and the finish had worn away in places, leaving gouges in the once-smooth surface. "You want to ask me why, but don't feel it's appropriate, I gather?"
It was perceptive enough an observation to make her shift uncomfortably. Being ignored by men who didn't care about her feelings had never been pleasant, but sometimes it made things less awkward. "It *is* an extravagant gift. I suppose I'm worried I can't repay your kindness."
"Have you considered that no repayment is necessary?"
He looked earnest. Handsome and godlike, and fully capable of benevolence toward mortals. She wanted to believe him. She imagined *every* woman wanted to believe him when he smiled at her.
She was sheltered, not stupid. "No. I'm afraid not."
It was his turn to laugh. "Probably the smartest thing, generally speaking."
A tightness between her shoulder blades loosened, and she smiled—a real smile, for once. "It's not personal. I hope you understand. But I don't know the rules here. A gift like this in Sector Five would come with...specific obligations."

59

kit rocha

"Mmm." He arched one eyebrow. "Tell me, Lili—do I strike you as someone who needs to buy women?"

"Not particularly," she conceded. "But most men of my acquaintance found it easier, whether they needed to or not."

"I'm not most men."

No, he wasn't. "Then...why? Why give me a piano?"

"Because the piano will mean more to you than the money did to me."

An unfathomable answer, the latest in a long line of things that made no sense to her. Maybe she'd never understand the rules of this place enough to blend in, but she had to keep trying.

Didn't she?

"Kindness, Miss Lili," he murmured. "It can still be found in the world. If this gift can show you that, it'll be well worth it."

Still. Her world had never held kindness. It was a fantasy, a dream, and the thought of it made her throat ache. She swallowed, trying to banish the threat of tears, but what had been a simple act of self-control with her heart insulated by the drugs seemed impossible now.

She had to feel it all, too bright and too raw. The sadness and the gratitude and the unfamiliar bite of hope. It wouldn't just go away this time, and she didn't know how to hide it.

Lili turned away from him and covered her awkwardness by touching the piano. "Do you play?"

"I'm technically proficient," he admitted.

"I don't know if I am." She brushed her fingertips over the keys, grounding herself in the familiar sensation. "But I love it. My mother taught me."

"That sounds lovely. And far preferable to my proficiency. I never really cared to learn, but it's expected of me."

"It is?" It was a curious enough statement that she

64

glanced back at him. "Why?"

He wasn't smiling now. "The ladies of Eden have cul-tured tastes. Or, at least, they like to imagine they do."

Lili studied him again. His strong features, all hard lines that seemed more severe without a friendly expres-sion to soften them. His perfect body and immaculate clothing, both as carefully maintained as hers had been. Not just carefully—*purposefully.*

Maybe that was what drew her to him, more deeply than the proper suits and polished shoes. He felt familiar because he was as shined and buffed as she'd always been, a person made up of all the talents and interests other peo-ple desired.

But it made sense for her. She'd been a wife, with all the attendant duties. Men rarely had to please anyone but themselves.

Jared tilted his head again. "You don't know."

Shame at her own ignorance was another feeling she was having to get used to. "Whatever it is, I'm afraid I don't."

"I'm sorry, I assumed someone would have told you." He shrugged. "That's my job—pleasing the ladies of Eden. I'm a whore."

"Oh," Lili said faintly, as if the words made any sense at all. Oh, the whores in Sector Five had hardly been re-stricted to women—even Lili knew that—but imagining that any of them were there to cater to a *woman's* pleas-ure...

He slid his hands into his pockets. "I've shocked you."

"No. I mean, yes—" Her cheeks weren't the only thing flushed now. Her whole body felt too warm, and she couldn't quite meet his eyes. "I'm..." *Surprised that a woman would pay for that.*

Maybe she shouldn't be. She'd been watching the O'Kane women for weeks, her certainty in their deception slipping bit by bit. But there was wondering if they were truly enjoying themselves, and there was *knowing.* Knowing could change everything.

"Horrified?" he supplied ruefully.

"No," she said forcefully. And now she had to tell him the truth, as humiliating as it was. "I didn't know women…sought out that sort of companionship."

"I see. Well, they do. Quite often, as a matter of fact." He said it as if it was an understood truth. Water was wet, the sky was blue, women often paid for sex. It was more than she could process all at once, more than she'd *ever* be able to process with him standing there, beautiful and tempting and representing a world of terrifying possibility.

But she needed him to know she wasn't judging him. She didn't know why it felt so vital, except that it wouldn't be fair to repay kindness and honesty with disdain. "I'm shocked. I'm a little confused. But I promise I'm not horrified."

There was that smile again—slow, easy. Knowing. "I've trespassed on your hospitality for too long. I should go."

She didn't want him to leave, but she had no reason to ask him to stay. "I know you said no repayment is necessary, but maybe I could make you dinner—" No, now she sounded like she was propositioning him. "Ace could bring it to you."

He arched one eyebrow. "As delicious as I'm sure it would be, I'd value your company more than the meal."

If it had been any other man, she wouldn't have dared consider. But surely a man like Jared wouldn't need *her* for sex. Perhaps he wanted the same thing she had longed for—companionship without demands.

Or maybe she was a foolish girl who wanted an excuse to believe he was safe.

"I could bring you dinner myself," she found herself saying without really deciding to—which might be all the proof she needed that he wasn't safe at all. But the words were out and she couldn't take them back. She didn't want to.

"I have a kitchen. And I'd love to see you in your element, Miss Lili."

The way he said her name made her shiver. "I'll have to check with Lex. She might not want me to leave the compound."

"Here, then."

"All right. How soon?"

"Friday night?"

Two days. Two days to second-guess her decision while anticipation made her skin too tight. Whatever Jared could be called, it certainly wasn't safe. But maybe he didn't have to be a threat to her.

She smiled and told him the truth. "I can't wait."

beyond innocence

 ace

A CE HAD ALWAYS had trouble warming up to prissy
rich girls.

It was easier to admit it now, with his name etched
across the two people he loved most. Self-reflection wasn't
as painful these days, though Ace didn't need to reflect
hard to come up with a reason for his distrust. Rich, prissy
women had tried to buy pieces of his soul for too many
years not to leave a mark.

He'd gotten over it with Noelle, but she'd been easy.
Just a wobbly-legged bundle of earnest horniness and
sweet affection, and it was hard to stay irritated at someone who got off so damn hard on being scandalized. But
Lili...

Lili wasn't eager. She wasn't horny. She was chilly,
brittle repression wrapped around enough pain and

65

trauma to be explosive. She was going to go off in someone's face without careful handling—and not in a sexy way, either.

And Rachel had adopted her as a pet.

Ace trailed behind them in the marketplace, his arm going numb from the weight of the purchases they'd already made. But Lili was taking her sweet time over the produce carts, examining vegetables like the fate of entire sectors depended on picking exactly the right fucking tomato.

Rachel slid one arm around his waist. "You're scowling."

Not anymore, he wasn't. He never was, once she touched him. "That wasn't scowling. That was seething with intensity. It's an artist thing."

"Mm-hmm." She steered him around the side of a stall, until they were half-hidden by hanging sacks of potatoes and braids of onions. "What's wrong?"

"It's nothing," he promised her, smoothing his fingertip over her collarbone. His name was there, in swooping, beautiful permanence, and it still didn't feel real sometimes. "Just...wondering what the hell is going on in Jared's head."

"Baffled or worried?"

"Do I have to pick one?"

"No." Rachel stared up at him, her eyes bright and smiling. "Maybe he thinks she could use another friend."

It was sweet, and no doubt exactly the reason she'd swooped in to tuck Lili under her wing. "Impossible. She's got you now."

Her only reaction was a pretty blush as she continued. "And *maybe* he wants to be more than her friend. Is that so terrible?"

Ace leaned past the sacks of potatoes to make sure Lili hadn't wandered off and found her peering at a row of herbs he couldn't have identified if his life hung in the balance. Her expression was so *serious*, as if, to her, it really was life or death.

"Not terrible," he murmured, looking back to Rachel. "Unless *she* doesn't want it. Men have delicate hearts, angel."

"Worried, then." She stroked her fingers through his hair, drawing her nails down his scalp to the base of his neck. "It can be worth the risk, can't it?"

Pleasure shivered down his spine, even at that simple touch. If they'd been alone, he'd be finding a secure alcove already, someplace to push her against a wall while he teased her with the threat of discovery.

He'd have to do it later. With Cruz's help.

She laughed softly. "I'll take that filthy look as a *yes*."

He had to scramble to remember her question. "Some risks are bigger than others. And Jared's never been big on the emotional ones. I don't want your little friend to end up hurting either, sweetheart. Lord knows the last few months have knocked her around pretty hard."

"Do you want me to talk to her?"

If Jared was working a slow, delicate seduction, barreling into the middle of it would go about as well as bothering Bren when he was elbow-deep in a bomb. Or maybe that was exactly what needed to happen. "I don't know. I don't know her as well as you do."

Rachel kissed him, just a quick brush of her mouth at the corner of his. "Do you trust me?"

"Always, angel."

"Then let it be. See what shakes out." She gazed up at him like he was the king of the world, and she was so damn adorable his chest ached with it. "You might be surprised."

"Oh, I'm sure I will be." He snuck his free arm around her waist and tugged her tight against his body. "She's lucky she has you. Don't make me *too* jealous."

"Of what?"

"Of having you." He brushed his lips over her ear and summoned his lowest, darkest whisper. The one he used for filthy promises of pain and ecstasy. "I know you have a big heart. But it's still ours."

Rachel shivered. "In my heart and on my skin. No one else, Ace, ever. Just you and Cruz."

"Damn straight." He kissed her again and reluctantly released her. "Let's go round up your little lost lamb, angel. Before any big bad wolves get ideas."

"Uh-huh." She took two of the bags from him and slung them over her shoulder. "You know she's likelier to be scared of you, right?"

"Me? I'm a tamed man."

"Doesn't matter." She turned to face him, her expression serious and her voice low. "She's from Five. She's spent her adult life—plus some—drugged and numb. I don't think anything can scare her the way *feeling* can."

Ace glanced over Rachel's shoulder again. Lili was tracing her fingertip over the curve of an apple now, tentative in that same brittle way she seemed to be about everything. But he *had* seen her the first night she'd dropped on their doorstep, doped so heavily her eyes were beyond blank.

The dead eyes were gone, but Rachel was right—it wasn't just repression that had taken over. It was restraint, a desperate grasp at controlling herself in a world where everything felt bright and intense after a lifetime of shadows and numbness.

Ace knew how that felt. "All right, I hear you, Rae."

"Do you?" She framed his face with her hands, smoothed her thumbs over his cheeks and jaw. "You make people feel—happiness, excitement, laughter. Love." A smile curved her lips, and she winked at him. "Must be an artist thing."

The warmth and affection in her eyes heated him more than her touch—and that was heating him up plenty all on its own. "Must be. I'll try to tone it down for her. Be really boring. Practice my Bren impression."

"Good luck with that, baby."

Ace suspected her of more than a little bias, but he took her to heart nonetheless. He'd tone down his scowls *and* his smiles and cut the girl a break. If Rachel saw someone worth caring for buried beneath all that armor, she was probably right.

He had to believe that now, because she'd been one of the first to see it in him.

beyond innocence

6

T HE STYLUS SLID silently over the tablet's smooth surface as Jared scrawled his signature, filling the final empty box of the contract. "There, it's done." For better or worse, he was now the owner of record of a grungy, unnamed—and illegal—underground club in Eden.

"You sure this is what you want?" Dylan Jordan was uncharacteristically sober as he accepted the tablet. "It's not exactly an easy retirement by anyone's definition."

"I'm not cut out for easy." He'd tried it. For the last five years, his life had been *easy*, with all the wealth and security he could ever want falling into his lap. Hell, he'd had the satisfaction of seeing his best friends well settled.

And none of it made him happy. He wasn't even content. He was drifting, as lost as all the rest of the people Dallas O'Kane liked to snatch up.

"Well," Dylan said slowly, "there's easy, and then

there's quitting your job to become a fucking *sp*—"

Jared shot out of his chair and clamped his hand over the man's mouth. "Don't say it, Dylan. Not even here."

He stared back at him, his eyes glinting, until Jared moved his hand. "Come on, lover boy. Don't tell me you haven't swept this place recently. No one's listening."

"That's not the point." Not entirely. He couldn't let that word get into his head—*spy*—or it would move the fuck in and live there. It would color everything he did, everything he said, and someone would figure it out.

Dylan caught his wrist, held it. "So what is the point? You want to pretend that's not what's going on here? That it's not what O'Kane asked you to do?"

Such a fine line, and so hard to explain to someone who didn't have to live it. But Jared took a deep breath and tried. "The best acting happens when you're not acting. You have to believe what's happening, feel it—even if it's just for a little while. So I'm going to run a club, the best damn club I can, and whatever comes of that is—"

"A happy accident?" Dylan sighed, twined his fingers with Jared's, and pulled him closer. "I understand perfectly. This isn't retirement at all, just a change of venue and clientele."

Maybe it was true, and he'd still be whoring himself, just in a different capacity. But they'd all reached a point where information was more precious than money, and Jared could trade in drinks and easy smiles just as effectively as he had in sweaty nights of earth-shattering pleasure. "It's worth it."

His fingers tightened. "It's dangerous."

"So is everything else in the sectors, Dylan."

"No." The hoarse word seemed torn from his throat, reflected in the darkness haunting his eyes. "Don't laugh it off, Jared. You think Dallas has *anything* on those motherfuckers in Eden? Sure, you cross him and he'll take an acetylene torch to your face, but that's clean. Physical. If

beyond innocence

you wind up in a little room in Eden where there are no windows and no cameras, you'll wish all they'd done was set you on fire."

The words were enough to elicit a shudder, but it was the hopeless, helpless tone of his voice that made Jared's blood run cold. The man they all called Doc had always had demons, as long as he'd known him, but this was unimaginable. Unthinkable. "Dylan..."

He broke away and took a step back. One hand closed into a fist, and the other lifted the tablet. "If you're absolutely sure," he said, his voice clear and steady, "then I'll have this delivered immediately. But be sure, Jared. There are other ways."

He thought of Dallas and Lex, who were trying so hard to keep everything together. Of Ace and Rachel and Cruz, who'd just stumbled into each other's arms—and deserved a lifetime or more to explore what that meant. He thought of the craftsmen and the people who relied on protection from the O'Kanes.

And he thought of Lili—of her shuttered blue eyes, and the millions of unspoken questions tumbling end over end behind them. She was just waking up, and if he could have a hand in making sure that the world she woke up to was a good one, a decent place where things made sense...

He had to.

"We've been on the fringes for too long," he whispered. "Safely on the outside. Pretty soon, that won't be an option. Do-or-die time, Dylan."

But the moment was over. "Indeed," Dylan said blandly as he bowed his head and took another step back. "Watch yourself out there."

The door clicked shut behind him, jarring Jared into motion. He finished his drink, grabbed his jacket, and headed out into the waning light. The sector was quiet, with the only real activity still bustling in the marketplace.

73

He skirted the square, sticking to the darker streets as he made his way toward the O'Kane compound. He rarely walked through the sectors anymore, let alone after dark, but he could remember when shots and screams had split the silence on a regular basis. When you didn't dare venture out without the comforting weight of a gun in your pocket, or three friends watching your back.

Dallas had changed that. Not overnight, and not completely, but the difference was stark—and a good reminder.

Dallas O'Kane might be a dictator, but at least he was a benevolent one.

The back gate was locked, so Jared rounded the block, to the main entrance of the Broken Circle. Six was working the door, decked out in leather and glinting knives that made a statement to those who hadn't seen her take a man apart in the cage.

Her expression had been fixed in a scowl, but it vanished when she saw him. "Hey, Jared."

"Good evening." From this spot, he could barely see the stage, just a glimmer of flesh now and then through the crowd. "Who's up tonight?"

"One of the new girls. But Jeni's about to go on." Six grinned. "Zan better get his ass down here before she does. Last week, she damn near started a riot."

"I believe it." Everything about seduction that he and Gia had been taught seemed to come naturally to Jeni, and she could do it all without saying a single word. "Say hello to her for me?"

"You got it."

He bypassed the bar and the crowded tables. The side door beckoned, and he made his way down the steep stairs and into the industrial-sized basement kitchen.

Lili was already there, chopping carrots at the kitchen island as chicken sizzled in a skillet next to her. She was wearing a little black dress with a pink and black apron,

and he couldn't see behind the island, but she was probably wearing high heels, too. The perfect picture of
domesticity, like some pre-Flare television show about
perfection in the suburbs.

Even her hair was up. Jared watched as she tucked
an errant lock behind her ear, and suddenly wished that
the image she presented *wasn't* so perfect. On her, it
looked like shackles, chains. Being forced into a box that
didn't quite fit.

He cleared his throat.

She looked up, surprise widening her eyes for a moment. "Jared. I'm sorry, I'm running behind."

"No, you're not. I'm early. I hope that's okay."

"As long as you don't mind watching me cook." She
nodded to the stools on the other side of the island. "Have
a seat. Can I get you something to drink?"

"Please." He unbuttoned his jacket and eased onto the
stool. She was in her element, perhaps, playing the hostess, but she was still nervous. On edge.

She poured two fingers of whiskey into a glass for him,
but nothing for herself. Her hand trembled a little as she
slid the drink across the steel surface. "I should have
asked what you like to eat," she apologized. "Ace said you
get enough fancy meals in Eden, so I picked something I
used to make for my brothers and sisters. But it's not very
sophisticated."

"Whatever you chose is fine." He reached for the glass
before she could draw her hand away. His fingers brushed
hers, and a sliver of heat kindled low in his gut.

Her breathing hitched. Her gaze dropped to the
glass—to their fingers—and her cheeks flushed lightly as
she gently drew her hand away. "Chicken pot pie," she
said, turning to the skillet. "Well, sort of. The children
didn't like the pie part, but they loved biscuits."

She said it almost conversationally, but pain lurked
beneath the words. "I was sorry to hear about them. And

75

your mother."

"Thank you." Her attention stayed focused on the skillet as she added more ingredients—flour and then broth, her movements so practiced as she whisked them together that it seemed like comfortable habit. "It's odd. It hurts to know they're gone, but I lost them the day I got married."

Losing contact was one thing. Knowing they'd been murdered was another. "Grief is an odd thing. It doesn't much care sometimes how many years have passed."

"I suppose that's true." She glanced at him, curious but undemanding. "My mother always told me I was fortunate. That people in other sectors often didn't have families to lose."

Surprising, the pain that lanced through him. "Everyone has a family. How long they get to keep it is the variable."

"I'm sorry," she said softly. "That wasn't very graceful of me."

"You don't have to be perfect all the time." He sipped his whiskey and tried to reduce the flood of memories to mere words. "My mother died a few days after I was born. Childbed fever. My aunt raised me on her own. Then she died, too."

"Your aunt was the baker?"

"Yes. A gang hit the shop where she worked for a shakedown. The owner hadn't been paying the extra protection money, so they planned to smash it up. But he'd left her in charge that day, so she tried to stop them."

Lili reached for his hand this time, resting her fingers lightly on his. "That's terrible."

"It's—" *It's life.* "It was a long time ago. And that's when I met Eladio—and Ace and Gia. They were my family, too."

"I don't think I've met Gia."

She wouldn't appreciate his smile, so he hid it behind his glass. "No, I can't imagine you have."

beyond innocence

Lili drew her hand away and returned to her cooking. "I take it she's not an O'Kane, either?"

"No. She runs the most profitable brothel in the sector."

If it shocked her, she hid it better this time. "An independent woman, then. I'd never met one before coming here."

"Plenty of them in Four. We all prefer it that way." Maybe she was getting used to how O'Kane ran things, after all. "What about you?"

"Do I prefer independent women?" She smiled a little. "I could, though I'm not sure I have the skills necessary to be one."

"Why not?"

She waved a hand at the stovetop. "This is what I do— *all* I can do. Cook dinner, play the piano passably well, and make conversation with people I cordially loathe."

"Ouch." Jared feigned an exaggerated wince. "Really, now?"

Lili wrinkled her nose. "This isn't making conversation. That's polite and bland and empty. We're *talking*, which is why I'm not very good at it."

He didn't hide his smile this time. "It's nice to know I merit the distinction. Friends always should."

"Friends," she echoed, returning his smile shyly. "Another thing I didn't know existed before coming here."

She'd always possessed a chilly, aloof sort of beauty, the kind they prized highly within the city. But here, warmer, softer, her apron smudged with flour and her hair falling from its chignon—

She was gorgeous.

"A toast, then." He lifted his glass. "To friends."

After a heartbeat of hesitation, she wiped her hands on her apron and poured a second drink. She held her own glass to his and inclined her head. "To friends."

She had to be nervous. She had to wonder what it all

kit rocha

meant—the gift of the piano, his attention, his offer of friendship. Things in the sectors were never free, and rarely worth the price you had to pay.

He could fix it all, maybe, with the truth.

He chose his words carefully, watching her as she drained her glass in several swallows. "Not many people know me. They know *of* me, who I am—well, what I do, mostly. It's a lonely way to be. I think you might understand that."

"I understand that," she agreed, setting the glass down gently. "That night at the party, you seemed familiar. Comforting, I suppose. Maybe even safe."

Safe. The thought might appeal to her, but it was laughable in the face of the days to come. O'Kane wasn't sending one of his warriors into Eden to lay the groundwork for his revolution. He was sending a man whose greatest claim to fame was as the living embodiment of whatever fantasy you held dear. A man so used to molding and remaking himself that sometimes he didn't know who he was anymore.

Lili looked at him and saw safety because that was what she *needed* from him. All she needed from him.

He avoided her eyes as he refilled their glasses and echoed her. "Safe."

Her whisk clinked softly against the bowl. "You don't blend in with them. And you weren't trying to. I wish I had that confidence."

It wasn't confidence, it was privilege. Dallas had been trying to recruit him for years, and joining up—for him— didn't mean having to blend in. Hell, no one even had to know. "Why?"

"Because I'm not sure blending in is an option for me."

"So don't." She'd earned her spot among the O'Kanes already, and Dallas wouldn't take that away.

Lili didn't answer. Her heels clicked on the concrete floor as she moved to the oven and silently transferred her skillet to it. She hesitated a little over the controls before punching in the time. The appliances weren't the shiny models currently popular in Eden, but more in line with Dallas's priorities—solid, well-made, with a minimum of technological frills.

"I don't know what else to do," she admitted finally, returning to pick up her drink. "I've been training my whole life to be something no one here wants."

"A wife."

"A trophy."

Of course. A strange ache overtook his chest, and he braced his elbows on the counter. "The things you've learned—does doing them make you happy? Or is it just all you know?"

She ran her finger through a dusting of flour left behind on the countertop, tracing absent lines. "The piano and the cooking. I liked both, when I did them for myself or for people I cared about. But they *are* all I know."

"Well, there's your answer." He leaned back, away from the urge to lay his hand over hers. "Sector Four has no need for trophies, but it can always use food and music."

She smiled and peeked up at him. "You're good at this. Talking. I'll have to cook you dinner again to thank you for tonight, at this rate."

She was teasing him, but, somehow, this *mattered*. Getting to know someone new, letting her know him. Something told him he might need these memories, fresh in his mind, before his time in Eden was finished. "I consider myself the lucky one."

"Now I think you're just flattering me." She lifted her glass higher and adopted a lazy expression and an icily precise inflection. "I'm a nice enough girl, but sector rabble shouldn't aspire to cleverness."

As far as impressions of proper Eden ladies went, it was spot on. He raised his own glass again. "To sector rabble."

Five minutes after arriving at the warehouse for fight night, Lili realized her dinner with Jared had made her dangerously overconfident.

She'd never tried this without the drugs. Without the *good* drugs, the ones that gave everything a dreamlike quality and coated her nerves with ice. She'd never tried to face it on her own, raw and stone-cold sober, and she'd been stupid to try.

The noise alone was overwhelming, even after she retreated to the comparatively secluded dais where the O'Kane women gathered. There were so many people, more than she'd ever seen in the same place before coming here. Men and women spanning all ages and ethnicities, some dressed in shabby, patched denim and some that gave the O'Kanes competition in finely crafted leather.

It was a jumbled, seething tangle of humanity and *life*, and Lili's pulse throbbed so loudly in her ears that she barely heard Rachel's greeting. "Over here!"

Lili tracked the sound and spotted Rachel on one of the couches. Relief flooded her, momentarily strong enough to overtake panic, and she moved away from the edge of the platform to join her. "Hi."

Rachel pressed a cold bottle of beer into her hands. "Where have you been?"

"I lost track of time." It was only a little lie. She'd spent a solid hour in front of her meager wardrobe, Jared's words still whispering through her mind even days later. In the end, she'd put back the leather corset and tiny skirt and had reached for the dress she'd worn that night.

Black. Simple. It wouldn't have been acceptable in Sector Five, but it was certainly tame by O'Kane standards, with a skirt that fell to her knees and lace covering

beyond innocence

her back and upper arms.

Caught between worlds, just like she was.

"You missed the first round," Trix said. "Some yahoo from Three *challenged* Bren."

"Idiot," Nessa drawled from her perch on the far arm of the couch. "A *big* idiot, because he thought he was winning until Bren got bored of playing with him."

Bren reminded her of one of her father's men—Ryder, the stern-faced, solemn bodyguard who had become Logan's right-hand man after her father's death. Hard, implacable and unswerving—the kind of man only a fool would cross. "Bren won, I assume?"

"Eventually." Rachel was drinking some red concoction with fruit floating in it along with the ice. She sipped it through her straw, then grinned at Lili over the rim of her glass. "No one cares about that, though. We want to know what happened the other night."

"With Jared?" Lili clutched her hands around the beer bottle. "It was just dinner. We talked."

Nessa clutched her heart and groaned. "Oh my *God*, you must be a saint."

The others made incoherent noises of agreement, and Rachel raised both eyebrows. "Even Cruz can barely be in the same room with Jared without getting *ideas*."

"It's the fuck-me eyes," Trix proclaimed.

"And the fuck-me voice," Lex chimed in from behind the couch. She leaned over it, her chin propped on one hand. "So?"

Lili would be lying if she claimed he hadn't given her ideas. From the first time their fingers brushed, her skin had prickled with awareness of him, an awareness that hadn't faded until long after he'd departed. "He's very appealing—"

Nessa cut her off with another groan. "She's about to break our hearts. I hear the *but* coming."

But I'm scared of wanting. No, true or not, those were

81

words she wasn't ready to share. "We agreed to be friends," she said instead. "I think that's all he wants from me, in any case. And I don't mind."

"He's a good friend to have." There was nothing salacious or sarcastic in Rachel's voice. "Ace has known him forever. They practically grew up together."

"That's what he told me. Ace and Gia?" Over dinner and drinks, she'd teased more of his past out of him, though not nearly as much as he'd coaxed out of her. Having her own conversational tricks turned against her could have been unnerving, but she understood now why they worked. Nothing felt quite like being the focus of someone's fascinated attention.

"Well, aren't you well-informed?" Lex teased.

"We just talked," Lili protested. "About our families, and about growing up in different sectors."

"It's cool." Lex climbed over the back of the couch and bounced onto the cushion beside her. "Flash and Zan finished off the leftovers you had in the fridge, by the way. You have to watch them. They'll eat anything that isn't nailed down."

Rachel snorted. "Or anything they can pry up with a crowbar."

"Don't be surprised if Tatiana comes knocking," Nessa added. "She spoils Zan rotten, but she doesn't cook. I bet you could trade her, though, if you run low on makeup. She makes the best shit."

Now that her head wasn't so foggy, the names were easier to remember. Tatiana was the one Rachel had mentioned the first day, the one who made soap and cosmetics. "I don't mind cooking for anyone who needs it."

Lex eyed her appraisingly. "Okay, then. I'll bite. Tomorrow night. We just got in a shipment of yellow squash." She leaned closer. "If you can figure out a way to get Dallas to actually eat it, you're in charge of the kitchens."

Lili couldn't hold back a bittersweet smile. "I learned

beyond innocence

how to cook by feeding toddlers and children. I can hide
vegetables in anything."

"Okay." Lex patted her knee before rising. "See you
then."

She strolled off without another word, leaving Lili to
look helplessly at Rachel. "Does that mean I have a job?"
The tiny blonde laughed. "Lex isn't much for cere-
mony."

"Or domestic bliss." Nessa propped her heeled boots
up on the low table. "Just the usual kind of bliss. The kind
Jared totally wants from you, even if he's playing it cool."

A week ago, the words would have sent her into a
panic. Now, they were unsettling. Terrifying and wonderful, and she didn't know which possibility was worse—that
he might want nothing beyond friendship, or that Nessa
could be right.

Trix elbowed Nessa lightly in the side. "Come on,
leave her alone."

"What? She should know." But Nessa grinned and
waved a hand. "But don't listen to me. I'm just jealous.
Jared still thinks I'm twelve or something, like every other
man in this sector worth climbing on."

"So find one who hasn't been here for years," Rachel
suggested. "Hawk's still available."

Nessa scoffed. "You only think that because you're too
busy being deliriously in love to notice. Hawk's *so* not
available. Ask Trix."

"Hawk's been preoccupied," was all the redhead would
say.

"He's got a crush," Nessa clarified, "and not on me. So
I'm going to live vicariously until someone promising
climbs behind those steel bars."

The reminder swung Lili's gaze toward the cage.
There were two men in it now, both strangers to her, slamming their fists into one another with the sort of gleeful
violence that still provoked a shiver of fear.

Rachel must have caught it, because she laid a comforting hand on Lili's shoulder. "I know it seems excessive, but there's no avoiding fights. The cage is how Dallas keeps things clean."

"That's clean?" As soon as the words escaped, Lili regretted them. She sounded sheltered and foolish, as if she hadn't lived her whole life with men capable of doing so much worse. But in Sector Five, cruelty and violence filled the dark corners and shadows. It didn't play out under harsh spotlights with everyone watching.

Maybe that was Rachel's point.

"Cleaner than where we're from," Trix added quietly, her soft voice barely carrying over the raucous din in the warehouse.

She might as well have screamed, because one word echoed loudly in Lili's ears. *We*, a word that granted Lili a solidarity she could never deserve. It felt so fragile, a truce so tentative, Lili was almost afraid to reply, to risk shattering it by saying the wrong thing. "It's more honest, I suppose."

"And potentially lucrative." Rachel ran her fingers through her hair, ruffling the shoulder-length strands. "If you know who to lay your money on."

"Always bet on Six," Nessa advised. "The odds against her are crazy, because these idiots still think she's on a lucky streak. She'll make you rich."

Lili's world tilted oddly, then settled while her mind continued to spin. Every time she was convinced she'd mapped out the boundaries of what her new life could be, an offhand comment shoved them outward again. Women could distill liquor and brew beer. Women could run businesses and have trades. Women could fight for money.

She didn't know if she wanted to do any of those things...

But now she knew she *could*.

7

"SO HOW LONG have you been spying for Dallas?"
Cruz's casual words startled Jared enough to
throw him off balance. He almost missed blocking the
man's next blow, and wood scraped over wood as their
staffs collided.

Jared spun around and tried to recover his composure.
As tactics went, this one was murderously lethal—throw
out something shocking, as boldly as possible, then take
advantage of your opponent's distraction to strike your
killing blow.

"You're a good soldier," he murmured, tightening his
fingers around his weapon. The staff was solid red oak—
deadly and perfectly balanced. "I bet you're an even better
interrogator."

"Not really." Cruz planted his staff on the floor and
met Jared's gaze squarely. "My psych evaluations were

consistently disappointing. I've always been burdened with an overabundance of empathy. The Base has plenty of soldiers not operating with that particular handicap."

"I'll keep that in mind." Wiping his face with his arm did fuck-all to clear Jared's vision, because every inch of his bare skin was dripping with sweat. He could make it through a solid hour of forms, no problem, but sparring with Cruz was a far more intense workout. "What gave me away?"

"Nothing obvious." Cruz shrugged one big shoulder. "I doubt anyone else will notice. But I know a lot of people inside Eden, so I hear the gossip. And I watch you."

"Good to know." He made a rush, swinging one end of his staff up toward Cruz's unprotected side. Cruz pivoted smoothly, his block effortless, his movements lazy as he flipped into a counterattack that pushed Jared back.

His next words were just as casual, just as easy. "I haven't talked to Dallas about it. I figured if he wanted me to know, he'd have told me. Unless something was stopping him."

"Not letting it go? Fine." Jared tossed his staff aside with a sigh, and it clattered to the floor. "Ace can't find out. That needs to be a promise."

Cruz hesitated only a moment before nodding. "The fewer who know, the safer you are. But *I* need to know. If something goes wrong, I'm the one most likely to be able to get you out."

"Bren's on it."

"Bren doesn't have my connections."

"Really, now?" So, quiet Cruz was the one with the friends in high places. "I'm impressed."

"I can't use them for information, not the kind Dallas needs. But if you get in trouble..." Cruz's expression stayed serious. "Don't underestimate how far I'll go to protect Ace's heart."

Not just a promise, but a warning. "You took the

words right out of my mouth. Which is why you need to stay the fuck out of it."

"I'm not going to trip you up at fancy parties—or your new club. But you need to check in with us regularly." Cruz swept up Jared's abandoned staff and tossed it to him. "And I need to make sure you can kill a man with whatever's handy."

"Your newest project, huh?"

"I don't want to get too soft living in all that O'Kane luxury."

It wasn't the high living on Dallas's compound that was bringing out all of Cruz's latent protective instincts— and that was exactly what this was, no matter how he tried to spin it. No, it was all that time he'd spent curled up between Ace and Rachel.

Caring. Once you let go and let yourself do it, it got to be a habit.

Jared kept his mouth shut for a few minutes, focusing instead on the careful coordination of his breathing and his muscles and the weapon in his hands, all moving in concert. But the words spilled forth anyway.

"It's not so different," he panted. "In my bedroom, or in a bar. Half the time, all I do is wait for them to say things they already want to say." That much he under-stood now—the compulsion born of secrecy, how silence was its own sort of prison. The relief that came with being able to tell someone, anyone, all those things you were supposed to keep locked up.

"People want to be heard." Cruz wasn't as breathless, but he wasn't moving so smoothly now, either. He blocked Jared's advance only inches from his ribs and broke away to regain space to maneuver. "The bar's a good idea. Eden's elite are getting bored and reckless."

Bored was one of Jared's longstanding clients tripling her number of monthly visits. *Reckless* was the time she brought two friends with her, both the wives of powerful, devout men. Of true believers.

Bored and reckless. Separately, they made people dangerous. But together? *Bored* and *reckless* had toppled empires.

Their staffs cracked together again, and this time Cruz held, his muscles flexing as he eyed Jared. "Watch out for the Special Tasks soldiers. They might not be under the Council's direct control anymore."

"Best news I've had all week." He shoved—hard—and it still barely put Cruz off balance.

The man stepped back instead of stumbling, and shook his head. "That doesn't mean they're on *your* side."

Jared would manage, as long as those Council assholes couldn't depend on them to be their attack dogs, either. "You're cute when you worry."

Cruz grinned. "Let's see if you still think that in an hour. Warm-up's over. Time to see what you're made of."

His humor faded. "Wait, what?"

Instead of answering, Cruz swept his staff toward Jared's lower legs. No time to block, so he jumped the sweep and lashed out quickly, before Cruz had time to finish his spin. His staff struck the man's ribs with enough force to rattle his arms, even though he held back on the blow.

Cruz grunted. "Goddamn, you're fast."

"As fast as I have to be." He spun the staff to his left and right as he backed away. "I think that's called surviving. I know how to do it."

"That's what I like to hear." Cruz's smile returned, wider this time. "Hit me again."

Jasper McCray was a second-in-command worthy of the title.

beyond innocence

Five years married to Logan had taught her all the ways a weak man propped up his power with symbols and demonstrations. Jasper's authority was quieter, but a thousand times more real. Lili saw it as they skirted the edges of the marketplace, watched it drift out in ripples as the people of Sector Four shrank away with wary expressions or drew closer with respect shining in their eyes.

Maybe he wasn't as intimidating a presence as Dallas O'Kane, but he still commanded more obedience than Lili's husband *or* father could have dreamed of—and he didn't seem the least bit interested in abusing it.

Not that he shrank away from using it. He led her down a narrow street, close enough to Eden's walls that everything stood in shadows even this early in the afternoon. He didn't knock when they reached the building at the end, just pushed open the door as if there was no place in this sector he didn't have every right to stroll into.

Lili wished desperately she shared his confidence. But *this* door belonged to Jared.

"Should be upstairs." The lower level of the building looked like a warehouse—except for the wide hallway encasing a polished wood staircase. Jasper climbed the stairs two at a time, barely pausing to knock as he shouldered through the door at the top. "Anybody home?"

No one answered, but the crash of wood crashing against wood grew louder as Lili stepped into an entryway so elegant, it felt like stepping into another world. Everything *gleamed*, clean and glossy and so, so expensive...

Then Jasper shifted out of her way, and her breath caught.

Cruz and Jared were fighting, though the word seemed insufficient to describe what was happening. They were dancing, flowing gracefully through attack and defense at such a terrifying speed that one misstep would cause devastation.

Her heart beat faster, the same way it did when her

fingers flew over the keys when memory and instinct over-took thought. But these stakes were dizzyingly high—a mistake here meant broken bones, not a few discordant notes. Which made the thrill shivering through her just as wrong as the way her gaze couldn't stop sliding over Jared's bare, flexing torso.

They stopped, all at once, and relief and disappoint-ment vied for control of Lili's emotions. Then Jared smiled and flipped the weapon he held up onto his shoulder in one smooth motion. "Hello."

Her hands ached from clutching the basket she'd brought, but she couldn't seem to relax her fingers or re-claim the ease with which she'd chatted with him over dinner. This wasn't a safe man or a mere friend. Her skin felt too tight, and she was sure they could all hear it in her voice. "I hope I'm not intruding."

Little droplets of sweat dripped from his hair onto his bare shoulders as he shook his head. "No, we were just fin-ishing up."

Cruz was watching her closely, a faint smile curving his lips. Lili stiffened her spine and reached for her icy composure—but even that melted a little as that droplet skated down Jared's chest, daring her gaze to follow.

She focused stubbornly on his face. "I brought some food. I can leave it, if you'd like..."

Jasper rubbed at his jaw. "Cruz, if you have time, I could use your help. We've got a property dispute just over the line in Three, and I'm mediating. Dallas figures the more muscle I bring with me, the less likely they'll be to argue with my decision."

Lili couldn't imagine *anyone* arguing with Jasper, but Cruz only nodded, set his staff against the wall, and re-trieved his shirt. "You'll escort Lili home when she's ready, Jared?"

"I can find my own way—"

Cruz cut her off with a shake of his head. "You're Rachel's friend," he rumbled. "Jared can explain what that means."

"On the walk home," Jared promised.

Cruz patted her shoulder as he eased past. In another moment, he and Jasper were both gone, leaving her standing awkwardly in Jared's immaculate entryway, trying not to stare at his immaculate body.

"I didn't know they were going to drop me on you," she said apologetically.

"You did me a favor." He swept up his own shirt and pulled it over his head. The thin white fabric dampened and clung to his body as he gathered the staffs and stowed them in a tall cabinet at the back of the room. "But you didn't have to bring anything."

"There were leftovers," she said, unable to stop staring at his back and shoulders. The shirt almost made it worse—it should be safe to look at him now, but one meager layer of cotton couldn't hide his strength.

He turned back to her, and she lifted the basket to cover the fact that she'd been staring. "Squash ravioli with goat cheese. Lex challenged me to turn the squash into something Dallas would eat."

"And did he?"

Lili found herself smiling. "Three servings."

"Congratulations." He lifted the basket, his fingers sliding over hers, and the tightness in her body expanded into a low ache. "Would you like a drink?"

One drink might help steady her nerves without compromising her judgment. "Yes, thank you."

He carried the basket into the kitchen, but unpacked its contents into the refrigerator instead of laying them out. Then he pulled a sleek black bottle from a shelf under the cabinet. "Wine?"

She hadn't seen a bottle of wine since she'd arrived in Sector Four, but nothing about this situation reminded her of her past life. Numbness was a distant memory. She was *alive*, so sensitive that the slightest shift of her dress over her skin made her shiver with each indrawn breath.

Just from *looking* at him. If he touched her again, she'd probably break apart. No one could survive so much heat after a lifetime of ice.

"Lili?" His voice had gone low, and it shivered up her spine.

"Wine," she said, too breathlessly. "Wine would be nice, thank you."

He uncorked the bottle with smooth, practiced movements and retrieved two glasses. "So. Is this a social call, or another demonstration of gratitude?"

It was a mistake, that's what it was. She'd been so flushed with success, giddy at the realization that the cost of her continued safety would never be more than a few hours a day in the kitchen. A feeling of dread she'd been living with so long it had become a part of her had vanished...

And she'd wanted to tell him. She still did, and the intensity of that need terrified her. "I am grateful, but not for the piano. You made me believe my skills might be worth something."

A slow smile curved his lips as he poured the deep red wine. "Good."

Her focus narrowed to his mouth. His lips. And, for the first time in over five years, she wondered what it would be like to kiss someone.

Bliss, wasn't that what Nessa had said? It seemed like childish fantasy to imagine that simple contact could produce such intense feelings—or it would have, if his smile alone couldn't make her flush all over.

She was staring at him. *Gawking.* She lifted her gaze back to his eyes, but his expression hadn't changed at all, as if he hadn't noticed her lapse. "I'm sorry," she said anyway, wrapping her arms around her body. "Some days are more overwhelming than others."

"That's understandable." He rounded the counter and offered her a glass. This time, his fingers didn't touch hers, which should have triggered relief, not a stab of frustration. "But they're normal, the things you feel."

"Are they?" She kept one arm wrapped around her middle, bracing the other to keep her glass steady. Without the counter between them, she wasn't sure what she wanted more—the safety of distance, or the indulgence of pressing close and letting *him* hold her steady.

"Very. Sex is one of the strongest drives we possess."

She sipped her wine to buy time, and was unsurprised to find it exceptional. Everything about this place catered to the tastes of the women who paid him to sate that particular drive. Strong, indeed.

It helped. Oh, it didn't banish the flutters, but she managed a shaky smile. "You're probably right. I suppose the O'Kane compound is a bit like being thrown into the deep end."

He didn't say anything, just *watched* her for so long that the intensity would have terrified her if being the focus of his attention wasn't thrilling in a different way. Finally, he sighed. "I don't know what to do with you, Lili Fleming."

Her heart lurched, and the words that spilled out were reckless—the most unguarded of her life. "What do you want to do with me?"

Again, the hesitation. "There are ways I could help you," he admitted, rubbing his thumb over the bowl of his glass. "Ordinarily, I would have already offered. But somehow it seems complicated now."

She watched his thumb make another slow sweep and couldn't *not* imagine it smoothing over her skin. That was what he was talking about—he *had* to be. Touching her. Showing her the things her body wanted, even as her mind shrank away.

kit rocha

"That's not why—" Her voice cracked, and she took a long sip of wine and wished it *was* whiskey. "I'm not ask-ing you for that. I don't know if I—if I could..." God, she couldn't even *say* it, her tongue tangling around the mild-est of euphemisms.

"I know you're not asking." He shrugged. "I guess that's what makes it complicated."

Because trades were simple. They never left you vul-nerable. And he hadn't really answered her question—he was so deft that she hadn't noticed. "What do you want to do?" she repeated softly.

Jared held her riveted, so completely that she barely noticed when he moved. She couldn't look away, even when he took the glass from her hand. Even when he laid his hands on her face, his fingers curled around her neck to hold her, and lowered his mouth to hers.

She'd imagined kissing. Mouths touching, lips brush-ing.

She'd imagined wrong, because Jared's tongue was the first thing she felt, hot and shocking, as if he knew it would make her gasp. Because when she did, he went deeper, his tongue finding hers.

It was too much. Too fast, too intoxicating. Her entire body throbbed along with her racing pulse, and her knees felt unsteady. She clutched for the only steady thing she could find, grasping his upper arms to keep from melting through the floor.

Then his hands tightened, tilting her head back, urg-ing her mouth open. His tongue swept over hers again, rough and rasping, and every tiny shiver of sensation built into an ache that settled between her legs. Not just an ache, a *need*, and she whimpered into his mouth.

Jared broke the kiss with a shudder and smoothed his thumb over her tingling lower lip. "See?" he whispered. "Complicated."

She closed her eyes and tried to catch her breath. "Not

sure that helped," she said, an attempt to turn it into a joke. It had to be, or fear and longing would crash together and vaporize her. "I'm feeling all sorts of things now."

"It doesn't have to stop." His hands trembled on her face. "But that's your choice to make."

An impossible choice—need or fear, pleasure or peace. And all of it shrouded in mystery, because she couldn't reconcile the O'Kanes' wild glee with her mother's whispered warnings to lie still so it would be over faster.

"I don't know." She forced herself to look at him, to meet his patient, waiting eyes. "I don't know *anything*. How can I make a choice when I don't understand what you're offering?"

"You're right." He smiled again and brushed her hair back from her forehead with a careful, gentle touch. "It's not exactly fair, is it?"

She was still clinging to him. Slowly, shyly, she eased her grip until she was touching, instead. His arms were solid, muscle flexing as she rubbed her thumb against his sleeve and wondered if he felt the same spark of sensation. "When I was on the drugs, everything seemed so clear. I thought they were all pretending. I didn't believe in pleasure."

"And now?"

Now it would be like not believing in water while she was standing outside in the rain. This wasn't some gentle mist, either. She was caught up in a storm, and she'd seen what heavy rain could do to the desert. The clay couldn't absorb the water, and the riverbeds couldn't contain it.

She wasn't made for pleasure. Too much would sweep her away. "Now I'm scared."

Instead of being surprised or offended, he nodded. "I'd never intentionally do anything to hurt you, but that's all I can promise. You should probably think about that."

It was honesty, and he deserved the same in return.

"I don't know if I'll stop being scared. Logan—my husband—" She squeezed her eyes shut and forced out the words that still felt like lies sometimes, because Logan had been quick to remind her that most women suffered so much worse. "He hurt me."

Jared's arms went rigid beneath her hands.

"Not in big ways," she clarified, the tightness in her chest making the confession come fast and unfiltered. "He didn't try to—he didn't want me like that. But he could be cruel. And I—I'm sorry. You don't want to hear this."

His only answer was to draw her into an embrace—slow, light, so easy that she could break away if she wanted.

Part of her wanted. But more of her wanted *him*.

Being this close to him was terrifying—and perfect. The lingering echoes of Logan vanished in the first moment, because he'd never touched her like this. Patient, gentle, offering strength without reminding her that strength was a threat.

Her heels made her tall enough to lay her cheek on his shoulder. She wasn't quite brave enough to bury her face against his neck, but she wrapped her arms around his back, digging her fingers into those beautiful muscles she'd been staring at earlier.

He was holding her, their bodies pressed together. Arousal hummed beneath her skin, and the world continued to spin.

"Lili." Just her name, two tiny syllables, but they rumbled out of his chest and ricocheted through her.

She kept her eyes closed. "I don't want you to help me out of pity. I don't want you to *touch* me out of pity."

"I'm not. I wouldn't. But I need—" He bit off the words.

"What?" Somehow, she found the courage to lift her head and open her eyes. "What do you need?"

He stared down at her. "To be honest with you. This is a bad time to get involved with me. I can't tell you why, but I need to know you believe it."

It could have felt like a brush-off, but it didn't. They were both too accustomed to navigating the expectations of others to be anything but up front about their boundaries and complications.

She couldn't give him easy. He couldn't promise her forever.

She reached up to touch his face, echoing his earlier gesture by pressing her thumb lightly to his lower lip. "I'm not looking for another keeper. Just...a friend. One who understands this world."

His eyes were dark. Burning. "I can give you that."

The words moved his lips, soft and teasing. Shivering, she rubbed her thumb slowly back and forth. "What can I give you?"

His breath blew across her skin, hot and faster now. He slipped his hand into her hair and gently tilted her head back, baring her throat.

"Jared?"

"Shh." He had leaned in, and the quiet exhalation skated over her throat—raising goose bumps on her arms, tightening her nipples to hard, aching points. Then his mouth, hot and open, grazed the base of her neck where it met her shoulder.

She dragged in a sharp breath and sank her fingers into *his* hair. It was soft and silky as she urged him closer, holding his lips to her skin even though it was already too much.

"No one's ever touched you like this," he said quietly. "With care. To bring pleasure, not fear."

"No one." She tilted her head back into his hand, trusting him to hold her.

"Feel it." His teeth scraped her flesh. "That's what you can give me."

No small request. She was already dizzy, drunk. She

could knock back shot after shot of liquor without blinking, but she had no tolerance built up for this. A few glancing kisses had swept her feet out from under her. She didn't know how much more she could take.

But maybe he did.

She flexed her fingers on his shoulders, reassuring herself. It was okay if her knees wobbled, as long as he was there to hold her up. "All right."

But he straightened, and she shivered at the loss of his heat. "When you're ready."

Lili leaned back against the counter to steady herself. "I'm not sure it's possible to be ready for you."

"Yes, it is." He smiled, just as slowly and easily as before, but there was an undeniable heat there now. "But that's quite the compliment. I'll take it."

She wrinkled her nose, hoping it counteracted the hopeless flush in her cheeks at least a little. "Does this mean I can invite you to go somewhere with me?"

"If you'd like." He reached around her, lifted her glass from the counter, and pressed it into her hand.

"There's a concert in Sector Three. Six's friend is playing. I was thinking..." She shrugged and sipped her wine. "It's not the music I'm used to, but new experiences are good."

"I'd be happy to go with you, Lili."

She believed him, which was the most unbelievable part yet.

8

"Well, it's official." Jared wiped his dusty hands on his pants, which probably cost more than all the tattered and busted furniture the previous owners had left behind. "I've bought a dump."

Not that that was entirely news. He'd been here before, when it was still operational, and it hadn't been much cleaner then. That was part of its branding, you could say—a chance for Eden's not-so-bold residents to feel like they were taking a walk on the wild side, without ever leaving the relative safety of the city walls.

Gia made a face and nudged a busted stool with the toe of one expensive shoe. "It needs work. Or a match and some gasoline."

"How *much* work is the question." He righted a table and grimaced when it left his hands coated with another layer of grime. "Do I pander to the low-rent fantasy or take it in the opposite direction? Give it a coat of naughty gloss and glamour?"

"Why choose?" Gia lifted her dress out of the dust as she stepped over a broken chair. "Pander, darling. Pander to all their ridiculous fantasies. Give them fake grime over luxurious gloss, and they'll pay double."

"A bit of Sector Four, huh?" It was dangerous, a little too much like hiding in plain sight, though Gia had no way of knowing that. Of course, the sheer audacity of it had the potential to push it over the line from foolhardy to brilliant.

After all, who would guess that the Eden bar owner pretending to be an O'Kane wasn't pretending at all?

'You're running a speakeasy," she replied with a wicked smile. "No need to be subtle. Subtlety is wasted on the ones who will make you rich."

"Truer words." Jared stepped into the main room. The only light shone, feeble and dim, from windows set high in the wall, windows that opened up above ground, at street level. "I need to talk to you."

"Of course." Gia followed him, picking her way meticulously through the trash on the floor. "What's on your mind?"

He couldn't tell her everything, but he could share enough of the truth that mattered. "Dylan thinks I'm making a mistake with this place."

"Doc?" Gia stopped next to him and slipped her hand through his arm. "Of course he does. Eden broke him. You can see it in his eyes."

"That goes without saying, but it's beside the point." He covered her hand with his, enjoying the gentle, capable strength in her fingers. A comforting touch, familiar and soothing. "Is he right? Does this damn place get us all, one way or another?"

"Only if you believe in it. Eladio tried to teach us better." She squeezed his arm. "It's a risk. Flouting the law always is. But we know too many secrets, you and I. Be-tween us, we could humiliate half the Council and discredit a third more."

"I'm not sure if I should be reassured or terrified."

"Reassured, love. If the Council gives you trouble, I can let the good people of Eden know which of their leaders pay me exorbitant sums for the privilege of licking my toes."

It startled a laugh out of him—not because he thought she was joking, but because he knew she wasn't. "You know what? I *do* feel better now."

"That's the spirit. And, Jared?"

"Yeah?"

"If there's some other reason Doc is worried, you don't have to tell me. It doesn't matter. If you need help, you'll have it, no questions asked."

It was the kind of moment where words weren't enough, so he leaned over and kissed the top of her head.

Gia patted his hand and surveyed the room. "You need a piano in here, now that you have a sweet little blonde to play it."

Oh *Christ.* "Ace has a big mouth," he muttered.

"That's hardly news, though it's amazing he still has time to make such liberal use of it." Gia quirked a perfectly groomed eyebrow. "Was he exaggerating?"

"Have you met him?" Jared hedged. A cleaned-up ver-sion of a sector dump wouldn't work for Lili. The dark leather, worn fabrics, and shiny silver looked out of place on her. No, everything would have to be opulent, the kind of grand, extravagant luxury that had pervaded the un-derground clubs and lounges of the early twentieth century. Polished wood, lustrous satin, low lighting. Tux-edos and heels, cigars and flowers pinned into meticulously curled hair.

And Lili—brilliant, glowing—in the middle of it all.

Gia released his arm with a soft laugh. "Oh, Jared.

None of us ever could resist a wide-eyed blonde."
He flashed her a sharp look and surveyed the room.
"Maybe I'll shine this place up and pitch it to Scarlet. I
could use a good torch singer."
"A better gamble than Tchaikovsky," Gia conceded.
"And maybe I'll borrow your Lili for a few of *my* parties."
She'd faint, love. The words died, unspoken, on the tip
of his tongue. Maybe she wouldn't—and wasn't that a far
more dangerous thought? He'd kissed her, after all. She
hadn't kissed him back, but she hadn't frozen up or shrank
back in terror, either.

The memory tightened in the pit of his stomach. He
could imagine all kinds of things now that had eluded him
before—the way her breathing would falter as he un-
dressed her, the soft noises she would make, growing
louder as her pleasure deepened. The color of her eyes,
blue darkened to midnight in the aftermath of too many
orgasms to count.

Gia was watching him with a tiny smile, so he shook
his head. "You're far too entertained by this, you know
that?"

"Of course. I know my own vices. It's allowed, you
know—to have a vice or two just for yourself."

"Sure." If you weren't on a mission. If your time was
your own.

He'd almost told Lili, that was the craziest part. For
some reason, standing there in his kitchen with her kiss
lingering on his lips, he'd resented the wall that his secret
had put between them. Only thoughts of her safety had
kept the words from pouring out, especially after she'd
made herself so vulnerable by sharing secrets of her own.

Gia's smile faded as she lifted a hand to his cheek.
"Oh, Jared. I shouldn't have teased. Ace made it seem..."
She shook her head. "It doesn't matter. I know his flaws in
that regard. I'm sorry."

"Oh Jesus, Gia. I'm not that delicate, am I?"

"Don't make me answer that." She patted his face gently and let her hand fall away. "I'll leave your girl alone."

"She's not—" But the denial would only make things worse. "Thank you."

"Mmm." Gia turned in a circle, her gaze sweeping the room. "Are you looking for investors?"

"Well, that depends."

"On?"

"Theme." He winked at her. "If I go grungy, I can pick up more furniture from the alley out back. But if I go for the glamour..."

"It fits," she said slowly. "I mean, that's what they want. The luxury. Mine get all the thrill they need crossing into the sectors." She walked to the bar and tapped a fingernail on the scarred surface. "You won't need grime, I suppose, when they're drinking under the MPs' noses."

Both ideas had merit, but the decision wasn't his alone to make. "I'll think about it."

"Let me know." Gia glanced up toward the small windows. "What do you think? Since I'm already here, should I scandalize a few ladies by indulging myself with a visit to the spa?"

They'd be talking for weeks, utterly horrified by the fact that Gia had invaded their territory instead of staying out in the sectors, where they could conveniently pretend she didn't exist. "I have a better idea," he said, throwing his arm around her shoulders. "Let's both go."

She laughed. "Oh, the poor little darlings. Do they cluck at me or coo at you? Should we wager?"

"A bottle of O'Kane's finest," he agreed. Afterwards, they could share it, and he might just find the words to explain how Miss Lili Fleming had managed to get under his skin.

Rachel hadn't been lying about Lili's ring. The tight roll of bills she presented to Lili seemed just shy of ridiculous, even after Lili had tucked most of it into the back of her drawer for safekeeping.

What was left was enough to buy her a new wardrobe for a new persona—

No, not for a persona, she corrected herself as she browsed a rack of pre-Flare dresses. This wardrobe wouldn't belong to a perfect wife from Sector Five *or* a fearless O'Kane. It would belong to Lili, a woman caught between worlds—and unashamed of it.

Trix was staring at her, her head tilted to one side and her nose wrinkled in an expression of deep concentration. "No, none of this is right."

Lili ran her fingers over the lacy skirt of the final dress in the row and shook her head. "It doesn't feel like me. But nothing ever has."

"You need something..." Trix turned and flipped quickly through another crowded rack before emerging with a flowing satin blouse. "Yeah, something like this."

"Oh, that's nice." Rachel grinned. "Very classic."

It was simpler than the clothing she'd owned in Five. Not *plainer*, just cleaner, with none of the ruffles and bows that had always made her feel wrapped up like a gift no one wanted. "Is there a skirt that matches?" she asked, moving to stand next to Trix. Most of the clothing on this rack wasn't just pre-Flare, it was *vintage*, undoubtedly scavenged from dozens of wealthy closets.

"No skirt." But Trix was laughing with delight as she pulled another hanger from the rack. "*These*."

It was a pair of high-waisted pants, wide and fluttery at the bottom, but fitted at the top. She'd never seen anything quite like them, but the elegant lines appealed to her almost as much as imagining her father's expression if she'd dared to show up to dinner in *pants*.

beyond innocence

The tiny shop didn't have a changing room, just a corner blocked off from the rest of the store by a curtain rattling on wooden rings. Lili retreated behind it, doing her best to ignore the fact that a good two inches of daylight stood between the curtain and the edges of the wall. Anyone could peek in on her. But no one would, not with Rachel and Trix out there flashing their O'Kane tattoos.

It was a rather nice way to shop, all in all.

The corner was too small for a mirror, but the shop owner had affixed one just outside the curtain. It was stained around the edges and broken in one corner, but tall enough for Lili to examine her reflection with growing wonder.

For the first time in a long time, the person staring back at her wasn't a stranger. Oh, she wasn't entirely familiar, either. Her dresses had always made her feel like a doll—a shadow of a girl, too insubstantial to support the yards of lace and flounce—but she'd been used to that.

Now all of the frippery had been cut away, leaving sleek lines and gentle curves, the body she would have grown into sooner without the constant pressure to starve herself.

Not a little girl. Not a doll. She was looking at a woman.

"Oh man, Trix. You were right. Old-school Hollywood, all the way." Rachel smoothed one sleeve and rearranged a curl where it fell across Lili's shoulder. "Girl, you look *good*."

Lili watched the color flood her cheeks this time, but it wasn't the pink that distracted her. It was her own eyes—bright and excited in a way she'd never seen. Makeup could fake a lot of things, but not this. Not life.

She'd stand out. In a crowd of leather and denim, it would be impossible to hide. But the thought didn't leave her queasy the way it should have.

"I like it," she said quietly, meeting Rachel's gaze in the mirror. "I don't know if it's me, exactly, but I want it to be."

"That's all it takes, isn't it?"

Lili traced a hand over her hip and found herself smiling. "Do you think we can find a dress like this for the concert? Jared's coming with me."

"Here we go." Trix reappeared with a jewel-toned dress of rich, deep blue. She held it up to the front of Lili's body and bit her lip. "It'll have to be taken in at the waist, but I can manage that. This is it, though. Anything else you want will have to be made."

The dress was modest enough in the front, though it would hug her breasts and skim her body so closely that maybe *modest* wasn't the right word. And then there was the back, which was cut so low most of her spine would be visible.

She loved it. "Can I pull it off?"

Rachel laughed. "Ace'll spend the whole night staring at your back—he can't resist a blank canvas—but you will look *fabulous*."

Ace's gaze wasn't the one she wanted to attract. It was too easy to imagine Jared's hand sliding over the skin left so brazenly bare, or—God, his mouth—

The memory did odd things to her body. It was awake now, starving, and she couldn't control her own responses. Even now, the silky slide of satin over her skin felt lush, sensual, as if the realization of one kind of pleasure had awakened an unknown world of sensation.

It was tempting to turn her back on it, to find a way to retreat to safety, to caution, if not numbness. But there were no half-measures in this, no baby steps.

She turned from the mirror with the dress clutched to her body and made her choice. "What do I wear with it?"

"Strappy heels and a smile," Trix teased.

And nothing else, was the unspoken message, scandalous enough to shock a laugh out of her. "I don't know if I can pull *that* off."

"You made it out of Sector Five." Trix folded the dress over her arm and nodded firmly. "Trust me, that means you can do anything."

She didn't remember coming to Sector Four. Everything about the last few days of her life in Five was blurred by a layer of detached terror, her defense against Logan's rage as it seeped closer and closer to the surface. And then grief, the night he came home and told her that the future of the Fleming family now rested in her hands.

To him, it had been that simple. Trimming inconvenient branches from the Fleming family tree. He'd dug bruises into her cheeks as he held her face and whispered the words against her ear, the last thing she remembered clearly.

Now there's no one left to distract you from your duty. We'll start tonight.

He'd left a guard to watch her while he went to face Dallas O'Kane, and he hadn't come back, because Trix's lover had killed him.

Someday, Lili would have to thank Finn for that.

"We all got out of Sector Five," she replied, shaking free of the memory. Pain, at least, was a familiar emotion now. She knew it, how to feel it and how to contain it. "And I'm glad I came here."

For a moment, Trix just stared at her, a look of understanding shadowing her eyes. Then she jerked her head toward the other side of the cramped shop. "Come on. Shoes."

The jumble of footwear was chaotic. Boots, heels, running shoes with mismatched laces, all in a dizzying array of colors and styles. So many *options*, and she wondered if the other people browsing the selection even realized how odd it was to be faced with choices every time you turned around.

It was thrilling but intimidating. Lili was grateful for Rachel's unflagging enthusiasm and Trix's instincts as she went straight for a pair of low velvet heels with T-straps. "Thank you both so much for coming with me. I would have been lost on my own."

"Everyone needs help sometimes," Rachel said.

It was as perfect an opening as she would ever get. Lili ran her finger over the strap on a pair of totally impractical sandals and gathered her growing courage. "I feel like I need a lot of it right now. I don't know how to do any of this. How to..." Did they even use the word here? It felt antiquated and silly, but it was the only one she knew. "How to date."

The two women seemed to consider that, and Rachel finally shrugged. "I'm not sure we know, either. I mean, it's a word with expectations, right? Those tend to get turned upside down around here."

"I've noticed." She glanced at Trix again, because even though they'd lived different lives in Sector Five, they came from the same place. "I thought I knew how the world worked. But now I think my expectations are broken."

"The world," Trix declared, "is a complex thing. But dating doesn't have to be. He likes you, you like him. So you hang out, maybe get a little naked. Get to know each other. Simple. People have been doing it forever."

People had. Jared had. But *she* hadn't. "I don't..." She wet her lips and looked down, suffering the hot sting of true embarrassment. "I've never gotten naked."

But Trix only sighed in relief. "That's the best news I've heard all week."

Startled, Lili glanced up. The look in Trix's eyes drove her point home well enough—better to be left neglected than to endure Logan Beckett's touch. "I wasn't one of my husband's vices," she agreed softly. "He had too many others, I suppose, to have room for me."

Rachel worried her bottom lip with her teeth. "Are you nervous about what Jared will think?"

"He must already know. I don't think it bothers him, but…" It bothered *her* to be so hopelessly out of her depth when Jared could read her secrets in every tensing muscle and indrawn breath.

Rachel and Trix waited.

She was going to have to say it. They were alone in their corner of the store, but she still lowered her voice. "All my mother told me is that it's terrible and over faster if I don't move. I don't know what to do."

They stood there, their anticipation melting into stunned silence. It seemed to go on forever, and Lili was beginning to wish she hadn't said anything when they stepped toward her in unison.

"Oh, God. Okay." Trix laid a hand on her shoulder. "Just—first things first. That's complete bullshit. Get it out of your head."

Trix came from the same darkness that had almost smothered Lili. She came from *worse*, because at least Lili had been insulated by her name and her station, her cage gilded from the day she was born.

There'd been no softness and luxury for Trix. No easy numbness to protect her. And there was no deception in her now, just firm, commanding truth.

She said it was bullshit, and Lili believed her. She swallowed past the lump in her throat and nodded jerkily. "Okay."

"All right." Trix gripped Lili's other shoulder and turned her slightly, so they were facing one another. "Now, Jared knows enough for the both of you—maybe enough for *all* of us—so if you trust him, he can show you. Right?"

"I trust him." To take care of her needs, at least. But trusting him to take care of his own was trickier. She, of all people, knew how habit-forming a lifetime of catering to others could be. "I just want to make him happy, too." "Well..." Rachel folded her hands together and rocked back on her heels. "If it's technique you're after, there are plenty of opportunities to...observe."

Opportunities Lili had been avoiding because of her confusion. She'd been struggling to find her footing, to reconcile the world she knew with the one she'd stumbled into. Her ironclad assumptions had already been cracking the night she'd met Jared. Now, all of her old understanding was gone, the last shards swept away by the firmness of Trix's words.

The next party she attended might make her every bit as uncomfortable, but in a very different way. A very *educational* way.

She nodded again. The ground solidified beneath her feet, and she felt steady inside her own skin. "Thank you. Thank you so much."

"Any time." Trix flashed her a grin, gave her a reassuring squeeze, then gathered their purchases and walked toward the clerk.

Rachel lingered. "You know, if you want advice about Jared? Ace knows him pretty well."

"They've been friends for a long time."

"And lovers."

Surprise froze Lili in place. "Oh."

"Uh-huh. Lots of personal experience." Rachel lifted one shoulder in a shrug, but her smile was soft and knowing. "Ace likes to tease me with it because he knows it's hot as hell, but there it is. No better source of information."

Hot as hell. Lili had a new appreciation for those words. She'd tasted that heat now, though her limited experience left her ill-equipped to imagine what Ace and Jared would look like with their hands sliding over each other.

Even trying to picture it left her feeling too warm. "I'll

beyond innocence

remember that." She returned Rachel's smile tentatively. "Maybe next time, I could cook for you guys, too?"

"That'd be nice." Rachel's voice was gentle, lower. Like they were both feeling too warm, and this moment wasn't as simple as an invitation to dinner.

The tension built until Lili ached with it, and she had to break away. "I'd better go make sure Trix doesn't try to pay for my things. Finn's always offering me money."

She hurried to the front of the store, not entirely sure she hadn't offered Rachel more than a simple meal—and embarrassingly intrigued by the possibilities.

111

mad

MAD HAD SEEN more of the sectors and beyond than most people knew existed. He'd visited pre-Flare cities left abandoned and gutted, every useful thing stripped away and buildings left like skeletons to decay and die alone. He'd seen miracles of human ingenuity and things that could only be the hand of a higher power—the vastness of the ocean, the beauty of the Grand Canyon.

He'd seen Scarlet a hundred times. He'd seen her laughing and angry, had seen her capacity for violence when she fought for her people, and her protectiveness in the way she handled Jade.

He'd seen so much of her, but before tonight he'd never seen her sing. And when she was singing, she was the most transcendent damn thing he'd ever laid eyes on.

It seemed like half the residents of Sectors Three *and* Four agreed with him. The crowd spilled out into the street, where speakers kept them from rioting and a makeshift bar kept them drinking, but the place closest to the stage had been reserved for the O'Kanes, giving Mad an unobstructed view of Scarlet as she cradled the microphone.

She was a rough-and-tumble woman, pierced and tattooed and often packing almost as many weapons as Mad himself. He'd expected her music to be the same—angry, sharp edges, loud and brash and unapologetically aggressive.

Not this. Not low and sweet, sliding over him like warm honey. Not so sensual his body stirred with the first notes and *throbbed* when she met his eyes from beneath her blonde bangs.

The first time, he thought it was a trick of the light. But her gaze returned, seizing his and daring him to look away.

He couldn't.

The lyrics blurred together, leaving her sultry voice and the steady, suggestive drumline. The music curled around him, tugged at him. Found an echoing darkness inside him, a pain too vast and old for anything to touch— and *stroked* it.

I understand, whispered the song, as Scarlet sang breathlessly about loss and need, a craving so deep it could swallow the world. *I know your pain. I know your heart. I know you. I see you. You are not alone.*

It was the lie behind music. You looked into it and saw what your heart desired, as if every note, every syllable, had been written just for you, instead of being the solitary work of some narcissistic creator who didn't care about the wounds on your soul.

A lie, and yet still truth. Scarlet might not give two shits about most of the people crushed in front of the stage, but—for the length of a song, a set—they felt less alone.

Believing the lie was enough. Hope healed in tiny increments, but it still healed.

Even him.

Scarlet's eyes drilled into his. Her body swayed in a hypnotic rhythm, one he'd seen before. Then, she'd had her hands on Jade's body, her hips rolling in a way that had left him uncomfortably hard. He'd blamed it on her dance partner at the time—Jade, who was made of mouthwatering curves, whose every movement was graceful to the point of absentminded seduction.

Softness, that had always been Mad's weakness. Sweet women who just needed a little tenderness to wake them up. Making them feel good made *him* feel good, and everyone walked away with fond, pleasant memories and mild feelings.

Mild wasn't always satisfying, but intensity was complicated.

Scarlet wasn't soft or sweet, and she didn't do mild. She could eye-fuck him from the stage all night, but if the two of them ever ended up locked in a room together, it wouldn't be warm honey and slow swaying.

They'd fight for the top. She'd play rough, fight hard. Fuck, she'd probably win. Not because he couldn't, but because the stakes were too damn high. It was one thing to shore up vulnerabilities that were already there, but when you *made* someone vulnerable, when you demanded their surrender—

You had to be worthy of it.

No, not just worthy. You had to be strong. Whole. You had to be unshakable, hard enough to protect them in their vulnerability, not be the one likely to shatter apart.

You had to be a fucking hero. And that was the one thing Mad had promised himself he'd never try to be again.

9

B REN AND SIX had worked miracles with Sector
Three.

Not long ago, the club had been a wasteland, just like
the rest of the sector. Its dancers had been overworked and
underpaid, and Christ only knew, but Jared had always
suspected some of them weren't there by choice at all. The
only damn thing the place had had going for it was Scarlet's music.

All that had changed. The club still looked mostly the
same, but it ran like a machine now, slick and efficient. It
was clean, well-stocked, and packed. The bartenders
worked busily, and—best of all—they still had the band.

Jared stood at the bar for their drinks, with Lili waiting for him in a darkened corner booth. The seats weren't
as nice as the ones the O'Kanes commanded, but tonight,
of all nights, he needed the distance. Too many people had

turned out for the music and the booze, and he couldn't afford to be seen as part of Dallas's inner circle.

He could barely afford for Lili to be seen with him, but he hadn't been able to resist her shy invitation—and now he was damn glad. She was dressed in head-to-toe silk that draped her body and hugged her curves, and he watched her as he headed back to the booth.

She smiled, her cheeks flushed with excitement and her eyes sparkling. It was a far cry from the last party, when only her determination not to appear weak had overcome her discomfort.

He placed one drink in front of her and slid into the booth. "So, what do you think?"

"It's amazing." She leaned into his side, her shoulder brushing his. "Scarlet's a beautiful singer. No wonder there's such a crowd."

"I had a feeling you'd enjoy it." There was raw emotion in Scarlet's performances, the kind he could never seem to work up for his perfunctory piano playing. Most of his clients couldn't tell the difference, but he knew somehow that Lili would.

"I wonder if she'd let me play with her sometime." Lili traced a fingertip around the edge of her glass. "Not like this, though, performing for so many people. I'd probably miss all the notes."

"I bet she'd love it." There was a difference between performing and doing something you adored for its own sake. Because you wanted to.

She flashed him another of those bright, joyous smiles. "Thank you for coming with me."

"It's not a favor." He found her other hand beneath the table and folded it into his. "I want to be here."

She leaned into him again and stayed this time, her body pressed all along his side. "This is the first time I've been out with the O'Kanes, you know. They're different...and they're not."

beyond innocence

That was true enough. There were parts of themselves, of their interactions, that they would only share
with one another, in private. The way the ladies liked to
tease Dallas out of his stern frowns, but never in front of
outsiders. Never in places where their defiance—as play-
ful and welcome as it was—would make him look weak,
like he couldn't keep his people in line.

Jared could even see it in Cruz. Out here, he played
the brooding dominant role to the hilt. He sat in one of the
O'Kane booths, watching Ace and Rachel as they danced,
their limbs entwined, bodies moving in perfect time with
the slow, languorous music. Every soft kiss and caress
looked like an invitation, and Cruz flashed a forbidding
glare at anyone who got too curious—or too close.

This was the game he'd play in public—hands off,
watching over them while they teased him. Waiting. And
when they went home, he'd have them both on their knees.

"It's about image," Jared murmured. "It isn't that
they're different people out here. It's that they only show
people what they know they'll understand."

"Their masks," Lili replied just as softly. "No wonder
I've been so confused. I kept trying to see through them,
kept trying to figure out what their game was. But it's not
a game at all, is it?"

"Not like you were thinking." He understood now, better than he ever could have dreamed. "It's about
responsibility. O'Kanes protect each other. And the best
way to do that, the most important way, is to protect the
gang."

"And when they're alone..." Her fingers trembled in
his. "That's who they are?"

"Yes." He watched as Ace whispered something in Rachel's ear, and she bit her lip to hold back a laugh. "That's
who they are."

Lili tilted her head to rest on his shoulder. "I don't
know if I'm jealous or terrified."

119

Ace grabbed Rachel's ass and dragged her up until she was riding his thigh, her dress hiked far enough to flash her bare hip. "Be like the rest of us," Jared advised softly. "Be both."

Lili shivered as she reached for her drink and took a bracing sip. "Is it like this for everyone?" she asked hoarsely. "Watching, I mean. Or is it just because I'm..." Raw and exposed? Or did she mean innocent? "I can tell you what—" His words died as Rachel shuddered through a moan. Her head fell back, and she made a pleading noise so unpolished and rough—so *real*—that his hand clenched around his glass.

Lili turned her face to his arm.

Not tonight. Not when she needed to see this. "Watch them, Lili."

"I can't," she protested, clinging to his hand under the table.

"Yes, you can." He squeezed her fingers. "This is what you wanted to know. It'll tell you everything."

She inhaled shakily and lifted her head, her gaze swinging directly to Rachel and Ace. Plenty of people were casting the pair covert glances as Ace licked the vulnerable arch of his lover's throat—but no one risked being caught staring, not with Cruz sprawled only a few feet away.

Ace kissed his way lower, following the loose neckline of Rachel's crimson dress. The strap fell off one shoulder, and the draping fabric slid down to catch on the tip of her breast. Ace nudged it aside, baring the luxurious glint of silver.

At first, Jared thought it was another piece of jewelry, the kind of gift Ace loved to lavish on Rachel—a delicate sterling shield, maybe, or a clamp that would heighten her sensitivity the longer she wore it. But then Ace tugged at it, twisting lightly. Rachel cried out, sharp and low, and Jared realized it was a piercing, a stylized barbell that ran horizontally through the rigid peak. Jesus Christ, no wonder Ace had been insufferably, blissfully happy. He had the perfect little submissive *and* the perfect glowering dom. Everything he'd ever wanted.

Lili was trembling now, her breaths coming quick and shallow. "I don't understand how I can be so confused and still so—" She shook her head. "My body knows things I don't."

"Yeah." Some things were instinct—survival, laughter, tears. Pleasure. "The only thing that matters is whether you *want* to know."

Blonde curls swung around her face as she nodded. "Help me understand?"

Heat prickled over his skin. He released her hand and reached for her dress instead, slowly drawing the length of satin up her leg. "Watch, sweetheart."

Ace dragged Rachel upright again, pressing her body to his. His hands guided her hips in a grinding roll in time with the music, and his lips found her ear. She shuddered again before shaking her head and taking his hands.

She pulled him back toward the booth, back toward Cruz, who was still watching them with protective heat blazing in his eyes. It didn't matter what other people saw when they looked at the three of them. Jared had been close enough to see the truth—more than anything else, Ace and Rachel belonged to Cruz. He was the one who guarded them, body and heart, who gave them the freedom to make themselves vulnerable.

Even like this. Ace hauled Rachel into his lap and guided her head toward Cruz's waiting kiss. No one else in the bar could see Ace's fingers as they crept between their bodies to settle unerringly on Rachel's nipple.

No one except Lili. "Doesn't that hurt?" she asked in a breathless whisper.

"Maybe it does." Jared's hand made contact—*finally*—with the smooth, hot skin of Lili's inner thigh. "Maybe she

kit rocha

likes it that way."

As if on cue, Rachel reached up. She covered Ace's fingers with her own and squeezed tight, forcing a rougher caress, one that left her trembling above him.

"Oh." Lili's legs came together, trapping Jared's hand—but only for a heartbeat. She gripped the back of his shirt, as if needing something to cling to, and inched her thighs apart.

"See?" He stroked her skin but didn't move any higher. Not yet. "Easy."

Ace and Cruz were kissing now, a lazy tangle of tongues while Cruz worked at Ace's fly. They'd fuck just like this, barely hidden by shadows, protected by Cruz's fierceness and their O'Kane ink.

Lili grasped her drink until her knuckles turned white, her other hand still clutching at his back. "Is that what you want to do with me?"

Jared glided his thumb a mere fraction of an inch up her thigh. "Baby steps, Lili."

Her breathing hitched. "I know you're not going to do it now. But would you *want* to?"

"Not like this. Something softer, slower." Another inch. "I'd lay you out on my bed, I think. Not yours—it would have to be mine. It wouldn't take long to figure out just where to kiss. Where to bite."

"Anywhere." Her leg trembled, and she pressed it against his to steady herself. "I don't think it matters. I feel so much."

"Shh." Too much, too fast, and she'd panic. "Watch."

Rachel was moving now, her dress spilling across Ace's legs in a token show of modesty, as if anyone could doubt what the slow roll of her hips meant. As they watched, Cruz sank his fingers into Ace's hair and hauled his head back.

They didn't have to talk, to coordinate. He and Rachel moved as one, each claiming one side of Ace's throat, and

122

Ace's groan of pleasure carried over the music, across the room.

Jared bit back a groan of his own. "What do you see when you look at them?"

The same question he'd asked her the first night, but her answer was different now. "Tenderness. Safety."

"And fucking." Jared slid his hand higher, until his fingers barely brushed her panties. "Tenderness and safety and *fucking*."

Lili's head tipped back, her throat working. "Jared—"

"They can have all three." He stilled his hand.

"Because they're O'Kanes?"

Because they had each other—but that was a complicated answer, one that hadn't yet been distilled to its essence. "Yes, because they're O'Kanes."

Her desperate grip on his shirt eased. Her fingers started to drift, up his spine and across his shoulders, before the soft tips feathered over the back of his neck, eliciting a shiver. "That's why they're all terrified of Dallas, isn't it? Because his people love him."

Wasn't that stronger than loyalty born of fear and violence? Mac Fleming's men had lived and died for him because it was required. Dallas's people did it willingly. Gladly.

"Love is strong," Jared whispered. "It can overcome anything else."

Lili traced circles on the side of his throat, echoing the way Cruz rubbed his thumb over the marks his teeth had left in Ace's skin. Jared took up the same rhythm, coaxing the damp fabric of her panties against the heated flesh beneath.

She was insanely responsive, shaking after only a few slow caresses, her breath coming quick and unsteady. Her nails pricked his skin, and she shifted her hips restlessly. Seeking.

Not yet. He pulled his hand away, and she sighed

softly at the loss even as she relaxed. "I wish I knew what to expect," she whispered, her voice edged with apology. "Maybe it wouldn't be so overwhelming."

Maybe she still expected something pleasant but manageable. Nothing like the toe-curling, muscle-clenching, earth-shattering release of a damn good orgasm. Like the kind Rachel was headed toward. She shuddered as she gripped Ace's chin, turned his head toward Jared and Lili, and put her mouth next to his ear. Too far to hear the words, but Ace groaned as his gaze locked with Jared's.

Whatever she said, it was filthy enough to turn the invitation in Ace's eyes into something deeper. Into a promise. Jared wrapped his hand in Lili's dress, drawing it higher, and leaned toward her. "What sorts of ideas did you put in Rachel's head, love?"

"I—I invited them to have dinner with us." She turned her face until her lips brushed his cheek. "I don't know if that was all I invited them to do."

"Yes, you do." He turned too, just far enough to graze her mouth with his. "Admit it, Lili. At least to yourself."

She closed her eyes, her voice dropping to a husky purr. "They'd let me watch, wouldn't they? That's why Rachel told me I could learn by observation. They'd let me watch."

Having an audience would get Rachel off, but he doubted it could put that lustful look in Ace's eyes. "I think they'd let you do more than that."

Lili's eyes popped open. She stared up at him, shock mingling with unmistakable fascination as the flush in her cheeks deepened. "What does it feel like? Giving someone pleasure, I mean."

Cruz was watching them now, lazily pumping his fingers in and out of Ace's mouth in a gesture so effortlessly obscene it had to be pure instinct. Jared responded the same way—without thought, without censoring his desires.

Without holding back. He reached for Lili's hand and pulled it down to her lap, molding her fingers beneath his. "Find out."

Lili's world was on fire.

It was wrong. Watching Rachel and Ace and Cruz, imagining doing more than watching, and now *this*, her dress pushed up to her hips and her fingers pressed between her own thighs. Everything about this was wrong, start to finish.

And it felt so, so right.

This was the source of the ache that consumed her every time Jared touched her. His touch had always been too much, illicit and skilled and intimidating. Her own touch was clumsy by comparison, but even that had her shaking in moments.

Something was simmering inside her, something that made every brush of her fingers—*their* fingers—more dangerous and more necessary.

Jared's breath blew over her ear. "You know this is what she wants, right?" He stroked his thumb over her cheek, guiding her gaze back to Rachel. "She gets off on being watched. And watching, I think."

It explained so much. The warmth in Rachel's eyes, the subtle tension in the store. Maybe Rachel hadn't wanted to push, but the willingness was there. To let Lili watch, to help her understand the O'Kanes and their reckless pleasure.

Lili even understood *gets off* now—it was the culmination of pleasure, the moment this ache inside her boiled over. The only question was how hot she had to get before it happened. Rachel had one arm wrapped around Ace's neck, her eyes drifting shut only to snap open again. She moved faster, her chest heaving, and she clutched at Cruz with her other hand, her fingers wound through his hair as he reached between her and Ace.

With a jolt, Lili realized what he was doing. Touching Rachel, the same way Jared was guiding her to touch herself. But not tentative and easy—even in faint light, the shifting pattern of his tattoos highlighted the flex of muscle. Rachel's response was immediate, her body arching as if the pleasure was so intense, she might fly out of her skin.

Blood pounding in her ears, Lili shifted her fingers, pressing more firmly. Sensation jolted through her, and she barely dug her teeth into her lower lip in time to hold back a moan.

The sharp sound of a zipper broke through her haze. "Do you do this when you're alone, Lili?"

Shaking her head, she sagged back in the booth. The vinyl was smooth and cool against all the skin bared by her dress, but her own nakedness was inconsequential. The table shielded Jared's movements from everyone else in the room—

But not from her.

He had freed his erection from his tailored pants. It jutted up into his hand, long and thick and impossibly big. It looked rough and delicate all at once, veined and throbbing but also soft, and she watched as he ran his thumb around the flared head.

Hazy nights spent at O'Kane parties had left her with a patchwork of blurry memories, of body parts and the ways they touched and came together. But she'd never wanted to look before. Now she couldn't look away. She watched his elegant fingers slide along his length, and felt an answer throb beneath her own fingertips, as if he was

beyond innocence

somehow touching her, too.

So wrong. And so good.

"Harder, sweetheart." He obeyed his own words, tightening his hand until his erection—his *cock*—jumped in his grip.

Her body was buzzing. Her nipples were tight, sensitive to the rasp of her dress, but she couldn't touch them without the whole room seeing. It was a game, the kind she'd always been so good at. Control her expression, project calm. Smile, like she wasn't brazenly touching herself beneath the table.

The thrill of it twisted her up. She let her thighs ease wider, until her knee bumped Jared's, knowing he'd be the only witness as she slipped her fingers beneath the thin fabric of her panties and sought out slickness and heat.

He froze and shook his head. "Take them off."

"What?"

"You heard me, Miss Lili." His voice was low, steady—and wrapped in unmistakable command. "Take off your fucking panties."

Her heart raced. Goose bumps prickled over her skin. She was more raw and open to the overwhelming sensation of this moment than every other second of her life combined, but, for the first time, she wasn't afraid.

Trix was right. He knew enough about pleasure for both of them, and the steel in his voice wasn't merely confidence—it was a promise.

Slowly, struggling to give nothing away to any curious onlookers, she edged the fabric off her hips and down. It was a torturous process that involved enough squirming to make her whole body ache, and she squeezed her legs together once she had the scrap of lace firmly in one fist.

He gathered the fabric in his free hand, his fingers gliding over hers as he took them. "Don't get shy. Our friends are waiting."

Startled, she looked back to Rachel. The blonde had

kit rocha

slowed her movements, her hips barely rocking as she stared across the space separating them. It didn't matter that the table shielded Lili's movements, or that the shadows should have protected her.

Rachel knew. When their gazes met, Lili was sure of it. She *knew*, and Jared was right. Being watched brought a feverish glint to the woman's eyes, and knowing Lili was taking pleasure in her enjoyment only enhanced it.

Only Jared could watch as Lili parted her legs again, but when her fingertips grazed her slick flesh, she couldn't keep her reaction from her face. Rachel smiled slowly, then closed her teeth on Ace's lower lip.

Shuddering, Lili looked down—not to Jared's hand but to her own, her fingers trembling over the one part of her body she'd done her best to ignore. Pain was all she'd ever expected, the pain of being taken and used.

Pussy. An insult in Sector Five. Not here. She wanted to form the word with her lips, whisper it. Scream it without shame, along with *cock* and *fuck* and all the other terrifying words that sounded thrillingly obscene when Jared whispered them in her ear.

She might have, if she could have dragged in enough breath. But that was impossible with Jared so close, his hand moving up and down, stroking his cock.

She tried to match his rhythm, but it wasn't enough. She *needed* something with a depth that drove her fingers in tighter and faster circles, until she'd centered on the spot that made everything in her tense with desperation.

It felt good. Good enough to make her gasp, to leave her clutching at Jared's free hand. But frustration intruded, sharp and brittle. Maybe this was it, this trembling heat and the pulses that made her shudder. It was already more than she'd known possible—

But there was something out of reach. Something she could almost feel, something that would turn *need* into *relief*.

128

beyond innocence

This time, there weren't just words in her ear. He whispered them, yes, but along with the barest hint of teeth on the sensitive shell. "Let it come."

She turned blindly into him, panting against his cheek. It was impossible to relax when her muscles wanted to tense. Every part of her was wound so tight that something had to snap or the pressure would destroy her.

Let it come.

She stopped trying to force it and *felt* the pleasure. The heaviness in her breasts, the trembling in her thighs, the bright little sparks, each one a promise with the potential to catch fire, but each wonderful on its own.

Between one breath and the next, she boiled over.

The surge of relief was the only warning. She crushed her lips to Jared's cheek, but that couldn't muffle her helpless moan. It was as if every one of those sparks had flared up at once, hot and pulsing, and nothing else in the world existed for long, exhilarating moments.

She wasn't made for pleasure. She was remade by it.

He captured her mouth, swallowing her second moan and her third, urging her to ride out her orgasm. He kissed her thoroughly, his tongue sliding over hers, until her body was sated and the only thing making her mind spin was his mouth on hers.

She broke away with a shiver and pressed her flushed cheek to his, her mouth close enough to his ear for her to whisper, "I understand now."

"Yes?" The word trembled, but it didn't sound like weakness.

It sounded like hunger.

She glanced down to where his fist curled around his cock with a rougher grip than she would have dared. But she knew the bite of need now, the sting of frustration when pleasure was close.

Without thinking, she reached for him, sliding her slick fingers over the base of his shaft. He was thick there, too thick for her fingers to meet her thumb, but the wetness made it easier to glide upward. "Like this?" His hand covered hers, squeezing tight. Tighter, until a groan rumbled free of his chest. "Wet," he murmured. "So wet, like you already came on my dick."

She squeezed her thighs together against an unexpected pulse of renewed heat. The dull ache inside her sharpened into a word—*empty*.

If she let Jared take her to bed, he'd work the hard flesh under her fingers deep into her body. The logistics had always seemed vaguely horrifying, but she knew better now. She'd melt for him, and he'd fill her. With pleasure, with satisfaction.

With his *cock*, and this time she almost said the word out loud. She could taste it on the tip of her tongue—which brought the vivid memory of the night she'd met him. Of watching Rachel, on her knees, Cruz's cock *literally* on the tip of her tongue.

Completely at her mercy. That was how Jared had described it, his whisper still vivid even if little else about that night was. And she finally understood. She squeezed her fist, and Jared's throat worked, his low sound almost as exhilarating as her own touch had been.

This was what it felt like, giving someone else pleasure. It felt like power.

"Faster," Jared growled, his hips twitching up with every stroke. "Christ, you're gonna make me come."

Yes, she wanted that. Not just his pleasure, but these drunk, dizzy moments where she was a creature capable of *making* someone as strong and unshakable as Jared lose his grasp on control.

She sped her movements, and he choked out her name. He swelled and pulsed in her hand, using her panties to catch most of the fluid that spurted from him in hot jets. It didn't stop it from dripping onto their entwined hands, tangible evidence of the power she'd claimed over

beyond innocence

his body, just as the lingering slickness on his shaft was proof of the power she'd claimed over her own.

He released a long, shuddering breath and turned his dark, dark eyes on her. He held her gaze as he lifted his hand to her mouth and pushed his thumb between her lips.

She tasted herself, tasted *him*. Salty and tart and impossible to separate, an arousing thought. Without thinking, she parted her lips for him, let him slip deeper, and touched her tongue to the tip of his thumb.

He echoed the caress, dipping his head to lick the top bow of her lip, then turned her head again.

Rachel wasn't trying to be subtle. With her head thrown back and her mouth open in a soundless cry, she rode Ace's hips with shameless abandon. Release—another word that finally made sense. So much pent-up need exploding outward at once, not just from Rachel but from Ace, who slammed his head back against the vinyl, his grimace more like agony than relief.

"He can't come yet." Jared rubbed his thumb over Lili's lip as he pulled it free. "Not until Cruz lets him."

At that moment, Cruz glanced at them, his gaze dark enough to evoke a purely instinctive shiver. Without looking away, he leaned close to Ace's ear and whispered something. The man's frustration melted into pleasure, and he gripped Rachel's hips and drove up with a moan Lili could *feel*.

Rachel rode his shudders with abandon, her open mouth pressed to his, her nails raking his chest through his shirt. Cruz held them both, his strength and protectiveness a tangible shield.

"They're the only ones in their world," Jared rasped. "But if they invite you in for a little while…"

"Not me," she countered. By herself, she'd be an outsider, however welcome. Alone, even in the most intimate moments. "Us."

131

"Mmm." Jared smiled, soft and slow. "Us."

Something fluttered inside her. Not low in her belly or between her thighs, but high in her chest, in the parts of her that had been frozen the longest.

Us was a seductive word. The most illicit one he'd whispered tonight, because *us* sounded like a future they'd agreed not to agree upon. One of tenderness and safety and fucking.

Lili barely understood love, but she already knew two things—it would be dangerously easy to fall in love with Jared, and the broken heart would be worth it.

10

THE FOOTSTEPS STARTED when he was halfway home, and Jared was damn glad he'd left Lili in her own room, drunk on good-night kisses and her first real orgasm.

At first, he chalked the steps up to his own footfalls echoing off the pitted brick walls of the taller buildings that comprised this part of the sector. The empty streets and bare alleys could do strange things to sound, play tricks with your mind. But when he varied the rhythm of his steps and the ones on his trail kept coming, steady but faster, he knew he was in a load of fucking trouble.

There was no time to swing back around to the safety of the O'Kane compound, and nowhere to lay low. So Jared kept his pace slow, slid one hand into his pocket to close around his knife, and waited for the steps to draw closer.

When they were right on his ass, he took a sharp left

into the nearest dead-end alley—if nothing else, no way would they be able to flank him. He stopped at the back of the alley and turned to face his unexpected company.

Three shadows spread out across the other end, back-lit by the moonlight filtering down between the darkened buildings. Jared saw glints of steel—the serrated blade of a knife in one man's hand, the wallet chain hanging from another's belt loop—but no guns.

Maybe he'd make it out of this all right, after all.

Then a fourth man rounded the corner, moving with broad-shouldered self-assurance. He took up more space than the other three combined, and Jared focused on him immediately.

The swagger meant he was their leader. The dramatic entrance meant appearances were important to him. He wouldn't tolerate being made to look bad in front of his crew—but Jared already suspected this was one fight he couldn't talk his way out of, anyway.

The leader spoke. "That's a nice watch."

Jared glanced down, turning his wrist as if appraising the item for himself. "Yes, it is."

The man drew back the frayed edge of his denim jacket, revealing the pistol tucked into his belt. "Hand it over."

Careful. "Why would I do that?"

The one with the knife snorted. "Because maybe you don't want to die?"

Jared stifled a sigh, torn between resignation and the rush of adrenaline coursing through his veins. "Maybe you're new around here, so let me explain. This watch was a gift. It means something to me. You could take it, but it wouldn't do you any good, because you couldn't unload it without winding up dead yourselves. So let it go."

A low, visible wave of unease swept through the three subordinate men. Only the leader seemed unaffected as he stepped forward, his hand now wrapped around the butt

beyond innocence

of his pistol.

He drew it as he stopped in front of Jared—and leveled it at his face. "I know how things work," he muttered. "No ink, fair game."

Oh, this fucking spy gig was going to kill him before he even got into Eden.

No more talking. No more *thinking.* Jared reacted in a quick flurry of movement—jamming his knuckles into the man's Adam's apple, knocking the gun out of his hand. Catching it. In the span of a heartbeat, he locked one arm around his opponent's neck and hauled him around, a human shield to protect him from the rest.

He squeezed off a shot, center mass, and one of the men dropped. The gun jammed on the second shot—cheap piece of shit—and he went for his knife instead, flicking it open as he jerked it from his pocket. He sank the blade deep into the leader's neck, twisting it when the man kicked and thrashed.

But it cost him precious time. White-hot pain slashed across his side and his upper arm, lightning-quick, and he kicked out in retaliation, driving this attacker back to stumble over his fallen friend. Something snapped, and the man screamed as he fell.

Jared dropped the dead weight of the man hanging in his arms just as the third mugger rushed him. The sheer force drove him back against the rough brick, and he struggled to keep the man's thumbs away from his eyes.

The guy was taller, bigger. Without the leverage to throw him off, Jared resorted to one of Ace's favorite tactics. He slammed his forehead against the man's nose, and his attacker broke away, howling and clutching at his face.

He was the one with the chain attached to his wallet. Jared jerked it hard, ripping it free of its loop, and wound it around the man's neck. A brutal twist tightened it, and he rode the man down to the ground, lodged one knee in his throat, and held it there until he stilled.

The last man took off down the alley, dragging his in-jured leg behind him. For a split second, Jared considered chasing him down, but the searing pain in his side was already blurring his vision.

His arm worried him even more. Hot blood ran down to drip off his fingers, striking his shoes and puddling under his feet. If he tried to make it home, he might wind up passing out in the street. And, with no way to gauge the severity of his injuries, passing out was dangerous. Maybe deadly.

But there was one place he could go. Gritting his teeth, Jared focused on putting one foot in front of the other and made his way to Gia's back door.

One of the guards answered, silently assessed Jared's injuries, and pulled the door open wide. "In her office," he said shortly, jerking his head toward the end of the hall-way.

One of the double doors at the end stood ajar. Soft voices came from inside, familiar even though he couldn't make out the words. He wasn't surprised to find Jeni perched on the arm of Gia's chair, both of them studying the screen built into her desk.

Gia looked up first, her eyes going wide. "Fucking hell," she snapped, rising swiftly to circle the desk. "What happened?"

"Got jumped." His tongue felt thick, and he stifled a rusty laugh. "The usual."

"Oh, is that all?" Jeni muttered. She stripped off her T-shirt, leaving her in only a thin tank top as she wrapped his arm. "Where else are you hurt?"

"Just my ribs." He began to list to one side. "It's not all my blood, you know."

Gia ducked under his good arm to steady him. "Come along, darling. Let's sit you down before you smash that beautiful face into the floor. Jeni, I need my med kit."

"Got it." She rushed out the door.

beyond innocence

"I'm fine," Jared protested, even though he knew he wasn't. Gia would understand—no matter how admirably you'd acquitted yourself in a fight, there was always more pride to salvage. More face to save.

Sometimes literally.

She maneuvered him onto the low leather couch along one wall and began unbuttoning his shirt. "Who was stupid enough to take a swing at you? Did you recognize them?"

"No." Suddenly, there were two Gias, and Jared blinked to clear his vision. "They wanted my watch."

Her eyebrows drew together as she jerked open his shirt, sending the final buttons pinging wildly to the floor. "I know it's sentimental, but Eladio would have whipped you for risking your life over a *thing*."

He nudged the locket nestled in the hollow of her throat and grimaced when he smudged blood over her skin. "Don't tell me you wouldn't have done the same for this."

"I wouldn't," she retorted, slapping his hand away. Her fingers were far gentler as she examined his side. "I wouldn't *have* to, because I don't go anywhere after dark without big guns or big men."

"Can't *always* have them around. Guns, bodyguards—" The room was spinning. "What if you're alone?"

"You're not alone now." Gia's hands were comforting and sure as she stripped off his shirt and wadded the fabric against his ribs. "When Jeni gets back with the kit, I'll send for someone to sew you up. Someone better with a needle than I am."

It was standard operating procedure—careful, skilled stitches and the liberal application of med-gel. No scars, because scars didn't belong on the blank canvas necessary to display a fantasy.

Fuck that. "You do it."

Gia gripped his chin and studied his face as if she

could see through him. Then she nodded. "An underground nightclub owner should have a scar or two."
    Jeni came back in with a standard med kit, as well as
Gia's black medical bag. "The other guys look worse,
right?" she asked as she gingerly prodded the sore spot in
the middle of his forehead.
    "Shit," he hissed. "Careful. I broke a bastard's nose
with that bruise. And yes—they look a lot worse."
    "Dead worse?"
    "Mostly," he assured her. "One got away."
    Jeni's jaw tightened. "Are you gonna tell Dallas, or
should I?"
    "Jared's not going anywhere tonight," Gia said firmly,
wiping her hands. "Get some painkillers into him. How
fuzzy do you want to be, darling?"
    He turned his head. "I hate those things."
    "You're eight kinds of wobbly," Jeni protested, holding
up two small tabs. "Come on. Under the tongue, or I'll have
to spray it up your nose."
    The painkillers dissolved under his tongue, and his
fingers began to tingle before the bitter taste even flooded
his mouth. It didn't deaden the pain so much as numb everything. It left him floating, buffeted between the strange
tugging pressure as Gia worked at his wounds and the
low, throbbing sensation of their words echoing in his ears.
    "Once we've got him cleaned up, one of the guards will
take you to see Dallas and Lex. I don't want you out there
alone right now."
    "I'm not stupid, Gia."
    "I know, love." A soft sigh. "Just...let me know if you
plan to stay there, or I'll be up all night worrying."
    Jeni's voice gentled. "If Jared's all right, I'll probably
stay."
    "Safer that way." The words were even, too even, hid-
ing the vulnerability only Jared and Ace knew was there.
    "It's too late now." Jared tried to pat Gia's hand and

wound up catching her hair instead. "Sorry."

Gia sighed and shifted her attentions to his slashed side. "What about your sweet little blonde, Jared? Should Jeni tell her?"

"Lili." The thought sent a pang through him, sharper than the heat blazing in his ribs. "No. She'd worry if she knew."

"The guard can bring her back with him," Jeni suggested, "and then she won't have to worry."

"*No*." That was even worse, because then he might tell her everything. The whole truth, and nothing could be more dangerous. "Promise me."

"Okay." Jeni ran her fingers through his hair, tugging lightly. "I promise."

Gia said nothing, just focused on her work until she'd smoothed med-gel over his ravaged flesh and bandaged both wounds. "Help me get him into my room. He can sleep it off in my bed."

Together, they propped him up on his feet. The whole room went dim and supernova white, all at the same time, and Jared had to laugh at the impossible dichotomy of it, the sheer silliness. "I hate those fucking drugs."

"I know, darling." Gia's office seemed miles wide, and it took forever to cross to the door on the far side. Her bedroom was equally big, but the bed was close. They guided him to sit on the edge, and then Gia knelt in front of him. "Don't you dare put your shoes on my silk sheets."

"Why not?" He laughed again. "My feet are only half as dirty as the rest of me."

Jeni slipped out, and Gia huffed as she tugged at his shoelaces. "I haven't heard you laugh this much since the night we stole Eladio's best bottle of brandy. When did we get so sober and serious?"

"When we stopped being young and stupid." When they learned what the world was really about—and how it never changed. You could escape the forthright violence of the streets, but all you'd find was that same rotten mean-ness, dressed up like a million bucks. "When we figured it all out."

Gia tugged open his belt and paused when her fingers brushed his pocket. A heartbeat later she lifted her hand, Lili's panties dangling from the tip of one finger. "My, you've had a *very* exciting night."

He snatched them from her. "Those are mine."

Her eyebrows shot even higher. "I'm not saying you couldn't pull off the color or style, darling, but they're definitely not your size."

"Maybe that's part of the allure." He shoved Lili's panties back in his pocket and waved Gia's hands away. "And I'm not five. I can undress myself."

"Then do it." She rose and headed for the bathroom. "*Without* falling on your face."

On second thought, maybe he'd just keep his pants on. He fell back on the mattress and watched the light fixture whirl around in sick, dizzy loops. "If you keep trying to hang on to her so tight, she won't come back at all."

The faucet cut off in the bathroom, and Gia returned to the bed with a towel in her hands. "If you're going to poke at sore spots, you should let me get drunk first."

"Just trying to help."

Gia pulled on a clean robe and stretched out next him. "I'm not a fool, Jared. Competing with Dallas O'Kane is hard enough. Competing with Lex is insane. Competing with them *both?*"

"Unimaginable," he agreed. He reached for her hand again, finding it this time automatically. "So don't compete. You shouldn't have to. What did Eladio always tell us?"

"You can't hold on to anyone," she quoted obediently. "If they want to stay, they will." Her fingers tightened too hard around his. "Does that mean we shouldn't try?"

"I don't know." Exhaustion dragged at him, and he

closed his eyes as the world floated away. "I don't know anything anymore."

The moment Lili stepped outside, she knew it wasn't a usual morning.

Too many people were milling about in the open court-yard between the O'Kane buildings. The sun hadn't even climbed above the hills to the east, and Lili herself was only up to get ready for breakfast.

The closest familiar face was Emma, Ace's assistant tattoo artist. Lili hurried across the pavement. "Is something wrong?"

"What? Oh, hey." Emma shrugged, then drove her hands into her messy, two-toned hair. "Crazy night. Did you miss the manhunt?"

After being kissed within a hairsbreadth of falling apart again, Lili had melted into bed for the soundest night of sober sleep of her life. That was new, just like the hazy dreams of heated skin and dark whispers.

But the word *manhunt* dispelled the remaining glow. "Who were they looking for?"

Emma opened her mouth, then abruptly closed it again. "Shit, sorry. A group of thugs attacked Jared last night. He's fine," she added hurriedly, "but one of 'em got away. Dallas had the guys out looking for the asshole all night."

Only years of practice kept Lili standing stiffly up-right with her stomach crashing toward her feet. "Where is he? Jared, I mean?"

"At Gia's place." Emma gripped her shoulders. "Lili, he's *fine*."

Her heart was pounding too hard. It was irrational, out of all proportion to Emma's words. Worry, pure and undiluted, the kind she hadn't felt in more than five years. She dug her fingernails into her palms until eight tiny pricks of pain flared. It helped. The roaring in her ears receded, and she managed an even breath. "Did they find the man who attacked him?"

"Yeah. Dallas is questioning the guy now. Hey." Emma smiled encouragingly. "Four on one, and Jared took out three. He did good. Don't be scared, be proud."

"Four on—" Panic threatened again, and she bit it back ruthlessly. At least, she *tried*. Maybe nothing would stop this but seeing him, knowing he was whole. "Oh, God."

"Come on." Emma wrapped an arm around her shoulders. "Let's get you a drink."

It was the comforting response. The easy one. All her life, shock and worry had been dulled by one thing or another. It would be easy to fall into that habit again, because if any place in the sectors had enough liquor to thoroughly intoxicate a Sector Five housewife, it was the heart of O'Kane territory.

But numbing the pain meant numbing the pleasure, and after last night...

Maybe here, the price wasn't worth it.

"Not a drink," Lili said, straightening with effort. "If people were out all night, they must be exhausted and hungry. I can cook."

"Oh, sweetie. You don't have to—"

"I *want* to." She squeezed Emma's hand. "People need to eat. This is something I can do."

"Okay," she whispered. "Okay, then I'll help you."

Lili's calm solidified, along with her sense of purpose. She could do this, put her skills to use and channel her fear and anxiety into something productive. She could be more than a trophy, more than decorative.

And, when it was over, she'd calmly, *coolly*, find out

where Jared was and examine every inch of him until she was satisfied he really was fine.

lex

NONE OF THE O'Kanes were related by blood. Some people thought that didn't make them family. Those people were wrong.

Somehow, it always came down to blood. They lived for it, fought for it. Sometimes, they died for it. And Dallas was covered with it by the time he came out of the cage.

Lex didn't speak until he had thrust his hands into the basin behind the bar and started to wash up. "I didn't hear any big secrets," she murmured. "Just a lot of screams."

"Don't think there are any secrets to hear," he replied, low and vicious. "Just a few greedy idiots from Three and freak fucking chance."

It made sense. A full-on fight was a sloppy damn way to execute a hit—and, judging from their prisoner's begging, he was no professional. "Punks looking for someone to roll? It sucks, but I'll take it over an assassination attempt."

"It's the easier solution." Dallas finished scrubbing his hands and started in on his forearms. "Jared did most of the work by killing three of them. Now we just need Bren to grind in the message."

People would get the message, all right—everyone in Sector Four was dangerous, even the fancy whores. But would it do any good? "Some days it feels like we're fighting a fucking Hydra. Cut off one head, get two more."

"And some days I'm glad it's only two."

"You're tired." She could feel it even before she touched him, the tension in his shoulders that rarely seemed to ease. She rubbed at the knots between his shoulder blades and dropped a kiss to the back of his neck, to the spot where he'd inked her name—her real name—into his skin. "But we're so close. You know that, right?"

"I know." Dallas clenched his fists. "If Jared can sway that councilman..."

"We'll have a real chance to change things," she finished softly. "But we can't count on that, Dallas. There's no—"

The door smashed open with a violence that had Dallas spinning around, one hand already reaching for his gun. But it wasn't an enemy striding toward them, his brown eyes hot with barely repressed fury.

She stepped between them. "Ace, calm down."

He jabbed a finger toward Dallas. "Him, I expect it from. He doesn't fucking know better. But you do, Lex. *You do.*"

Lex's own anger rose, and she slapped his hand away. "Watch it, Santana."

Dallas stood behind her, tensed to smack Ace down, but he didn't move. And Ace didn't look at him, either. The anger in his gaze was focused entirely on Lex—just like the betrayal. "Gia spilled the beans, not that she knew what she was saying. But she told me he bought that bar after all. And she's *hopeful*. She thinks he's getting out, not going down the fucking rabbit hole."

It hurt, more than Lex expected it to. More than she imagined it could. "Do you want to talk about this, or do you want to yell at me? I'm good with either, but I want to get it out there."

"I want to slap some sense into your boyfriend."

"No," Dallas replied, his voice dangerously soft. "You really don't."

It wasn't a threat. It didn't have to be. Ace shoved his fingers through his hair and took a step back—a carefully calculated retreat. "Then someone should *talk*."

"Out." Lex jerked her head toward the back room and took Ace by the shoulder. "You and me, come on."

Dallas stood in their path long enough for his silent battle to be obvious. In the end, he stepped aside with a harsh look at Ace. "I'm not coming in there to save your ass if you piss her off."

"No one's getting his ass kicked today." She steered Ace toward the back room, winding her arm through the crook of his as they walked. "Right, honey?"

"Sure, sweetheart," he drawled, not sounding convinced at all.

"Don't be a dick, Ace." She lowered her voice. "There are things you don't know."

He waited until the door had closed behind them before breaking away to pace the room. "I'm sure there's a lot of shit I don't know. But I know Jared."

"Yeah?" She'd bet everything she owned that he didn't know it all, not the way he thought he did. "So it won't surprise you to learn that Jared came to us."

Ace came to an abrupt stop and turned slowly. "Maybe, but Dallas planted the idea in his head. Jared told me about the bar, right before all that shit with Finn went down. And he said he wasn't interested."

"I guess he changed his mind." So many things she could tell Ace, so many truths she could lay on him...and none of them were hers to share. "Take a minute and think about *why.*"

Ace rubbed his side—and froze, his fingers lingering over the scar left behind by the wound that had nearly killed him. "Shit. Tell me this isn't my fucking fault, Lex."

Any reassurance would be a lie, so she held her tongue. It *was* his fault—because he'd almost died, because Jared had spent years being stupid in love with him. Because Jared would die to protect not only Ace, but everything and everyone Ace cared about.

Ace swore roughly and sank onto the edge of a spare table. "Is that why he got jumped? Because he's spying?"

"Dallas and I were worried about it," she admitted, "but it wasn't a hit. It was random." But that wasn't the whole truth, was it? "This time. He *will* be in danger in Eden, that's unavoidable. We can be careful, but it won't change facts. We know that, and so does Jared."

"It's gonna hurt him either way." Ace squeezed his eyes shut. "That girl's getting to him, Lex. Maybe she's not the love of his fucking life, but she's making him feel shit. And if he goes into Eden like that..."

Bless the fucking O'Kanes, who even kept bottles handy in storerooms. Lex raided the cabinet in the corner and poured two shots of whiskey, then handed one to Ace. "Dallas wanted him any way he could get him. The undercover shit was Jared's stipulation."

Ace sipped his drink, his gaze fixed on the wall. "So if he decided he wanted to join up the regular way, Dallas would be okay with that?"

"He *has* joined up, Ace. Everything but the ink. He's one of us."

"Bullshit, Lex. Look me in the eyes and tell me that."

She stepped up, right in his face, and squarely met his gaze. "You think Dallas would have had our guys out all

beyond innocence

night, scouring two sectors, if it wasn't true?"

"You can pay for bodyguards. You can pay for beatdowns." Ace didn't waver. "He needs the shit money can't buy, and he's not getting it."

"It's his choice. I can't make it for him. Maybe—" She bit off the words, then forged ahead, because Ace needed to *understand.* "Maybe, someday soon, we can convince him that he deserves it."

Ace sighed and finally broke eye contact. "Who else knows? Bren? Jas?"

"Yeah." She'd eat her favorite leather corset if Cruz hadn't figured it out by now, but that was another tale that wasn't hers to tell. "We good?"

Ace bumped his forehead against hers. "We're always good, sister. Even when I want to throttle you."

"Same here, Santana." She couldn't help a laugh as she set aside her empty glass and cupped his face in her hands. "A little bit of advice?"

"Depends on if I'll like it."

"Doubtful."

He groaned. "Fine, lay it on me, love."

"The truth." She stroked her thumbs over his cheeks. "If you want to know what's going on with Jared, talk to him. Not *at* him, okay?"

Ace huffed. "Says the girl who tattooed Dallas's name on her instead of sitting him down for a nice chat."

"Never said I was perfect, honey. But I love you—*all* of you—and I would never, ever ask a single one of you to do anything that I wouldn't do if I could."

"I know." He kissed her cheek before straightening. "Gia won't share her secrets with Dallas. But if Jared's in trouble, she'll burn the city to the ground. Keep that in mind."

"Good. He can always use more backup."

"Only if he needs it," Ace cautioned. "She'll blow up if you tell her now, and that is *not* the way I want to see you two go at each other."

She'd heard more convincing, less desperate flirta-
tions from Ace, but he was *trying*. So she took his whiskey,
finished it off, and winked. "Cross my heart, Santana.
Only in case of emergency."

11

LILI WALKED TO Jared's home by herself.

It was a small victory, but it felt like an honest one when Lex regarded her seriously before granting permission. She made it all the way to the marketplace before she realized the truth—there hadn't been much risk in letting her wander through the sector so soon after the O'Kanes had swept through, reminding everyone of their power. Today, anyone could walk unmolested this close to the compound.

Even her.

She slipped through the downstairs door of Jared's building without knocking and paused at the base of that polished staircase to settle her protections into place. She had the right to her concern, out of sheer friendship. She had the right to fuss over him a little.

Check his wounds. Express her delight at his safety.

Leave before she wrapped her arms and legs around him and clung until the fear of losing him stopped being an icy splinter in her heart.

She had more leftovers—pancakes with blueberries from a hothouse farmer who sold them for more than most people spent on food for a week, with thick honey and fresh butter—and she clutched the basket to steady her hands as she ascended the stairs.

Cool. Friendly.

It all fell apart when he opened the door—shirtless, with bandages on his side and wrapped around his upper arm.

"Oh, God." She reached out, her fingertips hovering just shy of his arm. "Are you okay?"

He sighed and rubbed a hand over his face. "I told them not to tell you."

Lili jerked her hand away, stung so badly she didn't think before speaking. "Why not?"

"Because of this." He stepped back and gestured to the basket, then to her face. "Because you'd worry about me, about this, and I can't—" He broke off and looked away. "I can't let you worry about me, Lili. Not right now."

It should have hurt, but *he* was hurting, and it strengthened her resolve. "You can't stop me."

His voice softened, and he opened his arms. "I know. Come here."

Without hesitating, she wrapped her free arm gently around him. "Tell me if I hurt you."

He took the basket from her other hand and dropped it to a low table beside the door. "I'm not weak. I won't break."

"Weak people don't break," she whispered, tracing the edge of the bandage around his arm. His skin was warm above it, clean and smooth and unmarked. "Strong people do."

He slid both arms around her waist and buried his

beyond innocence

face in her hair. For several heartbeats, he only stood there, breathing deeply. Then he shook his head. "I haven't been straight with you. Before anything else happens, I need to be. I need to tell you something."

"Anything, Jared."

His grip on her loosened just enough for him to pull back and study her face. "What do you know about me and the O'Kanes?"

"That you've known Ace for a long time." And that no one else seemed to know him at all. "That's it, really."

"True enough," he confirmed. "That's how it was for a long time, but not anymore."

The words were firm, his eyes serious. His hands trembled the tiniest bit. She let the words sink in, let their meaning follow.

He'd only been friends with Ace. But...

Not anymore.

She followed his arm down to his wrist and pulled it up between them. "But you're not an O'Kane."

"I don't have the ink." He twisted his wrist, caught her hand, and tugged it to his chest. "It wouldn't really fly in Eden, after all. And that's where I'll be—gathering intel for Dallas."

"Oh." She spanned her fingers wide, over the only tattoo he *did* have, but she couldn't even focus on the pattern. All she could hear was the word he hadn't said, the dangerous word that had lurked beneath every gentle warning.

Spy.

"Oh," Jared echoed with a sigh. "I should have told you. I should have told you before...everything."

Oddly, it made her smile. "That wouldn't make you a very good spy."

His expression remained sober. Grave. "Maybe not, but it might have made me a better person."

He was giving her a chance to leave, but not sending

153

her away. And, in the end, the truth changed nothing—he hadn't promised not to hurt her. He hadn't promised her something lasting.

Except now she understood just how badly he needed a friend.

She freed her hand from his and returned to the bandage. "Do these need to be checked? I know basic first aid." "They're fine." He slid his hand into her hair, his fingers tangling in the strands.

Every individual tug at her scalp set off a shiver. Pleasure, sweet and warm, and so, so different from the times Logan had wrapped his hand in her hair.

Trust, that was the difference. Trust and intent.

Jared stared down at her, his eyes locked with hers. "If you need to go, I understand. But I wish you'd stay."

When he stared at her like that, nothing else existed. Her stupid, immature heart gave a funny kick, and her voice came out breathless. "I made pancakes."

The corner of his mouth curved up. It was a slow smile, a *knowing* smile, one she could vaguely understand after the previous night. "Thank you. But I don't want pancakes."

He wanted *her*. And, for the first time, she wanted to be wanted.

Careful not to put any pressure on his wounded arm, she rose slowly on her toes and brushed her lips over his.

He didn't keep it careful or light. His hand clenched in her hair, and he pulled her head back, giving him deeper access to her mouth. And he took it, kissing her hard, with a rough edge of desire eroding his usual polish.

Passion, unchecked and unrehearsed. Her heart raced, and she pressed closer without thinking, sliding her hands down and around his body. Her fingers encountered the bandage on his side and she froze, then broke away. "Jared—"

"Shh." He pressed his thumb to her lips to silence her

protests. "If you want to go, I'll walk you home. But if you stay, no holding back."

Somehow, it was easier to trust Jared to be careful with her body than with his own. She ran her hand past the bandage to stroke his back and whispered a compromise against the pad of his thumb. "I want us both to feel good."

"We will." He moved forward, guiding her to step back. "I'm not scared of pain. It can coexist with pleasure. The only thing that *can't* is... Well, you know, don't you, Lili?"

Oh yes, she knew. She knew in her bones, the bones that had once been ice and steel and were now melting along with the rest of her. "Numbness."

"Mmm." He was still moving, and he bent his head to lick the corner of her mouth. "In order to feel good, you have to feel, and that's terrifying all on its own."

She nearly stumbled. She caught his shoulders, steadying herself as he coaxed her back another step. "It's so much, and it's so new. I never know how much I can take."

"I do, though." His hand slipped from her hair to cup the back of her neck. "Is that enough for you?"

She didn't even have to think. "Yes."

His fingers squeezed tight in silent, imperious command. "Then trust me."

Shivering, she closed her eyes. "Yes."

They moved again. When she opened her eyes, they were in a dark room—sparsely furnished, with a wide window along one wall that looked out onto the bright lights of Eden. You could see the wall, the giant stone-and-metal structure separating the city from the sector, impenetrable and unforgiving.

The bed was a sharp contrast to the stark, chilly stone. Wide and soft, with no headboard, it sat on the far side of the room, surrounded and framed by curving, abstract pieces of metal wall art.

Shadows softened Jared's perfection. So did his disheveled hair and the stubble that covered his strong jaw. He wasn't a cold, aloof god anymore, but a flesh-and-blood man who could bleed, hurt. *Want.*

And he wanted her. Lili's hands trembled with the knowledge as she lifted them to the top button on her blouse.

Jared sank to the edge of the bed and watched her through heavy eyes, his fingers curling and relaxing in the plush duvet. "Slowly."

She didn't have a choice. She was clumsy, and the silk shirt Trix had found for her felt slippery and uncooperative. It took forever to work the first three buttons free, and her cheeks heated as the fabric parted to reveal her plain white bra and the tops of her breasts.

"Keep going."

She did, slowly pushing each button through the fabric with a rasp that was audible in the otherwise quiet room. The shirt slipped from one shoulder, and she let it fall away with the last fastening, sliding to pool on the floor.

Desire blazed in his eyes, but his voice was pure patience. "You're not naked yet, love."

Oh, *God.* It was exhilarating and intimidating at the same time. Naked wasn't a dress pulled up or pushed aside, frantic touches in a dark corner. It was stripping off every layer of armor, one scrap of clothing at a time, and showing him every usually concealed imperfection.

She took off her shoes first, robbing her of the additional inches of height. Then the pants, revealing her wide hips and soft thighs, the curves that had grown more pronounced without fear of Logan controlling how often or how much she ate.

She couldn't meet his eyes as she fumbled with the clasp on her bra. Nerves made the tiny hooks impossible to maneuver. It took three tries to unclasp them, and her uncertainty kicked a notch higher as she worked her panties down.

Braced against seeing disappointment in his eyes, she stepped free of the last bit of her clothing and looked up at him.

He rose, silent and intent. He circled her, his fingers brushing her skin—her shoulder, the small of her back, the top of one thigh—in quick, glancing caresses that left her hypersensitive and shivering.

"Jared?" she whispered.

"Shh." He knelt, so close that his jaw brushed the curve of her hip as he spoke. "Beautiful, Lili. I love that word, but it's not enough for you. Not nearly."

Self-consciousness vanished under the warmth of his words. For so much of her life, she'd struggled to make herself look better, *perfect*, all to benefit men who never really saw her.

Jared looked at her flaws and still saw perfection. "Thank you."

"You're welcome." He touched her again, his knuckles gliding up the back of her leg, from her ankle all the way to her ass.

Swaying, she dropped one hand to his shoulder to steady herself as each touch built on the last. Not a fast plunge into overwhelming pleasure, but a slow fall that let her feel the prickles over her skin, the little jolt along her spine.

He stood, so close to her that she could feel the heat of his body, the brush of fabric against her legs, the rough graze of gauze against her back. It was illicit, standing there naked while he was still half-dressed.

Even more illicit when he slid one hand around her waist. It came to rest low on her belly, just above her pussy—and the fact that the word came to her so easily was the most illicit part of all.

She let her head fall back against his shoulder. She

felt smaller like this, without high heels to bring her height closer to his. Her head fit neatly under his chin, and his body curled protectively around hers.

Smaller, but safer.

"How far does this go, Lili?" he asked softly. "Tell me now."

"As much as I can take," she replied, covering his hand with her own. "I trust you."

He spun her around—slowly, but with hands that were a little rough. Needy. His mouth descended on hers, another deep, demanding kiss full of teeth and tongue, one that went on forever.

She barely realized they were moving again, not until he pressed her back against his bed. She moaned into his mouth and clutched at his hair, the dual sensations of his hot skin above her and the cool sheets at her back heightening everything.

Like his fingers. They skimmed her shoulders, tugged at her hair. Tickled the end of one curling lock over the aching tip of her nipple until she wanted to sob at the slow burn.

She forced one hand open and slid it down, indulging herself by running her fingertips over his strong shoulder and the flexing muscles of his back. "You're beautiful, too."

He huffed out a short laugh. "Can't count the number of times I've heard that." His hand drifted lower, stroking the bottom curve of her breast and the sensitive skin over her ribs. "You're the first person I've believed in a long time."

She tightened her grip in his hair, pulling his head back so she could meet his eyes, suddenly needing to know he understood. That he knew *she* understood. "I see you."

"Yes." He dropped a kiss to her collarbone. "You do."

His mouth drifted lower, and she sucked in a breath when she realized each meandering kiss brought him closer and closer to her taut nipple.

beyond innocence

Warm air. Soft lips. She squeezed her thighs together, squeezed her eyes shut, but it didn't help. Her body pulsed when he closed his mouth around the tip, wet and hot and then rasping as his *tongue* grazed her, and she let out a helpless noise and writhed on the bed, half sure they'd already reached her limits.

Touching herself felt good. *Him* touching her was... So much. Almost too much.

"Hands above your head," he whispered.

She struggled to obey, clutching at the sheets, barely noticing when she caught her own hair in her trembling grip.

He touched her knee, then his fingertips skimmed up to the sensitive spot where her thigh met her hip. "Keep them there, Lili. I'll know when you've had enough."

She still had her legs clenched together. She could promise again that she trusted him, but pretty words were hollow compared to action. Exhaling shakily, she eased her knees apart.

"Good girl. So sweet." He sucked her nipple into his mouth again, drawing on it sharply as his hand slipped between her thighs.

Her body twisted tight. She didn't have to hold back her cries this time, but she couldn't stop herself from digging her teeth into her lower lip as a lifetime of training in smothering her reactions kicked in.

She had to *contain* this. But she couldn't—his fingers slicked over her pussy, and she shuddered at how wet she was, how nakedly needy.

His leg slid over hers, urging her legs wider, and he raised his head. He braced his free arm beside her head and tangled his fingers with hers, holding her arms in place. "So close to ready," he murmured.

She clutched at the only thing she could—the hand pinning her down. It should have been frightening, being naked and vulnerable, trapped and *open* to him in every

159

possible way.

But there was such tenderness in his body. In his voice. In his touch, as he soothed her trembling with slow strokes that eased the sharpest edges of her nervousness.

"Ready for what?"

He answered with his body instead of words, pushing one finger against her.

Into her.

It stretched awkwardly—not quite pain but not pleasure, either—and that was oddly reassuring. It let her suck in a breath and find her equilibrium for the brief moment before he withdrew and worked it back in, deeper.

It stretched more now. She might have shifted her hips away, but the strong leg over hers held her in place, and there was nothing to do but shiver and *feel*.

Jared sought her gaze and held it, his dark eyes locked with hers as he eased a second finger inside her. Moving, pumping slowly, twisting gently, until the almost-painful pressure gave way to something even more maddening.

Heat.

"Jared." Arching into his touch was as impossible as flinching away, and she whimpered with frustration. "I need..." Something. *More.*

"I know." He pushed deeper, then pressed the pad of his thumb to her clit with just a whisper of pressure.

She couldn't hold back her cry this time. It tore free of her throat on a pulse of white-hot bliss, and she writhed in a futile attempt to buck up.

He stilled with a soft noise. "Careful, love. Not too fast."

Incomprehensible words. Everything was fast and desperate now, anticipation magnified a hundred times. It had been so *easy* with her own touch, easy to center her fingers precisely where the ache was worst, easy to relieve it before it could become too overwhelming.

"Why?" she pleaded, digging her nails into his hand.

beyond innocence

"Why can't it be fast?"

"Because you want us both to feel good," he reminded her of her previous words. "I may not be scared of pain, but it doesn't belong here. Not your first time."

Nothing hurt anymore. But she knew the first time probably would. It was supposed to be painful and abrupt and over with blessed speed—except if she'd still believed any of that, she wouldn't be here.

His thumb grazed her clit again, jolting her into another whimper before she managed to speak. "I feel good. Too good."

"No." He nuzzled her cheek, then licked her lips. "Not yet. But you will."

She leaned up to catch his mouth, kissing him clumsily, *desperately*, as his fingers twisted inside her, not only gliding in and out now but stretching again.

As the pressure built, she understood. He wasn't just trying to make her feel good, he was trying to make her *ready*. Teaching her body to accept him, building sensation until she wasn't even embarrassed at the slick sound of his thrusting fingers.

"See, Lili?" He whispered the words against her mouth, breathing them into her, an intimate connection almost painful in its intensity. "Your body is waking up, learning what it wants. What it needs."

"You." Too revealing, but she wasn't embarrassed, not with release so close she could taste it.

But not reach for it. She didn't have to. Jared knew what she could take, and he gave it to her—his fingers plunged deeper, and the slick pressure on her clit turned into a demand.

When she gave in, it wasn't like before. Not the sweet flash fire that burned through to her core and left her limp. Her body clenched tight around his fingers, a pulse that expanded and expanded until she shattered outward with a hoarse cry.

"Fucking—" He bit her ear, closing his teeth on the lobe with a shudder as he rocked his hand. It dragged out the pleasure, turned her orgasm into a series of throbs instead of echoes that faded away. *Too much.* Nothing could feel like this and be real. She dug her fingernails into his hand, unable to stop herself when the world was buzzing and she couldn't move, couldn't breathe, couldn't do anything but shudder through it.

Jared whispered her name, soothed her with soft kisses and gentle flicks of his tongue—over the line of her jaw, her cheek, the spot where her neck met her shoulder.

She gasped in a breath and turned her face toward his. "That was..." Amazing. Beautiful. Life-altering. The O'Kanes weren't a mystery, not anymore. If this was what it felt like to share your body, they'd found a high far easier to manufacture than any drug her father had ever developed.

"Just the beginning," he promised.

She whimpered.

Jared eased from the bed in graceful, smooth movements, as if he wasn't injured at all. He unbuckled his belt, his gaze still locked on her, and opened his pants.

The black boxers he wore couldn't hide his erection. She'd seen it before, touched it, but now she knew how completely he could fill her with only two fingers. No wonder he'd taken his time to prepare her.

She watched, hypnotized, as he pushed the fabric down his powerful legs, freeing his cock. He stood there, completely confident and unashamed of his nudity, as she let herself stare.

A sculptor couldn't have created something more perfect. Smooth skin marred only by the bandages was otherwise free of scars or marks. He had muscles, but not huge and bulky like Zan and Flash, or even solid like Bren. He was strong but lean, his broad shoulders sloping into well-defined arms. Her gaze drifted down his chest and stomach to his narrow hips—

His cock stood as proud and shameless as he did, and she remembered the way she hadn't been able to encircle the base with her hand. She should be terrified, braced for the pain of taking him into her body.

But she trusted him so much that she reached out. "Come back. I want to feel you."

He climbed back onto the bed, this time with the lean bulk of his body looming over her. One leg nudged between hers, and he smiled slowly as she obediently parted her thighs to make room for him.

When he was close enough, she reached up to cup his face, pressing her thumb to his lips. "I never thought I could want this so much."

"You've been locked away." His voice was low, a little rough. "But now you're free—to be who you are, do what you want. Free to *feel.*"

Who she was—that was still a mystery. Right now she was fluid, liquid. The world was alive with potential, and Jared was right. Whatever form she solidified into would be *her* choice, and no one else's.

This was her choice. To hook one leg around his hip, to tug him closer so she could feel him pressing her into the bed. She was safest like this, with him holding her together while pleasure broke her apart. "Show me."

His hips settled into the cradle of hers, and he braced his elbows on the bed on either side of her head, careful not to catch her hair as he held his weight above her. The hair on his body rasped over her skin, a delicious tease, but nothing compared to the hot, slick glide as the shaft of his cock nestled against her.

Jared sucked in a sharp breath that turned into a groan. "You feel so damn good."

That was what she wanted. *His* pleasure. That noise that started deep in his chest and sounded as needy as she felt. "So do you."

He flexed his hips, rubbing against her, and groaned again. "I should wait, but I don't know if I *can.*"

He could. She knew that in her gut. If there had been the slightest bit of fear left in her, he would have touched and stroked and soothed it all away, no matter how much he suffered for it.

She arched up, shuddering when it only intensified the dizzying pressure against her clit. "You could," she gasped. "But you don't have to."

His eyes went darker. "I know. You want this." He rolled his hips, circling them in one slow, controlled movement that brought her back to the edge. "You want it so much I can't even imagine how hard you'll come on my dick."

Words so obscene, she squeezed her eyes shut against the shame of *loving* them. "That's—"

"Hot?" He bent his head and nipped at her ear again. "Say it, Lili."

"Dirty," she whispered. "Good."

"How good?"

She moaned, but he didn't relent. Her cheeks burned as she hid her face against his. "I want more. I want to know the dirty words for all the things you do to me."

"Like how I'm going to pound your pussy?" He nudged her chin, forcing her gaze to his. "How I'm going to fuck you until you scream?"

Harsh, rough promises—and they did harsh, rough things to her. The word that had balanced on the tip of her tongue unspoken last time spilled free. "With your cock."

"That's right, love." He thrust against her again. Harder. "With my cock."

She grabbed his shoulders as a shudder rocked her. She was close again. She knew it now, knew what was coming. "Now, *please*, Jared."

His fingers slid into her hair again—twisting, tangling—but he hesitated. "Were you on any other drugs, Lili? Fertility drugs?"

The sweet edge of safety slipped away at the reminder. "Y—yes. Only for a couple of weeks, but I don't know if that means..."

"What kind? Implants?"

"Pills."

He stroked her temples with his thumbs. "The effects should have worn off by now. But I have condoms, if you want to use one."

An unfamiliar word, but she could imagine the purpose well enough. To save her from her mother's fate, from ending up with a child that might trap her. "Please."

He leaned past her and retrieved a small packet from the table beside the bed. It contained an odd little circle that didn't make sense until Jared lifted himself and fitted it against the head of his cock. His strong, graceful fingers moved hypnotically, dragging her gaze down as he unrolled it onto his shaft.

"See?" He reached for her hand, lifted it to his lips for a quick kiss, then wrapped her fingers around his sheathed erection. "Safer now."

Touching him brought back need. He was so hard under her fingertips, as ready for her as she was for him.

And he'd keep her safe. Safe enough to be brave. "I want you." She tightened her fingers. "I want this."

He climbed over her again with a shudder, moving too carefully to slide free of her grip. He seemed to relish it, a pleasure she understood when he grinned, dark and dangerous. "Show me where."

It took a moment to realize what he wanted. Not for her to lie passively, but to *take*. Slowly, without looking away, she guided his cock to press against her. Jared took over the movement, his muscles taut and trembling as he braced himself above her and flexed his hips.

The pressure was intense, but it wasn't pain. Not until she rocked up, taking more of him, but even that was manageable. An aching sting, and worth it for the way his teeth sank into his lower lip as his brow furrowed—as if holding back was an agony more intense than anything else.

"Jared." She wrapped her leg around his hip again, digging her heel into his lower back. "I'm not afraid of pain, either. As long as I'm feeling."

"It's not for you." His lips brushed her cheek. "For me."

Because he didn't want to hurt her.

That ache in her chest expanded. She turned her face to his, finding his mouth in a slow, sweet kiss as she relaxed and let him work deeper, bit by bit, moment by moment, until the pressure nearly overwhelmed her.

He whispered softly, words that made no sense, words that weren't *supposed* to make sense, because all they meant was that he was there, that he had her. That they were together.

When his hips settled against hers, he was so deep that was all she could feel. Him, filling her so completely that the slightest shift of her hips set off a riot of friction. She moaned into his mouth and clung to him, afraid he'd pull back if she let go.

"I'm not going anywhere," he murmured, because he understood. Of course he did.

"I know you have to..." She rubbed her cheek against his and closed her eyes. "I don't want to be overwhelmed. I want to be here with you."

"Look at me."

She did.

The friction slammed into her again as Jared flexed his hips, nudging deeper before retreating just a little. He did it again, and again, turning friction into heat with each slow roll, until she was digging her nails into his back hard enough to break skin.

And, through it all, his gaze never left hers. When the tension threatened to sweep her away, he held her with his eyes, forced her to feel, to *savor*, to claim each new sensation as his pace increased.

"Don't," he whispered. "Don't slip away, love."

She met his next thrust with a moan. "When do you fall apart?"

"When it's enough. If it ever is." He drove into her again, harder this time.

It jolted through her. Her toes curled as something vast rushed toward her, something she needed with a desperation that left her breathless. "Jared—"

He covered her mouth with a noise caught between a laugh and a groan, and did *something* with his hips, something that hit every spot so perfectly she couldn't even scream when that wild tension snapped.

It wasn't like the first time. It wasn't even like his fingers. There were so *many* ways to fall apart, and this was the most intense yet. He rode every wave of pleasure, driving into her hard enough to spark the next cascade, and the next, while her body clenched tight around a cock that felt larger and harder by the second.

He went rigid above her, and she held him as he shuddered. He throbbed inside her, quick, hot pulses echoed and answered by her own body.

Together. She sank her hands into his hair and dragged his head up so she could watch his face, just like he'd watched hers. His parted lips, his furrowed brow, the hazy, dangerous hunger that even an orgasm couldn't touch.

A new emotion stirred inside her, nothing so gentle as affection or even as vulnerable as love. It was dark, dangerous, something that made her tighten her fingers as satisfaction overtook them both.

Mine.

kit rocha

Beethoven woke him.

The apartment was dark, and Lili had left his bed. Jared followed the soft strains of the piano out into the living area, and his dick went hard. Again.

She was sitting at his piano, naked. Her hair spilled across her bare back, and the only thing touching her skin was the scant light bleeding in through the windows. Her face was in shadow, so he stood and watched her fingers move over the keys.

She hit a wrong note from time to time but didn't stop. Not technical proficiency, maybe, but there was no denying she *felt* the music, so much that she was oblivious to his presence, even after the last note died away.

"You play well," he murmured.

Lili half-turned on the bench. "I'm sorry, I couldn't resist. It's such a beautiful instrument."

"By all means." He crossed the room and leaned against the cool wood. "Why did you choose that piece?"

She lifted one shoulder. "I always liked it. When I was on the drugs, I didn't feel, not really. But sometimes the music made me come close."

"Moonlight Sonata. *Quasi una fantasia.*"

"Is that...French? Italian?" She smiled self-consciously. "I'm better with cooking vocabulary."

"Italian." It fit this moment, even better than she realized. "Almost a fantasy."

She turned back and slid her fingers over the flawless, polished wood of the piano. "It's a lot of work, isn't it? Being almost a fantasy."

"Too much work." He didn't regret his life or his decisions, but it would be facile—maybe delusional—to insist that playing sex god to the repressed women of Eden hadn't left its mark on him. "But everything is a cost-benefit analysis, isn't it? 'Do I want this badly enough to pay the price?'"

"I suppose it always is. 'Is the chance that tomorrow could be better worth living through today?'" She smiled up at him. "Now I'm glad I paid the price."

His heart thumped, and he looked away. "You have another analysis to make, now that you know the truth about me."

The bench creaked, and she touched his arm. "I made it before I took my clothes off, Jared. I'm not going to change my mind now."

She wouldn't be the first. Hell, he wouldn't blame her. "Things happen, Lili. People say things in the heat of the moment, and I'd be some kind of asshole if I held you to them without giving you a chance to think."

She rose, standing so close that her hair tickled over his shoulder and the smooth curve of her breast brushed his chest. But she moved before he could, sliding behind him to rest her cheek between his shoulders as she wrapped her arms gently around his waist.

Her skin was warm against his. It would be easy to accept her acceptance and ignore the anxious pressure in his chest. He could lose himself in her, even tell himself nothing else mattered right now.

Easy...but not right. Jared turned and grasped her hips, holding her just far enough away to maintain the illusion of decency. "I mean it. My life right now is dangerous. I need to know you've considered that."

Her blue eyes weren't soft now. They were frozen and ancient, just like her expression. "I know I must seem sheltered, but I didn't grow up in a fairy tale. And I'm not trying to turn you into one."

"I wasn't implying that you were." He tightened his fingers on her hips. "And I'm not trying to get rid of you, either. But there are things I'm only now realizing about my situation, so I'd be damn surprised if you'd managed to wrap your head around it all already."

Lili covered his hands with hers, holding them in place, and took a step back toward the bed. "Then talk to me about what you have to do, and maybe we'll both understand better."

"What I'm already doing," he corrected. "I've been passing information to Dallas for a few months now."

"About the leaders in Eden?"

About everything—leaders, followers, society, and politics. Economics and backroom deals. Anything and everything a woman might complain about over wine...or whisper into his pillow. "You never know which things will be useful."

She nodded, still backing slowly toward his bed and drawing him with her. "Is it hard? Harder than it was before, I mean?"

"Which part?"

"Being almost a fantasy."

"It's—" Yes and no. Trying to explain, that was the hardest thing of all. "At least I knew how to sell sex, you know? The fantasy? And I never pressed for secrets—anyone who spilled them, all I did was listen. It was passive, just...handing over whatever I might have learned. This thing now—the bar, being in Eden—it's different. I'm not an observer anymore. The information I get won't be incidental."

Her eyes widened slightly, and then narrowed. "And that makes it more dangerous."

Jared nodded. "If one of my clients let something slip, she'd have a vested interest in not pursuing it if that information made it out of my bedroom. The people I'll be spying on won't have that holding them back."

"What will happen if you're caught?"

If you wind up in a little room in Eden where there are no windows and no cameras, you'll wish all they'd done was set you on fire. Dylan's words echoed in his head, and Jared shook them away. "I don't know, Lili. I honestly don't. But I think we can safely say it wouldn't be pretty." She stopped as her legs bumped into the mattress. "For you. You're the one in danger. You're the one who needs to be protected. Not me."

"That's a simplistic way to look at it." He couldn't suppress his smile as he sat on the edge of the bed, pulling her along with him. "You wouldn't be the one facing down the barrel of a rifle, but you can't say it wouldn't hurt you. I know it would hurt me, sweet Lili, if our positions were reversed."

She leaned against him and closed her eyes. "Would I be worth it?"

The question was low, hesitant, as if she needed the answer but wasn't sure she could bear it. "Absolutely, love."

She exhaled softly and slipped her hand into his. "So are you. So stop asking."

"All right." Her hand was small, her fingers delicate, and he gripped them tightly. Desperately. "It's easy to lose yourself when you're always playing a role. I've never had someone I didn't have to pretend with, ever."

"Neither have I. I'm not even really sure who I am. Who I would have become, if I'd had a choice."

"Who you *will* become," he corrected softly. "You have that choice now. Dallas and Lex will make sure of it."

She smiled and shifted, sliding one leg over his until she perched on his lap. The light from outside was softer here, glinting off the wild curls that tumbled over her shoulders and down her back, leaving her face in gentle shadows.

In silence, she traced her thumb over his nose and across his cheek. When she reached the corner of his mouth, her smile widened. "Thank you for trusting me with your secret."

He'd trusted her with more than that. With every-thing—his hopes, his passions, all the things he'd spent too many years not considering because they were second-ary to work. To the person he needed to be in order to be an ideal.

With Lili, he didn't have to be perfect. He just had to be Jared.

beyond innocence

12

I T WAS AMAZING what enough money could do in a
relatively short period of time.

The bar was coming together quickly. In the end, his
chat with Gia about the benefits of grungy sector pastiche
versus opulence had led him to his obvious answer—*de-
cayed* opulence. If the people of Eden wanted a speakeasy,
he'd give them one. A real one, just like the underground
bars that had popped up in cities across the country back
when Prohibition reared its ugly head.

The ceilings were low, and it helped that the location
was literally below ground. Exposed stone, dark wood, red
wallpaper, and ornate gilt-framed mirrors completed the
look. Anyone who walked through the doors would feel as
if he'd walked into the past, into a place of secrecy and illicit thrill.

Which made it perfect for his purposes. A dim place

made entirely of secrets was exactly where clandestine meetings happened. And he would be right there, listening.

He was supervising booth placement when quick, decisive footsteps raised the hair on the back of his neck. Military police.

"Mr. Capello." The voice was low and lacking in inflection, possibly because the use of Jared's little-known last name was threat enough. "I'm here to escort you to City Center, on Council orders."

Jared took his time setting aside his clipboard. "Concerning?"

"That's beyond my purview, Mr. Capello. I'm sure everything will be explained."

"I'm sure." He held out both hands. "Well, I'm at your disposal, Officer...?"

"Ashwin Malhotra." He paused, his dark eyes studying Jared's face. "Lieutenant."

"Ah, yes. Russell Miller's replacement." He allowed himself a small smile. "How are you enjoying your promotion, Lieutenant?"

Ashwin didn't return his smile. "Most loyal citizens wouldn't know who Russell Miller was."

"Most loyal citizens don't get shaken down for bribes every fifteen minutes." He rocked back on his heels. "Or do they?"

"Not the loyal ones." Ashwin pivoted. "This will go more smoothly if you come willingly."

Of course it would. But Jared still got the feeling Lieutenant Ashwin Malhotra wouldn't mind shooting him in the fucking head, so he followed the man out the back, to the cramped alley behind the building.

A black SUV was waiting, and Jared squinted at the thick divider between the front and back of the vehicle as he climbed into the back seat. "Nice ride."

beyond innocence

Ashwin slid behind the wheel. A moment later, the vehicle rolled smoothly and silently down the alley. No painstakingly manufactured biodegradable diesel for Eden's elite—just solar power and clean electricity. And tech. In spite of the thick polycarbonate wall between them, Ashwin's voice came to him clearly from invisible speakers. "There won't be any more bribes."

"Really?" That was damn ominous. The ability to pay off the MPs to look the other way as you conducted necessary business was one of the lynchpins of Eden's economy. Ashwin guided the SUV onto the street before meeting Jared's gaze in the rearview mirror. "Miller used to drive bars out of business and then have to waste resources fetching spoiled rich kids out of the sectors. I don't have time for that. Don't draw my boss's attention, and I won't notice you."

"How reassuring." If there was one thing he'd always been terrible at, it was *not* drawing attention.

"Reassurances are also beyond my purview."

"I bet. So." He leaned forward, close to the divider, propping one arm on the frame. "Who is it, exactly, who commands my presence this afternoon?"

"Councilman Nikolas Markovic."

The new guy, the same one Dallas had his eye on as a potential convert and ally. Jared sat back on the seat and resolved to think of this less as a shakedown and more of an opportunity. "I don't believe I've had the pleasure."

Ashwin glanced at him in the mirror again. "Is that what you consider it?"

Jared shrugged. "Until something or someone proves otherwise, why not?"

"It's not the reaction I'm accustomed to."

"No?" The SUV passed through the market district and headed straight for the cluster of glass and steel buildings that housed the city's shriveled political heart. "No, I imagine most of the *loyal citizens* you drag before the

Council would have good reason to be shitting their pants, wouldn't they, Lieutenant?"

He shrugged one broad shoulder, but it was stiff, as if he was mimicking proper body language instead of expressing himself. "Loyal citizens don't know I exist, either."

"I'll keep that in mind." They pulled to a stop outside of the towering Civic Building, and two uniformed officers stepped forward to escort Jared through the door.

At least we're not going in the back, he thought dourly. If you planned to beat someone to death and dump his body in the reservoir, you wanted as few witnesses as possible, even here in Eden. Even if you were part of the Council.

One silent elevator ride later, the lieutenant left him alone in a small corner office, staring out the windows that overlooked the outer edge of the city, as well as a large part of Sector Five.

He didn't have long to wait. The far door opened, and Nikolas Markovic stepped through.

The newest councilman looked a little younger than Dallas, but even more harried. His suit hung just a bit big, and his dark brown hair was overdue for a trim. His strong jaw was stubbled, though it was too early for five o'clock shadow.

In a place that valued appearances as much as Eden did, Markovic was an unlikely leader. And his expression said he knew it. "Have a seat, Mr. Capello."

"Jared." There were two chairs in front of the desk, both canted slightly to either side. He pushed one to the middle, squarely facing the desk, and sank into it. "My name is Jared."

"If you insist." Markovic settled into his own seat and studied Jared. "It's not as if the name attached to your bar code was originally recorded by Eden, was it?"

"That sounds like a rhetorical question."

beyond innocence

"Just an acknowledgment." He waved his hand to take in his office. "We could be having this conversation some-where less comfortable. But I don't consider you an enemy."

The words meant more when they didn't come hard on the heels of a veiled threat. "What do you consider me?"

Markovic pressed his fingers together and considered the question. "Impressive," he said finally. "You've navi-gated between worlds for more years than most people manage. Worlds with contradictory demands."

Jared grinned. "You didn't have your pet Special Tasks soldier haul me out of my bar to talk about my flex-ibility, did you?"

Suggestive words, and they worked. Markovic flushed and sat back, gripping the arms of his chair. "No. I thought you deserved a warning."

"I find it hard to believe that your fellow Council mem-bers could begrudge my change in profession. After all, it means I won't be fucking their wives anymore."

Flustered or not, the man held his ground. "On the contrary. You were harmless while you were...catering to their wives' idle curiosities."

"Was I."

Markovic inclined his head. "My colleagues have their blind spots. But Dallas O'Kane isn't one of them."

"I see." The man could be dismissive of Jared's job, of his clients' happiness—hell, of sexual pleasure altogether. But he couldn't overlook the O'Kanes. The realization was a powerful one, one that meant everything. "The real point of this visit."

"There's been talk," he agreed. "They're saying that O'Kane is tired of crumbs, and you're the one he's sent to steal dinner."

The urge to laugh overwhelmed him, and Jared gave in to it. "I don't know Dallas very well, but I can tell you one thing—whatever you bastards here in the city have, it's the last fucking thing he wants."

A muscle in Markovic's jaw twitched, and he leaned forward again. "We have plenty to offer. Plenty that we should be—" He ground his teeth together. "Whether he wants it or not is beside the point. *They* think he does. And if someone questions you again about your associations with him, it won't be in an office."

"No, it'll be in one of those rooms downstairs that no one talks about." Jared rose and reached for the top button of his shirt.

Markovic's eyes widened. "What are you doing?"

"Answering your question, Councilman." His shirt fell open, and he began to loosen the cuffs. "O'Kane inks all his men."

Flushing, the man averted his gaze. "This isn't necessary."

Jared stilled his hands. "It's your call, Mr. Markovic," he murmured. "You're the boss."

The flush deepened. Markovic's hands flexed on the arms of his chair, then he leaned forward and swung his gaze back to Jared's. "If you don't think Cerys has tried worse on me, you're not as impressive as I thought."

Cerys could spot repressed dominant tendencies from fucking orbital space. It was her favorite thing to exploit, the shaky, desperate need that had yet to find its focus. She could play to that need, coax it to life with the perfect sweet young thing—and then snap her trap shut right on the poor bastard's balls.

Jared arched one eyebrow. "Fair enough. You're not interested in me, and I'm officially retired from the whoring business. So why don't we be straight with each other? I just want to run my bar, Markovic."

"Your *social club*, I'm sure you meant."

"Whatever helps you sleep at night."

The councilman almost smiled. "Better relations between Eden and the sectors would help me sleep at night.

I have a feeling neither of us can survive forever on our own."

Every so often, some bigwig from Eden would start talking about *better relations* between the city and the sectors. Usually, it meant they wanted a piece of the sector action under the cover of a humanitarian crusade. But Jared got the strangest feeling that Nikolas Markovic was sincere.

It would make him exactly the ally Dallas wanted. And it would get him killed. "You want my advice on how to handle facilitating those relations? Don't."

One eyebrow swept up. "Don't? At all?"

"Unless you just can't wait for your colleagues on the Council to get rid of you, then yeah."

"Save your concern. Your current position is even more precarious than mine." He waved a hand and averted his gaze. "And button up your shirt."

"Yes, sir," he murmured, busying his hands with the task. "There's something you should know, since you're thinking about climbing into bed with O'Kane."

Markovic didn't bluster or deny. "And that is?"

His next words could get Dallas exactly what he wanted—or put him on the chopping block. So Jared chose them carefully. "Dallas isn't tired of crumbs. He's tired of the bullshit, the hypocrisy. Your buddies might think he wants what's theirs, but the truth is much more danger-ous."

After a moment, Markovic inclined his head. "That would be valuable information for someone interested in aligning himself with O'Kane. Which neither of us are, of course."

"Of course."

"I'll relay your lack of associations to my colleagues. But, Jared?"

There was a lilt of warning in the other man's voice. "Sir?"

"Now would not be the time to convince them you were never harmless."

"Sure, I was," Jared replied softly. "I still am. Completely harmless. A brainless pretty face with a big dick and plenty of O'Kane's finest whiskey, right?"

The words earned him a tightened jaw and slight frown. "If you keep poking for a reaction, someone's going to give you one you don't like."

"Relax." Jared carefully rearranged the chairs into their proper places. "I don't poke where I'm not wanted."

"Kindly get out, Mr. Capello."

Jared allowed himself a smile as he turned for the door. "Yes, sir."

Rachel got very, very excited about hops.

"They have greenhouses, right?" she asked Hawk, the words tumbling over each other. "Hops need moisture. You can't just grow them in the desert, they'll be useless."

Lili hid a smile by looking down at her notes, where she'd plotted out her wish list of herbs and spices. Rachel was always exuberant, but now she was domineering, too, leaning in with a confident focus that left Hawk a little flustered.

"We can do greenhouses—"

"And trellises," she went on. "They do better with more exposed surface area. If you train them up trellises, you get a better yield."

"I'm sure we can figure something out," Jade said, stepping smoothly into the conversation and gently diverting Rachel's attention. "Finn and Bren have recovered so much in the way of building materials from Three that we can create anything you'll need for a stable, consistent crop."

Rachel blinked at her. "I'm doing it again, aren't I?"
"A little. But it's charming." Jade smiled and gestured
to Lili's tablet. "What about you, Lili? What else do you
need to expand the kitchens?"
Lili glanced down at her list again, as well as the idle
doodles spiraling down the side. There was a *weight* to sitting at this table, a responsibility, even if it was merely
about herbs and vegetables. People with the power to
make sweeping changes were consulting her.
What she said could change things. "Just the herbs,
which should be easy. But I'd like to grow extras. As much
of everything as we can, so I can dry it."
"We use solar dryers on the farm," Hawk said.
"Wouldn't be hard to make a couple more."
Jade nodded. "Rachel? Anything else you need him to
consider during the construction phase?"
"No, I'm good." She snapped her stylus into her tablet
and rose. "But I'm late for opening shift." She waved at
Hawk and stopped to brush a kiss over the top of Jade's
head, then Lili's. "Have fun."
"Wait." Lili swept up her own tablet with a smile for
Hawk and Jade. "I'll walk over with you."
"Sure." Rachel waited until they were nearly to the
access door for the roof before slinging her arm around
Lili's shoulders and leaning close. "Tell the truth—I scared
Hawk, huh?"
Lili laughed. "I think we all scare him a little, even
me. He seems more comfortable with the men."
"Less intimidated, you mean." She lowered her voice
further. "I get the feeling Hawk doesn't have a lot of experience with women."
"He's from Sector Six, isn't he?" The little she knew
about the farms painted them as sprawling families where
men took half a dozen wives, each one expected to have as
many children as her mother had. Lili had grown up surrounded only by her siblings. Hawk had likely been the

same.

"Yeah. Related to practically everyone around him on the farm." She paused. "I wonder if that's why he wanted to stay."

"Maybe not the only reason." Lili looped their arms together as they started down the stairs. "Once you get used to it, it's hard to imagine leaving."

"Right on." Rachel grinned, pleased. "Something's different about you today."

Everything was different about her today, and it had nothing and everything to do with the blissful night she'd spent in Jared's bed. The pleasure had been sweet, but not as sweet as letting go of fear.

The world still might break her. But it might *not*, and the potential in every breath was exhilarating. "I think I'm finally fully awake."

"It must have been one hell of a night." Rachel squeezed her arm. "Good for you."

Lili didn't blush, though maybe she should have. After the first time, she'd all but demanded he take her again, and he *had*, deep and slow and whispering filthy promises of the things they could do to each other, things that must be sin on either side of the wall and nonetheless heated her blood.

If he'd appeared in front of her, she would have dragged him straight to her rooms to try a few of them. "It was...eye-opening."

"With Jared? I bet."

"Is it always so—?" She bit her lip, suddenly uncertain. Nessa and the others had been relentless in their teasing demands for details, which meant frank discussions had to be common, but Lili hadn't shaken free of all of her repression overnight.

"Intense?"

"All-consuming." She paused in the stairwell at the second floor so she could face Rachel. "And still confusing.

beyond innocence

Even the parts that should have been terrifying...weren't."
"Yeah, because Jared's not a selfish asshole." Rachel
tipped one shoulder up in a shrug. "You wanted him to
have a good time, right? That goes both ways."
It was so simple, and yet still the most profound reve-
lation of her short life. "Not everywhere."
Rachel winced. "Right, not everywhere. I'm sorry. I
forget."
"It's all right." They continued down the stairs, and
Lili tucked their arms together again. Casual affection—
something else that might take time to feel natural. The
O'Kanes were only standoffish with outsiders. Absent
touching meant belonging, and Lili was beginning to un-
derstand how much she wanted to belong.
"Before I came here," Rachel went on, "when I lived in
Eden, my parents expected me to marry a certain type of
man. A politician, someone who would wind up on the
Council someday."
Having met plenty of those men, Lili could imagine
what Rachel's life would have entailed. "I'm glad you came
here, then."
"So am I. But I do know that if any of those men had
treated me badly, my father would have put a stop to it."
She hesitated. "That's why it's easy for me to forget how
awful things can be. Sometimes I need reminders, you
know?"
If she could forget at all, she truly was one of the elite.
Not because she'd been born to wealth or in a certain sector, but because she'd had the rarest of all things—a loving
parent with the power to protect her.
They stepped into the sunlight together, and Lili
squeezed Rachel's hand. "I don't want to remind you of bad
things, and I don't want to remember them, either. We're
here. And I like it here."
"Dallas and Lex will be glad to hear it."
With Rachel's ink under her fingers, the question

hung in Lili's throat, so obvious, so fraught with the potential for rejection. Taking in a broken girl out of pity and obligation was a far cry from wanting her. "Do you really think they will be?"

"Yes, I do," Rachel said firmly.

"Enough to let me join, some day?"

The shorter woman sighed as she came to a halt in the middle of the courtyard. "Someday, tomorrow—you know they will, Lili. And you know why. Because we're not so different, the two of us."

It seemed laughable, but Rachel didn't look amused, so Lili didn't smile. "We're not?"

"Not at all. And I should have thought to tell you, because I know it matters. It did to me." Rachel folded her arms around her body. "We're both here because we gave Dallas something he wanted. You gave him testimony in front of the other sector leaders. I saved his supply lines into Eden."

It came back to Lili in a rush, all the furtive meetings between her father and her husband. Meetings involving men from Eden, men trying to move liquor and beer. She remembered hiding in a pantry while those men discussed betraying their leader.

Liam Riley. Rachel's father. "How did you do it?"

"It's a long story, but Eden was looking for someone to hang, and I took the fall. It kept Dallas and my father in business, so Dallas took me in."

"And made you a member." And *now* Lili understood. Her defensive posture, the faint sadness, all the little hints that echoed Lili's own unease. It was that discomfort that had driven her to Rachel to begin with, searching for some purpose or value that wasn't rooted in the worst day of her life.

"Yeah. And it took me a while to figure it all out. The truth." Rachel looked away, then pinned Lili with a pointed stare. "They *had* to let me in. But that doesn't mean they can't love me just as much as everyone else."

Lili nodded, even though the situations weren't the same at all, in the end. Dallas O'Kane had everything to gain from keeping Rachel happy and safe, especially if her father could sever business ties over her poor treatment. There was no one left in the world to protest Dallas turning Lili out into the streets.

Except he hadn't. Not on that first night, and not on any of the drugged, useless nights that followed. Because by some inexplicable miracle, the leader of Sector Four *cared*. "You're pretty easy to love, Rachel."

Rachel blushed. "Not everyone agrees, but thanks. That means a lot."

Spontaneous affection, it turned out, was something you never forgot. She hugged Rachel, and it didn't feel awkward at all this time.

Not that it was the same as hugging family—there was a warmth there, an awareness of the sensual pleasure of touching someone else. It didn't burn as brightly as Jared's touch, but when they broke apart and resumed their walk, Lili knew Rachel had felt it, too.

Which was good. It distracted them both from what Lili hadn't quite said, the darkness beneath her compliment.

You're pretty easy to love. But I'm not.

13

"WELL, BROTHER, YOUR pretty little flower sure is blooming now."

Jared should have known it was coming. All through dinner, Ace had been on his best behavior, with barely a word or a look out of place. Now that Lili, Rachel, and Cruz had cleared the dishes and left to take them back down to the kitchen, it was his chance to pounce.

Jared avoided Ace's gaze by pouring out five generous glasses of whiskey. "The fish was lovely. It must have cost Cruz more than money to get enough."

"Thank Hawk for it." Ace grinned. "Knowing a gang of smugglers in fast cars can come in handy. And plenty of people in Six and Seven will trade a hell of a lot more than fish for a few bottles of O'Kane whiskey."

"Being one of Dallas's men has its benefits, I suppose."

"Mmm." Ace picked up one of the glasses. "You'd

know, wouldn't you?"

Fuck. "Who's been telling tales, Alexander?"

"You, brother, when you sat in my chair and told me Dallas was trying to turn you into a spy." Ace pinned him with a hard look. "Gia told me you bought that fucking bar. Don't worry—I didn't tell her what it really means. Couldn't bring myself to break her damn heart. Plus, she'd murder you."

"Probably." Jared drained his glass and set it down gently, taking a moment to compose himself before continuing. "I'm surprised at you, though. You've been after me to join your happy little band of brothers for ages."

"Yeah, so you could live with us and drink with us and fuck with us and always fight with someone at your back. That's what it means. Not this—this *bullshit.*" Ace waved a hand at the wall, as if gesturing toward Eden itself. "That place is toxic. I wanted you away from it, not up to your eyebrows in its muck."

"I see." He refilled his glass, and added more to Ace's, as well. "You wanted me on your terms."

"I wanted you to be *safe*," Ace countered hotly. "Being an O'Kane can be dangerous, but that's not all it's supposed to be. You're *only* getting the dangerous parts."

"Safe," Jared echoed. "You mean like running enforcement operations or collections? I'm safer doing what I know how to do, Ace. What I'm good at."

Ace struggled with it for a long moment, then relented with a scowl. And he *had* to relent—there was no other choice with his own scars so fresh. "Fine, but what about being alone? No one knows, Jared. And they'd love you if you let them."

"No one? Let's see." He ticked off the names on his fingers. "There's Dallas and Lex, obviously, I'm pretty sure Jasper. Bren." *Cruz.* "Lili knows."

"Lili? Dallas and Lex told *Lili?*"

"No, I did. She deserved to hear it from me."

beyond innocence

Silence. Ace stared at him forever before snagging the whiskey bottle and pouring himself another generous shot. "Fuck, man. We're going to be drunk by the time they get back."

Jared allowed the possibility with a short nod. "I asked Dallas not to tell you. I made him swear it, actually."

"Dallas is a big boy. He can handle my irritation." Ace snorted. "Almost punched me out over it—that's how I know he still likes me, by the way. The *almost* part."

"Of course he does," Jared whispered. Ace was the embodiment of O'Kane, sometimes even more so than the man himself. He was a living, breathing symbol of how they functioned—not just the fucking, but the fighting. The brotherhood.

And that was what Jared needed to protect. Not Dallas or the rest of the O'Kanes—not even Ace, not really—but the *dream*. The idea that something like this could exist, and no one could kill it, no matter how hard they tried. The O'Kanes had survived turf wars and territory disputes, hostile takeover bids and political maneuvering—hell, even assassination attempts.

With Jared's help, they could survive Eden.

Ace slid his hand over Jared's wrist, curling his fingers over the skin where all the other O'Kanes wore their loyalty in ink. "How can I help?"

No time to deflect with suggestive words—not that they would work on Ace anyway. "Honestly? I need you to promise you'll take care of Lili."

"We'll all take care of Lili," Ace said without hesitation. "She may not be an O'Kane yet, but she *is* blooming. I wouldn't have guessed she had that spine in her. But you and Rachel saw something there."

"So will you. Give her a chance, Ace."

"Hey, I *like* the spine. And her cooking." Ace's sudden grin was familiar and wicked. "And how hard Rachel gets off on having her watch."

"Filthy bastard." Jared shoved his hand away with a chuckle. "Don't blame it on Rachel. I was there. I saw you getting off just as hard."

"Oh, Rachel's full of delicious fantasies about your girl." Ace paused deliberately before arching a brow. "If that's what she is. Yours."

"Mine." He tried the word, just to see how it flowed off his tongue. "I've never had anyone I was able to keep before."

"Is that what you want to do with her?"

"Yes." The timing was horrible—worse than horrible—but he couldn't deny the way she pulled at him with every breath. It didn't matter whether she was aware of him or not. When Lili was nearby, he knew it. He knew it in a visceral way that only seemed stronger now that he'd been inside her.

Ace smiled in sympathy. "It's unsettling as hell, isn't it?"

"Certainly nothing Eladio ever taught us how to handle."

"No fucking kidding. But hey, you've watched me and Gia screw things up left and right. Learn from our mistakes."

"I'm not sure that's how mistakes work." Their missteps would always be theirs, and he would always have his own that he had to stumble through, because it was all about pain. Realizing that the hurt was there before you could ever dream of crawling over it.

Ace lifted his refilled glass. "Keep her, Jared. I like seeing you happy."

"Same." Jared met the toast and finished his drink. "How many is that?"

"Enough to get the blood pumping." Ace slammed his glass down. "You know why Cruz is taking his time with the cleanup, right? He's giving me a chance to see how you

beyond innocence

feel about an encore performance of the night at the con-cert."

Jared snorted. "And here I thought the ladies had this all figured out already."

"The ladies are sweet and earnest and eager enough to make my dick hurt." Teasing words, but Ace's tone was as serious as his eyes. "And I don't think either of them have considered that you might want to keep Lili all to yourself."

He had no claim on her, certainly nothing as strong as an O'Kane claim—collars and ink and forever. "Sex is sex," he murmured. "If I couldn't separate having a good time from love, I'd be a terrible whore, wouldn't I?"

Ace stilled. "Is that what we were talking about, then? Love?"

If they were, Ace wasn't the person who needed to hear it. "We could be."

"Damn." Ace tapped his glass absently against the ta-ble. "Do you want to keep her all to yourself? And no bullshit evasion this time, brother. That's the only way this works."

"No." There were worse things than freedom. "Lili's had enough of other men controlling her. She can have whatever she wants."

Ace nodded slowly. "Think she knows what that is?"

Jared could hear voices drifting through the door, and he pushed his glass aside. "If she doesn't, she'll soon find out."

Cruz was the first to come in. His gaze swung straight to Ace and lingered as Lili followed him, holding a plate of brownies.

She smiled at Jared. "I brought us something sweet."

Rachel laughed. "Lili throws around baked goods the way Nessa gives out manicures."

"I got one this afternoon." Lili set down the plate and held up one hand, showing off pale pink nails with white

191

tips. "She's an artist. My lines are always crooked when I try to do this."

It was easy to imagine her hands on his skin, those nails raking over his arm, down his side. Up his thigh. Jared took her hand, drew it to his mouth, and kissed her knuckles.

Lili's smile softened into the one from last night—shy, sweet, and just for him. As if they were the only people in the room, she slid her free hand into his hair, her nails teasing lightly over his scalp. "You got into the whiskey without us."

"Not too much," he assured her. "Just enough."

Lili reached for a glass, but Ace leaned forward to cover her hand, trapping it. "Before you go tipping liquor past those pretty lips, you've got a decision to make."

Her brow furrowing, Lili turned to face Ace fully. "What decision?"

He tilted his head toward Cruz, who already had one arm looped around Rachel's waist, his fingertips edged under her shirt. "Me and Cruz? We're going to strip her naked and do filthy, filthy things to her. And to each other. But, if you want, we'll keep our clothes on until you're gone."

Lili still had one hand curled around the back of Jared's neck, and her fingers tightened as she studied the other three in silence. Then she tugged the glass from under Ace's fingers and lifted it to her lips.

She didn't slam the drink back. Instead, she sipped it, letting the liquor linger on her tongue before her throat worked. And when she bent to capture Jared's mouth with her own, he could still taste it.

He wanted to pull her into his lap right there—but there were better vantage points in the room, like the wide couch that directly faced the bed. So he rose, gathering her in his arms as he moved, and crossed to sink into the plush cushions.

Low voices murmured behind them, too soft for the words to be distinguishable. Lili cupped his face and pressed her forehead to his. "We can leave whenever you want."

He brushed her hair back from her face. "That's my line."

"Lines are rehearsed." She turned her face into his hand, her lips brushing his palm. "I don't want to be."

"You're right." He stroked his fingers over the delicate line of her jaw. "No more lines."

"Just what feels good." She tilted her head, smiling up at him with big eyes brimming with trust. "You know how much I can take."

A curious concept, one he hadn't concerned himself with in years, but it fit. She was still learning—not just to feel in her heart, but with her body, as well. "That's why we're here, isn't it?"

Her cheeks flushed, pink spilling down her throat as she glanced over his shoulder. He didn't have to turn—a moment later, Ace backed Rachel around the couch. Her shirt was already gone, and Ace twisted one hand in her hair as he slid the other into her pants.

"Goddamn, angel," he groaned as her back collided with one solid bedpost. "Were you this wet all through dinner, you dirty girl?"

"No." She arched her back and sank her teeth into her lower lip. "*Yes.*"

Ace withdrew his hand and slicked his fingers over her lips before dipping his head to lick them. "What are we going to do about this filthy girl, Cruz?"

His voice rumbled from behind the couch. "Take off her clothes so everyone can see."

Rachel shivered, the movement echoed in slow motion as Lili trembled. This was the moment where expectation collided with desire, and they discovered what came next—confusion and awkwardness, or explosive pleasure.

In her jumbled, drug-fogged memories, Lili had a dozen moments like this. Moans and skin and clothes falling away as she tried to avert her eyes, tried to block out the sights and sounds and the way both made her feel, even when she barely *could* feel.

Tonight, she didn't have to avert her eyes. She wasn't *supposed* to. As unfathomable as it was to someone who'd spent her life hiding, her attention was the entire point. Watching as Rachel came alive under Ace's hands and Cruz's words heightened the other woman's pleasure.

Knowing she had that power heightened Lili's own.

A low growl rumbled up in Jared's chest. "This reminds me of a story I heard once, Ace."

"Yeah?" Ace tugged Rachel's pants over her hips, guiding them down as Cruz crossed the room. "Was it a good story?"

"The best. A story about the first time your angel there decided to cut loose."

Ace grinned against Rachel's waist. "She always comes prettiest for an audience. Sometimes Cruz sits right on that couch and watches me work her over until she's begging to stop coming."

"Begging to stop?" Jared's thumb made slow, breathtaking circles on the inside of Lili's knee. "I don't believe it."

"Neither do I," Cruz whispered, stopping next to Rachel. "She begs, but she doesn't mean it."

He curled his fingers around her throat, and now Lili could see all the little details she'd missed by averting her eyes. The way his thumb rubbed slow, tender circles just below her ear, echoing Jared's shivery touch. The way his stern expression was ruined by the softness in his gaze, and the fact that her sharply indrawn breath was pure excitement, without the slightest edge of fear.

They were carrying on entire silent conversations in the nuances, and she finally understood enough to see them.

"Please," Rachel whispered, the hitch in her voice one of sheer anticipation.

Lili's own body tightened in response. Jared's hand was already under her skirt, his fingers warm on her skin. He wouldn't have to slide much higher to brush her panties and discover how swiftly she was reacting.

She struggled not to squirm, but Ace was tugging at Rachel's underwear now. He dragged it down a few teasing inches and paused to bite the newly revealed skin. She whispered again, another plea that trailed off into a breathless moan.

"See?" Cruz was so tall he had to bend to brush a kiss to Rachel's temple. "She begs when she doesn't mean it."

She reached for him, but Cruz made a chiding noise and tapped the bedpost above her head. "Hands, sweetheart."

She leaned more heavily against the bedpost, as if her knees had gone weak, and raised her arms. It lifted her breasts, and light glinted off the metal decorating her nipples. In the bar, distance and shadows had obscured anything beyond the fact that it was there, but now Lili could see the delicate hoops.

They weren't simply attached. Her nipples were *pierced*, and the memory of having a needle jabbed through her sensitive earlobe made Lili want to cross her arms over her chest.

Apparently, her discomfort showed. Cruz slid his hand from Rachel's throat down to cup her breast, his thumb teasing just below the adornment. "Tell her about these."

She sucked in a sharp breath. "My nipple rings?"

"Mmm." He nudged the ring lightly, and Lili did squirm this time.

Rachel clenched her teeth and rubbed the back of her head against the bedpost. "It hurt," she admitted. "I didn't know how much it would. I have so much ink, and I thought it would be the same. But Ace is soft with his nee- dles. This...felt like being bitten. Hard."

Ace ran his hand up the inside of Rachel's thigh. "But it was worth it, wasn't it? Now it hurts just the way you like."

Another moan. "Yes. Sometimes they catch on my clothes, and it feels like someone's touching me."

Lili knew the swimming, dreamy warmth of Jared's thumb stroking away the tight ache in her nipple. She tried to imagine feeling it every time she moved too fast. "How do you not go crazy?" she rasped, forgetting until the words were out that she was meant to be *watching*, and maybe that meant silence.

But a slow smile curved Rachel's lips. "Who says I don't?"

As if to demonstrate, Cruz caught one silver ring and tugged until she shuddered. Lili felt the same reaction building in her, but then her brain skidded to a halt as Jared's fingers brushed her nipple through her shirt.

There was no darkness to hide her shivers this time. No music to swallow her gasp. She clutched at Jared's arm, as acutely aware of being watched as she had been of being the watcher.

In the bar, it would have been too much. Even a party might have scraped her nerves raw—so many eyes, so many near-strangers. But this was different. Intimate. She was protected.

Safe.

Cruz pulled on the ring again and murmured a soft command. "Ace, get her present."

Ace rolled to his feet, leaving Cruz to stroke his fingers

beyond innocence

down Rachel's trembling body. "That's right, sweetheart. He's been shopping again."

Her only answer was a moan, and Jared leaned close, his mouth next to Lili's ear. "Ace loves to decorate her—tattoos, jewelry. Anything that will get her off."

Her skin *was* covered in ink—Lili had seen it before, but she hadn't really looked. In addition to the intricate work on her throat and the O'Kane logo nestled between her collarbones and breasts, she had a breathtaking piece on her side of an angel in a dizzying dive, the wind whipping at her hair and ribbons from her gown flowing behind her with movement Lili could almost touch.

Digital art was popular in Eden, as well as with the sector families who aspired to Eden's luxury. Huge, expensive frames that showed whatever you wanted on a given day. Flat and uninspiring, because there was no risk in artwork where mistakes could be so easily undone.

Ace marked people forever. Now she understood why they let him. "The tattoos are beautiful."

"I know," Ace replied, coming back around the couch with a box in one hand. He stopped to trace his fingertips over the angel on Rachel's ribs. "She's a terribly behaved canvas. Gets so hot and bothered. Ten minutes under the needles and her pussy's so wet it'd be cruel not to fuck her."

Rachel's sleepy eyes widened, flashed. "You love me for it."

"One of many reasons." Ace set the box on the bed. "Cruz, get her hair."

They moved in concert, Cruz gathering Rachel's hair as Ace lifted a web of delicate, bejeweled chains. It was impossible not to remember that last party, the way Lili had stared in horror, struggling to understand why any woman would want to suffer the needs of two men.

Tonight, she was the center of their world. Every touch, every word, was about her. Even Jared and Lili's

197

presence was the answer to another need—to be seen, to be watched as they fastened one delicate chain around her throat.

It could have been a necklace, except the focal point was a thin piece of silver twisted into an intricate, looping design that hung low, between her breasts. Lili didn't understand why until Ace lifted one of the dangling chains and hooked it to the ring through her nipple. Jewels dripped from the hook, dancing with every one of Rachel's uneven breaths.

With a smile so wicked it stole Lili's breath, Ace tugged the chain firmly.

Rachel jerked with a sound that was half-whimper, half-laugh. "More?"

Cruz hooked the other chain in place with a soothing noise. "So many ways to give you more. Maybe I'll ask Jared what they'd like to see."

"Why me?" Jared ran his hand lazily down the length of Lili's arm, then back up again. "She's the one watching every single breath, every touch. Drinking it all in. Learning what she wants to do. Right, love?"

The words should have shamed her, but there was such naked approval in them. And that was when she realized she'd been wrong—this wasn't just about Rachel's fantasies and Rachel's pleasure.

It was about hers, too.

Her pleasure, her curiosity. Her comfort. And it was the answer to the secret fear she'd barely admitted to herself—that Jared could only cater to her ignorance and innocence for so long before it began to feel like work. He, of all people, deserved a lover willing—*able*—to cater to *him*.

Ignoring everyone else, Lili sought Rachel's eyes. They were beautiful, a dreamy blueish hazel, and full of unashamed lust. Rachel was open, unafraid. Brave enough to help Lili understand. "How much pleasure can you take before it's too much?"

"The one question without an answer," Rachel whispered. "All I can do is show you."

Lili found Jared's hand and wove their fingers together to hide her nerves. "Please."

Cruz touched Rachel's chin, tilting her face up to his. "Help me undress."

She reached for his shirt first, her fingers tangling eagerly in the fabric as she drew it up, up, as far as she could before he had to take over and strip it away. His body was as intimidating as Lili remembered, wide and hard, every line perfectly formed. He had tattoos, too—dragons winding around one arm and down to his wrists, the creatures so vivid they seemed alive when his muscles flexed.

An appreciative rumble vibrated through Jared's chest. "I'm not sure how either of you manages not to lick him all the goddamn time."

"It's not easy." Rachel demonstrated with a quick flick of her tongue over his ribs as she sank to the floor at his feet. She worked the laces on his boots, her head bent to her task, her movements slow and reverent.

Lili tensed. She couldn't stop herself. There were too many echoes, vague memories of evenings spent kneeling at Logan's feet in chilly silence as she unlaced his shoes and counted down the seconds to her escape.

Breathing faster, she grasped for the nuances. And they were there, so clear when she made herself look. Rachel's flushed skin and the smile only half-hidden by her hair. Cruz's protective stance. The gentleness in the way he reached down to stroke the back of her head, murmuring soft compliments that only made Rachel flush harder.

The echoes might be the same, but the details made it different. Beautiful.

When his feet were bare, she closed her hands around his belt. The buckle clicked, and leather hissed against denim as she pulled it open, pulled it free, and handed it to him.

"Good girl." Cruz folded the belt slowly. His fingers caressed the leather in a suggestive way that made Lili tighten her grip on Jared, but after a moment he tossed the belt aside. "I don't think we need it tonight. Ace?" The other man reacted like it was a command. He sank to his knees behind Rachel and slid a hand down to cup her pussy. She arched against him, sinking her fingers into his hair, and Ace groaned. "Fuck, if she gets much more wound up, she'll come if you *breathe* on her."

"Not yet, Rachel." Cruz caught her chin. "You're not done undressing me."

"I know." She ran both hands up his thighs, over the prominent bulge in his jeans, all the way to the button. She undid it delicately, then tugged at the zipper with the same slow dedication.

All at once, uncertainty seized Lili. Jared's body was a comforting warmth against hers, silent security and support. Staring as another man's erection was revealed felt wrong—and not just the delicious sort of wrong that made her knees weak.

She averted her gaze, sneaking a look at Jared's face. He was tense, all right, but with anticipation, not dread.

He caught her eye and smiled slowly. "Ace talks about Cruz's cock like it's a true wonder of the world," he murmured. "What do you think, Lili?"

The slightest shift and she felt *his* cock against her hip, hard and big and tangible proof that he was as aroused as she was. "I think he's probably biased," she replied in a whisper. *Like I am.*

"Definitely," Jared agreed, "but that doesn't make him wrong."

"I'm never wrong." Ace's voice dragged Lili's attention back to the trio, and her whole body clenched at the sight of them. Cruz, naked and unashamed, almost as perfect as

Jared but in a different way. He was like a statue of a warrior god, and Ace and Rachel knelt before him in supplication.

Well, Rachel did. The wicked glint that never left Ace's eyes shone as he reached up to grip the base of Cruz's cock. "It's glorious, all right. The only thing more perfect is watching Rachel try to swallow the whole damn thing."

"I can't." Rachel met Lili's gaze, her tone one of gleeful, secret confession. "Unless Ace makes me."

Oh *God,* that was wrong, too. The good kind, the kind that made her skin prickle and her voice waver. "Do you like it when he does?"

"More words?" Instead of answering, she leaned in, her eyes still locked with Lili's, and traced her tongue up the length of Cruz's cock, from Ace's hand all the way to the tip.

Yes, she liked it, and Lili didn't have to wonder why anymore. Cruz's groan was the answer. She could understand the concept with her mind, but her body was the part that reacted viscerally to the sight of Ace twisting a hand in Rachel's hair, pushing her forward.

Making her take Cruz's cock. But there was no force, just her glee and eagerness as she parted her lips and Cruz rocked deeper. Ace's other arm flexed, his fingers still pressed against her pussy. The blowjob muffled the volume of her moan, but it couldn't dampen the sheer pleasure in the sound.

"Enough," Cruz grated. Ace immediately urged Rachel's head back, but he didn't stop working his fingers between her thighs until Rachel whimpered and Cruz gave him a stern look. "Ace."

"Tease." Ace withdrew his hand and gave Rachel over to Cruz, who lifted her from the floor and carried her to the bed. Ace had already shed his shoes. As Lili watched, he stripped his shirt over his head, revealing hints of light brown skin and a riot of color—tattoos covering his arms, his chest, his stomach, and his entire back.

He paused and smiled. "You two are overdressed, brother."

"Yes, we are." Jared locked his arm around Lili and rose. He set her on her feet, then turned her and captured her mouth in a blistering kiss. His fingers skimmed over her silk blouse, searching out the buttons with skillful ease.

Another set of hands caught at the fabric, tugging it off her shoulders, and Lili broke from the kiss, panting for breath and off balance.

"It's okay, blue-eyes." Ace's voice was as soft as his touch—though he wasn't touching her at all, really. Just her shirt, teasing the silk against her skin as he worked it down her arms. "Everyone here has got you. Tell her, Rae."

"Yes." She was watching from the bed, propped up on one elbow as Cruz traced the tattoos around her throat with his lips. "Everyone."

It wasn't just watching now. In her gut, Lili had known it wouldn't be. She'd seen how easily the O'Kanes traded touch, traded affection.

What she hadn't realized was how intoxicating it could be to be one of them.

When Ace freed her hands, she lifted them to the top button on Jared's shirt. "Everyone's got me," she echoed, staring up into his eyes. His dark, beautiful, *hungry* eyes. "And I've got you."

He smiled down at her and nodded slowly, briefly touching her hand before turning his attention to the front clasp of her bra. "This is lovely. Trix?"

"Yes." It was hard to keep her fingers from trembling when his were brushing her breasts with every movement. She freed the first button and the second, but fumbled with the third when Ace's touch returned, sinking into her hair and lifting it from the back of her neck.

"Fucking hell." It was just one fingertip, but the way

he dragged it down her spine made her shudder. "All this naked skin. When are you going to let me put something on it?"

"I told you." Affection and laughter suffused Rachel's voice. "He can't resist a blank canvas."

Lili found herself smiling, too. "I don't know if I'd like the needles as much as you do."

"You don't have to." She turned her face toward Cruz, nuzzling his jaw as he trailed kisses up to her ear. "It's not about sex. It's about art."

Ace nudged one of Lili's heels with his foot. "Anyone who walks around in these things all day can handle a tattoo. Plus, it's usually the big manly men who cry."

Lili bit her lip and undid the next two buttons, revealing perfect skin and Jared's tattoo. "I can't tell if he's teasing me or not."

"Ace? Always." Jared cupped the back of her head and drew her closer, so close that her lips almost touched his chest.

So she closed the distance and tasted him. His skin was warm beneath her lips, but his shirt frustrated her. So she jerked at the fabric and sent buttons flying to ping on the floor, the sound nearly drowned out by Ace's delighted laughter.

Lili was too busy sliding her hands over Jared to care. "This is my favorite shirt." His hand twisted tight in her hair. "Rip it again."

Only two buttons left. She flexed her fingers and tore the edges apart. Her bra slipped to her elbows, and there was nothing between them as Lili pressed herself to Jared's chest, so hot she was burning up.

They were moving. Lili was only vaguely aware of it, the sensation lost in the tumult of every other wild thing she was feeling—until her legs hit the edge of the bed.

The last line. She kicked off her shoes and fumbled for her pants. But Ace's hands covered hers and guided them back to Jared's chest. "Trix will murder me if I let you rip *your* clothes," he murmured, which was when she realized *he* intended to help—and that she didn't care.

She explored instead, sweeping her thumb over Jared's nipple, entranced when he sucked in a sharp breath and released it shakily. "Harder, Lili." Fabric caressed her thighs, creating another layer of sensation as Ace drew her pants down her legs. Through the fog of want, she remembered the sharp satisfaction of Jared's mouth and echoed what he'd done to her the first night, leaning in to close her teeth lightly around his nipple.

He groaned, and the sound was still vibrating through her when a soft, wet tongue touched the small of her back and traced up her spine.

Not Ace. He was at her hip, guiding her to step free of her pants. Rachel, then, or maybe even Cruz, but it didn't matter. It felt good, and she wanted it.

Silky hair brushed her shoulder as that long, endless caress reached the base of her neck, and Rachel's hand slipped around her body, down her arm, to Jared's skin. "I've never seen him like this before," she whispered, her lips against the side of Lili's throat. "He's always so composed, but not right now. He's burning."

"Good," Lili replied just as softly. Their joined fingers caressed his chest before dropping lower, over the firm muscles of Jared's abdomen, low enough to brush his belt.

"Take it off," came Cruz's voice from behind her, an order that wasn't just for Rachel this time. She'd ventured into Cruz's domain, the place where he held power as firmly as Dallas held Sector Four. Ace and Rachel belonged to him.

Tonight, so did Lili and Jared.

Rachel's lips found the sensitive spot behind her ear, and she shuddered and tilted her head farther, silently begging for more as she slipped Jared's belt free of the buckle.

It wasn't just Rachel who gave it to her, licking and biting and kissing her neck and shoulder. Jared bent to the other side and did the same, until she wasn't sure *which* way to tilt her head for more.

They answered for her when Jared drifted lower, palmed her breast, and sucked her nipple into his mouth. She cried out, abandoning his belt to clutch at his head. Her back arched, and she would have fallen without Rachel there, warm and soft and nothing like being pressed against Jared's hard body.

His teeth scraped her nipple, but only for a brief second before he lifted his head. He searched her face, then the corner of his mouth curved up. "You're curious about pleasure, but not just your own."

Because her own blurred the world. Even now, thoughts slipped through her fingers, and she knew that later she'd struggle to remember them, to remember anything beyond the urge to wrap her legs around his waist and squirm. "I want to understand."

He grasped her shoulders and turned her around to face the bed—and Rachel.

She was beautiful. Gentle curves and flushed skin and all that ink. Lili reached out to trace the chain lying across her collarbone, down to the design nestled between her breasts.

Power. The O'Kanes valued it, exchanged it. Effortlessly, casually, following rules Lili barely grasped and couldn't have appreciated before she understood she held it, too. But she knew who held the power in this room, so she glanced past Rachel to where Cruz sprawled, watching them.

He answered her silent question with a nod. "Ace, show her what Rachel likes."

A second body pressed in behind her, and Ace's hand covered hers. "It's easy," he rasped against her ear as he drew her fingers along the chain that lay between Rachel's breasts. It shifted with every one of her uneven breaths, the blue jewels catching and refracting the light.

"She likes being adored," Ace continued, curling her fingers around the chain. "And that's the easiest fucking thing in the world, because she's goddamn adorable."

Rachel squirmed. "Cruz—"

He came to his knees behind her and hooked his arms through hers, trapping her. "You can be patient," he murmured with a kiss to her temple. "You know how good it is when you're patient."

"Any other night," she murmured, "and I would. You know I—"

His hand locked around her throat, but his gaze caught Lili's. "She likes to squirm. She likes to beg. But she doesn't want you to give in, because she needs the kind of pleasure you can't give yourself. The kind that wipes everything else away."

The kind that both terrified and called to Lili. Letting everything go, knowing she'd felt the extreme edges of pleasure and could take it.

She wet her lips and met Rachel's glazed eyes. "Show me?"

The other woman melted into a shudder that made the chain dangling between her breasts jingle. "No wonder none of you bastards can resist a pretty face."

"It's the big eyes." Ace cupped Rachel's chin and rubbed his thumb over her lips. "Seeing all those filthy thoughts pile up behind them. Watch those big eyes, Rae, when I tell her how many fingers you want filling your pussy."

He didn't even have to. Lili's eyes must have been huge already, because the words were raw and sinful and shocking all on their own—but not shocking enough to stop her from tugging lightly on the chain.

Rachel arched, her lips parting on a gasp as she pulled

against Cruz's grip. He held tight, and she gasped again. Jared stretched out on the bed, his face inches from Rachel's trembling thigh, his hand hooked beneath her knee. "It doesn't have to be about denial," he told Lili. "Just expectation. If she gets off on not being obeyed, it's easy. If she asks for fast, you give her slow."

And soft. Lili leaned in to let her breath feather across Rachel's adorned nipple, relishing the whimpering sounds it elicited. But it was her turn to whimper when fingers plunged into her hair, twisting expertly, just shy of pain. Her scalp tingled, and the tingling spread when Ace growled, "Tongue, Lili."

She liked this, too. All the power of giving pleasure and none of the uncertainty of not knowing how. She parted her lips and traced the tip of her tongue over the tight peak and the ring decorating it.

Rachel jerked, twisting beneath her, her nipple growing even harder as each writhing movement rubbed her flesh against Lili's mouth. "More," she whispered.

Jared moved closer, licked the corner of Lili's mouth. "You have to watch your teeth with these." He bent to Rachel's other breast, nudging the ring until she whimpered. Then he caught the ring with the tip of his tongue—and tugged.

Rachel's response was instant, electric. She moaned another plea, nearly unintelligible in her desperation, and Cruz soothed her with one big hand splayed across her belly. "Almost, sweetheart. Tell them how good it feels."

"I can't. They might stop."

"Never," Jared promised. Then—carefully, delicately—he closed his mouth around the tight, pouting peak.

So Lili did the same.

"Fucking *hell*," Ace breathed as Rachel cried out. "Oh, angel, they're tormenting you something good, aren't they?"

She made a soft noise of agreement—of supplication—and parted her legs.

Ace tugged at Lili's hair, urging her to look up into Rachel's flushed face. "She's so pretty when she's desperate, isn't she?"

Not just pretty. "Beautiful," Lili corrected. Her whole body ached with sympathy now, with a hunger for things she had only just begun to understand. That she might not fully understand until Rachel found release.

Cruz's rough, calloused hand was still splayed across Rachel's middle. The difference between strong fingers and soft skin was entrancing as Lili stroked down, lower. "How do I give her what she needs?"

"She wants you." Jared was breathing fast as he sat up and wrapped one arm around Lili. His hand came to rest on her side, just beneath the curve of her breast, and he caressed her skin lightly. "It doesn't have to be perfect, not yet. It just has to be *you*."

Oh God, she wanted to believe that. That clumsy fumblings and hesitant touches could be enough, that *she* could be enough. She inched her fingers lower, until they encountered soft, hot flesh. She caught her breath when Rachel's hips jerked, as if even that was overwhelming.

Ace groaned, so low and rough it was its own sort of embrace. "How wet is she?"

So wet. So sweet and desperate, straining her hips toward Lili's touch. "Very."

"Show me."

She could still be startled, and she stared as Ace leaned in closer. "You heard me, blue-eyes. Get that sweetness all over your fingers and *show me*."

Jared wrapped one strong hand around her wrist and guided her lower, sliding her fingers over Rachel's pussy. As he dragged them up again, Rachel whimpered at the loss.

"Good girl," Ace whispered, and Lili didn't know which

of them he meant. Then she didn't care, because his tongue was on her fingers, licking Rachel's arousal from them as each swipe tugged at that place low in Lili's body, until she squirmed restlessly in Jared's grasp.

"Ace is greedy, but lazy, love." He touched Rachel again, rubbing his thumb slowly over her clit before pumping one finger inside her. Her hips tried to follow as he withdrew his wet finger and lifted it to Lili's breast. He circled her nipple, slick and careful. Maddening. "There are better places for him to lick you."

Ace bent his head, and Lili realized what he was about to do a heartbeat before his mouth closed around her nipple. He didn't just lick—he *sucked*, hard, and it felt so good Lili's knees wobbled.

Rachel and Cruz both watched, entranced. Jared gathered Lili's hair off one shoulder and nuzzled her neck before raising his mouth to her ear. "Giving pleasure and taking pleasure—it isn't one or the other. When it's good—when it's *right*—they're so mingled you can't tell them apart. Taking without giving is selfish. And if you can give pleasure without taking it in return, then it's just a job or an obligation. Or worse."

Lili groped for Jared's free hand. "Show me," she rasped, dragging their tangled fingers back to Rachel's body. She shuddered at the first touch, and Lili shuddered, too, because Jared was right. "Help me."

He bent her over until her body was pressed against Rachel's, their entwined hands still caught between them. His chest was against her back, trapping her. Hot skin brushed hers with every breath, every tiny movement—

He guided her fingers into Rachel, into slick, clenching heat. Just two, but tight enough for Lili to feel every pulse and flutter of reaction. Then a slippery pressure nudged her deeper—Jared, fucking his own fingers in alongside hers.

"Give and take, love," he whispered, rocking against

her ass. It pushed her forward, driving their fingers into Rachel—hard.

"Oh, *fuck*." Tension wreathed every word, every breath, and Rachel shivered through another vicious curse before reaching for her, cupping her hand around the back of Lili's neck, and drawing her in for an open, ravenous kiss.

Lili moaned into her mouth, overwhelmed but still *there*, in her skin, every sensation sharp and bright. The bite of Jared's open belt against the small of her back, the heat of his skin and the commanding confidence of his touch. The soft roughness of Rachel's tongue, the rasp of the chains trapped between their bodies.

And the *tightness*. Every time Rachel squirmed, every time she gasped, Lili *felt* it, felt her body clench, felt the heady power and the driving need for more. More gasps, more clenching. She wanted to drive Rachel over the edge, watch her scream—and have the courage to follow her.

Rachel's hands roamed her body, exploring the dip of her waist, the curve of her ass, even the tiny, sensitive spot just under her jaw. She cupped Lili's breasts, cradling them in her hands before closing her fingers tight, pinching her nipples.

Not soft, the way Jared had. It was almost pain, a confusing shock that arched her back and drove a moan from her. Her pussy clenched, her pulse pounding so strongly in her ears that she barely heard Cruz's chiding words. "Not so rough, Rachel. Not yet."

"Yes, sir," she whispered wickedly, releasing Lili with a softer, soothing touch. Then she slid one hand down, between them—

"No." Cruz caught her hands and dragged them back. "This, you don't get to control, sweetheart. This you just have to feel. Jared?"

Jared straightened, pulling Lili with him until they were standing, their fingers still buried deep in Rachel's pussy. "Watch."

Ace was already moving, dropping teasing kisses down Rachel's body, kisses that turned into sharp little nips that had her twisting against Cruz's grip. Lower and lower until Lili could feel the heat of his breath against her fingers.

"Look at you, angel," he murmured. "So full. Do their fingers feel good?"

"*Yes.*" There was a different sort of tension twisting her voice now, something less like discovery and more like anticipation. "Please."

"But you still want my tongue, don't you?"

"I need it." A ready confession, with no hint of shame.

"I know." But he brushed her with his thumb first, the slightest touch that still had her tightening around Jared's and Lili's fingers. He rubbed in a slow circle, murmuring tender obscenities that Lili could barely hear. It didn't matter. She couldn't tear her attention away as he gently parted Rachel's folds and drew his tongue across her clit.

She bucked. The more firmly they held her down, the louder and shakier she got, until she was trembling all over, begging, *begging* Ace to let her, please let her—

"Let go," Cruz whispered against her cheek, as Ace sucked her clit into his mouth. She went rigid, her cry building into a scream as her inner muscles clenched, released, over and over, throbbing with the force of her orgasm.

No—*orgasms.* Because Jared rocked their fingers deeper and Ace redoubled his efforts and even Cruz released Rachel's hands in favor of cupping her breasts, his fingers toying and tugging with the silver rings until she sobbed with it.

Overwhelmed. Rachel was overwhelmed in every sense of the word, and it wasn't bad or shameful or terrifying. It was transcendent.

Dazed, Lili lifted her free hand to stroke the woman's flushed skin, letting her fingers rest on the racing pulse in her throat. "She's perfect."

"Yes, she is," Jared agreed. "Here, now. Like this. We all are."

All of them. Even her. "I want to let go, too."

A rough breath left him, and he gently pulled their fingers out of Rachel, who made a soft noise—not of protest but approval—when he wrapped both arms around Lili. "Your wish is my command."

"*Our* command." Rachel eased up the bed, into Cruz's lap. "Right?"

Ace crawled after her, catching her mouth in a hot, lazy kiss before glancing back at them. "Get up here."

Jared released Lili, all but one reassuring hand on her hip.

Cruz and Rachel and Ace looked like an invitation to sin, sitting at the head of the bed, trading lazy touches as they watched her. Lili rested one knee on the mattress, knowing she had to cross this final boundary by choice.

But not alone. Jared steadied her as she slid onto the bed, and Ace reached for her, coaxing her closer with his fingertips on her shoulder. She settled on her knees just short of Rachel, acutely aware of her own frustrated arousal—flushed skin, tight nipples, the slickness when she pressed her thighs together.

The other woman smiled and opened her arms, welcoming Lili with a soft laugh and skin sliding over skin. "Tell me what it's like."

If the words were supposed to make sense, she was too muddle-headed to figure out how. "What what's like?"

"Fucking Jared." She tilted her head back to Cruz's shoulder. "I'd ask Ace, but somehow I don't think it's the same. Not the way you look at each other."

Lili turned slowly in Rachel's grasp, until she was facing the foot of the bed. Jared had his hands on the

beyond innocence

fastenings of his pants, but when his eyes met hers, Lili answered the question—for him. "It's like being awake for the first time. And it should be terrifying to feel everything, but it's not. Because he knows if it's too much."

"I only know the truth." He tugged down his zipper. "There's no such thing as *too much*, not really. There's only *never enough*."

He hooked his thumbs in his pants and his underwear and pushed them both down.

His cock was hard and big, and she wanted it. Under her hands. In her mouth. Inside her. Lili clutched Rachel's hand and tried to remember when she'd become a creature made of nothing but *want* and sinful hunger so dirty she bit back a whimper.

"Do you want it?" Rachel brushed her hair away from her throat and pressed a kiss to her overheated skin. "All you have to do is say yes."

Let go. "Yes."

Rachel crept forward on her hands and knees, stopping just shy of the edge of the bed. "Ace remembers," she whispered. "Do you?"

Jared grinned down at her. "Remember? I thought you were going to drop-kick me off the fucking roof for touching what was yours."

Rachel grasped Lili's hand and pulled her closer. "He's exaggerating. A little."

Lili had to tilt her head back to meet Jared's eyes. "Tell me the story."

"It happened a while back, during one of O'Kane's parties." Jared wrapped a firm hand around the base of his erection. "An open party, not one of the filthy, private ones. Rachel caught me sucking Ace's cock up on the roof."

"And stayed for the big finish," Ace murmured as the bed sank on the other side of Lili. "Your turn, brother."

Lili wet her lips and dropped her gaze. The head of Jared's cock was so close, and his words came back to her.

213

It doesn't have to be perfect. It just has to be you.
So she parted her lips and licked him.

He dropped his head back with a groan. "Again."

Savoring his moan, she dragged the flat of her tongue up his shaft. She shivered when she reached the tip and found a drop of wetness with the taste she remembered from the bar—bitter and salty and *right.*

Ace's fingers closed over Jared's. "That's right, blue-eyes. Lick him all over. Make Rachel help, if you want. She's panting for it."

Lili tilted her head back again, seeking Jared's eyes before she tested the boundaries of her newfound brazenness. "Do you want us to suck your cock?"

"Yes." He slipped his thumb between her lips, gliding it over her tongue, urging her mouth open. "Think about my face in your pussy. I want to see it in those big, big eyes, love."

The thought alone made her moan. Jared's clever, taunting tongue soothing away every pulse of need until she shattered in relief. Maybe he wouldn't stop this time. Maybe Cruz would hold *her* arms down, and Jared wouldn't have to hold anything back.

"That's it." His eyes blazed, and he gave a short, decisive nod.

A warm hand slid over her hip. Big, rough, but so *gentle*—Cruz's touch would have been unmistakable, even if he hadn't been the only one behind them. "You two help her with Jared, since you can't be trusted not to play too rough with her."

"But not you. Mr. Control." Rachel's teasing words blew hot on Lili's earlobe. "You can watch him lose it, too. Later."

"Later," Cruz agreed, stroking the back of her thigh this time before urging her to rock forward. She shuddered and gave in, and it was simple. Effortless. Ace guided Jared's cock between her lips, and she was rewarded by

Jared's shuddering sigh.

Rachel licked a path ahead of Lili's conquering lips, leaving Jared's rigid shaft slick and hot. In seconds, Ace had joined her, dragging his tongue up to hers as she tried to take more, only to meet with frustration as his size threatened to choke her.

"Shh." Ace tugged at her hair, easing her back. "Swallowing a dick is hot and all, but it's not the only way to get a guy off. Lips and tongue, that's all he needs. And suck, Lili."

That was simpler. Rachel and Ace had already made it easy. Their tongues tangled, stroking over Jared, over each other, over Lili. They left Jared's shaft so slick that her lips glided effortlessly. She swirled her tongue, almost used to Cruz's soft touches now. They were one more spark of warmth, one more step toward a goal she could sense now. It was rushing toward her, big and bright and beautiful. And she wanted it.

Seeking out Jared's gaze again, she sucked.

His eyes went dark, and he licked the corner of his mouth. "So pretty," he breathed. "These gorgeous pink lips stretched around my cock."

"She's sweet." Cruz's fingertips skated higher up her inner thigh. She was so empty, so *aching*, that she inched her knees apart, silently begging for relief.

"Mmm." Jared's soft noise melted into a groan, and he sank his hand into Lili's hair.

She had to close her eyes against the visual. His fingers twisted in her hair, answering the silent voice inside her that didn't want to be sweet anymore. She wanted to be wild, rough, dirty—

Cruz cupped her pussy, and she moaned in relief. But that was all he did, his other hand gripping her hip to still her when she would have squirmed in search of a firmer touch. "She's responsive, too. How easily does she come?"

Jared used the hand in her hair to pull her head up.

kit rocha

"Answer the man, love."

As if she had anything or anyone to compare herself to. Only Rachel, who had endured endless tormenting before succumbing. Lili doubted she would last more than a few glancing touches. "Easily. So easily."

Rachel moaned as she turned her head and bit Jared's hip. "Christ, that's hot."

Ace pumped his hand over Jared's cock. "C'mon, Cruz. Put us all out of our fucking misery."

"Impatient," Cruz chided, his fingers rocking just enough to make Lili whimper. "You know better. You're the one who taught me. Before you can go hard, you have to go..."

He trailed off—or maybe he didn't. Maybe he was still speaking, but Lili couldn't hear. Because he'd spread his fingers, and the tip of one had found her clit. He rubbed with a firmness she'd been craving *forever*, and the world started to fracture around her.

She gasped in a breath and forced her eyes open, staring up into Jared's familiar, dark gaze, the only solid thing as her body throbbed. "Jared—"

He gripped her jaw. "Give and take, Lili."

"Is this the give or—or—?"

Take.

Pleasure crashed over her, and she took it. Took every pulse, every clenching wave, and she gave in return. Her hoarse cries, her shudders, her pleas. "More, please, *please*—"

Rachel guided her head forward, licking a slow path over Lili's lips a split second before Jared drove between them, into her mouth. The taste of him filled her, the last puzzle piece in an exhilarating tangle of bliss.

She moaned around him when Cruz began to ease a finger into the aching emptiness of her body, and she whimpered when he stopped with a groan of his own. "Goddamn, she's so tight. Rachel, if I let you touch her, can you behave?"

Her chest heaved, shaking the chains draped on her body. "Not a chance in hell, baby."

Don't behave. She couldn't say anything, not with Jared filling her mouth, so she moaned and arched her back, begging Jared with her eyes.

And he knew. He stroked shaking fingers over Rachel's cheek and nodded. "Go."

Rachel smoothed her palm down Lili's back as she moved, over the flare of her hip and the curve of her ass, until her hand reached Cruz's. "Not so easy," she urged. "Give it to her."

"Brat." Cruz's touch vanished, but then Rachel's fingers were there, smaller, softer, but still so good, and somehow she *knew* Cruz was guiding her, controlling her, even before his voice washed over them all. "Give her as much as she'll take."

"Don't tempt me." But Rachel's voice was all sweet, trembling submission as she traced her fingertips over Lili's outer lips, down her slick thigh, and up again. She worked two slender fingers deep, deeper, all the way in-side—and sighed, a sound full of shivering lust. "She'll take it all, and beg for more while she's still coming."

It should have been enough to tip Lili over the edge all on its own. But it wasn't, no matter how much she squirmed, and Cruz's fingers rested stubbornly shy of where she needed them again. She made another pleading noise as Ace licked Jared's shaft a final time before kissing his way up Jared's chest, all the way to his ear.

His strong fingers circled Jared's cock again, and he stroked from the base to Lili's lips. "Look at her, brother," he rasped, as if Jared hadn't been holding her gaze hos-tage all along. "So eager, so hungry to please you. Two seconds from coming on Rachel's fingers and she's still try-ing to suck you off. You want him to come, don't you, blue-eyes?"

So much. More than she wanted to come herself, even though need was a sharp thing, twisting inside her. Lili made another eager noise and nodded as much as Jared's grip in her hair allowed.

"Make him." Rachel turned her hand and curved her fingers inside Lili, sparking a dark, throbbing pressure to life. "You can, you know."

Ace's fingers tightened. Rougher than she would have been, but Jared gritted his teeth, and his hips jerked, driving him deeper into her mouth. "Come on her tongue, and then make her come on yours."

"Jesus *fuck*." Jared's fingers knotted in her hair, pulling sharply as he cupped the back of her head. Not the gentle guidance from before, but a desperate demand. "Harder. Suck me harder."

Finally, *finally* he wasn't catering to her. He wasn't building a fantasy. He was trapped in his own, and she was part of it. Central to it. Her head spun, not just from Rachel's thrusting fingers, but from the knowledge that Jared was letting go, too.

She obeyed.

"That's it," Ace rasped, stroking faster. "He's going to come in your mouth, Lili. Do you know what that means?"

That what had happened the night in the bar would happen again—but Jared wouldn't be spilling over her hand this time. She tried to nod, but his fingers were tangled too tight, and the tug on her scalp made her moan.

Jared drove into her mouth, into Ace's fist, and shuddered his release, spurting in hot jets across her tongue. She struggled to swallow, to take everything, reveling in the wild look in his eyes.

But she only had a moment to savor it before Cruz shattered her focus with a rough nudge on her clit, timed perfectly with another thrust of Rachel's fingers. Her body lurched, her toes curling. Her elbows buckled, until only Jared's fist in her hair held her up. Then he lifted her, dug his teeth into her jaw, and growled her name.

Everyone else fell away. It was just Jared, Jared's hands dragging her up the bed, Jared's body pushing her back until she was sprawled on the sheets, boneless and shaking. He loomed over her, his fingers demanding as he guided her legs up against her chest.

The position left her completely open, completely vulnerable. But all that mattered were Jared's hands under her knees, his lips on her inner thigh.

The slap of skin against skin drew her attention. Ace had his hand on Rachel's hip, rubbing a reddened spot. "Go give her something to hold on to, angel. She'll need it when he gets his tongue going."

Rachel slipped one hand into Lili's and stroked her damp hair back from her forehead. "Jared's a tease," she murmured, "making you drift down first."

As if there was any *down*. She was still floating, the tension close to unbearable but unimportant. Jared would soothe it. Her faith was so absolute that even her frustration had vanished. "I listened," she whispered, turning her face to Rachel's. "I trust him."

The other woman's smile wavered in and out of focus as Jared finally touched Lili, gliding his tongue over her wet flesh. So wet that every slick caress was heightened, pleasure and anticipation of *more* pleasure crashing into one another in deep, throbbing waves.

The edge of her tiny, safe world loomed in front of her. The boundary marking *too much*, more than she could take. More than she could hold in herself and still hold on to herself. And, even though she was steeped in trust, fear made her heart race.

Fear would always make her heart race until she knew what it was like to feel everything.

She closed her eyes and clutched Rachel's hand. "More," she pleaded. "Give me more than I can take."

"Haven't you figured it out, love?" Jared's words feathered over her, far away and dreamy. "There's no place I can't take you. Nowhere you won't go. Nothing you can't take. That's what this is."

He put his mouth on her again, and there was nothing slow or careful about it. He ravished her, with his lips and his tongue and even his fingers. Everything shrank to just the two of them, to frozen moments of pulsing pleasure where nothing else existed.

One thought crystallized as all others fell away. A truth. Jared had been right all along. There was no such thing as *too much*. Just *never enough*—

And she could never have enough of him.

After a lifetime of bliss, the pleasure gentled. She floated in warmth and safety, only vaguely aware when careful hands wrapped a blanket around her. A solid weight settled next to her—Jared's body, curling around hers as his fingers brushed her cheek.

Her eyelids felt too heavy, so she turned her face into his hand. "Jared."

"You with me, love?"

She smiled against his palm. "I don't know."

"Good. That's how it should feel."

She could *hear* the smile in his voice, and that gave her motivation to open her eyes. He hovered above her, beautiful and smiling and so very, very *smug*, though she could hardly blame him. "It feels like a different world." A world where she was made for pleasure after all, and her laughter was as much relief as delight. "I'm not the desert."

He leaned closer, until he filled her field of vision. Her entire world. "I think you're a little delirious, Miss Fleming."

"It makes sense," she protested, reaching up to trace his lips. "The first time you kissed me, I felt like the desert, and you were the rain. So much rain, I thought you'd wash me away. But I'm not the desert. I'm the flowers."

"So you're blooming." His mouth moved under her fingertips, like a kiss. "And you're beautiful, Lili."

She wanted more than almost a kiss, and she wasn't afraid to take it. Sliding her fingers into his hair, she tugged him down until his lips met hers, utterly unafraid of the way her body reacted to the first touch of his tongue.

She'd always known she could tolerate pain. Now she knew she could survive pleasure.

With Jared at her back, at her *side*, she could survive anything.

14

THE BASTARDS HAD smashed up his bar.
Jared stood in the open doorway, numbly surveying the damage. Every chair and stool had been either destroyed or defaced, and the smooth vinyl seats of the booths had been slashed so that the stuffing tufted out like the insides of a child's teddy bear.

The bar itself had been gouged, and messy red letters splashed across its surface in paint that was still wet. The same paint had been splattered across the wall, over spots where the wallpaper had been torn away, forming ugly letters that his brain mercifully refused to coalesce into words.

He stepped forward, over shards of wood and sparkling, shattered glass. "Mind the chandelier," he murmured.

Gia edged around it and stopped next to him, her gaze

fixed on the bar. "Well, that's just amateurish. They can't even spell *whore*."

"Yes, they can." Jared righted a chair and sighed when it pitched over again immediately. "They just want me to think they can't."

She quirked an eyebrow. "You know who it is?"

"I know who it *isn't*." Random thugs, the kind that weren't supposed to exist in the city. The kind that would trash a place to send a message, or just for the sheer, exhilarating joy of it.

There was no joy in the destruction around him. Beneath the mess, there was a pattern to it all. Precise and methodical devastation, wreaked by soldiers with orders, not criminals out looking for a good time.

The acrid scent of urine drew him into the other room, and he wrinkled his nose as he surveyed the ruined carpet in the center of it. "Boot prints." He gestured to the impressions at the edge of the dark, damp spot. "Military issue."

She pressed her lips together. "So it's not amateurish. It still stinks of fear. Little men and their little insecurities."

Little men who wanted him to stay in his proper place—which meant Markovic was right. Jared posed a threat just by daring to think he could step outside the mold they'd created for him in their ordered world. Everything else was secondary—his plans, his abilities, even his possible association with Dallas O'Kane.

The rest of it would get his new business trashed. The last one would get him killed.

He turned and eyed Gia with a tense shrug. "At least I haven't stocked the booze yet. Can you imagine all those busted bottles? Not even the cost, but the sheer goddamn waste?"

"Some things are harder to replace." She shrugged off

her expensive coat and draped it over the edge of an over-turned table. "Tell me you have cleaning supplies, at least."

"I'll take care of it later, Gia."

She was already unbuttoning her silk blouse, revealing an equally expensive camisole. "I said the same thing to you more than once, and it never stopped you from sweeping up broken glass or scrubbing dog shit off my front door. And I never forgot what you said to me, either."

You can quit, but I'd much rather see you take all their fucking money. "It doesn't exactly apply anymore, does it?" But he rounded the bar anyway and reached for a broom with a broken handle. "We're already rich."

"They still have plenty." She stripped off her rings and tucked them into her pocket. "And you'll do better things with it than they will."

He passed her the broom and began to roll up his sleeves. "Like buy pianos for sweet young things?"

Gia laughed as she started sweeping up the chande-lier. "That was a little extravagant, even for me, darling. But it seems to have worked, so I shouldn't doubt you."

Jared grabbed a bucket and sponge from beneath the bar. "It wasn't a play. If it was, I think I'd consider myself a much smarter man. But I just wanted to do something nice for her." He paused. "Is that pathetic?"

"Absolutely. As pathetic as me buying a closet full of that soap from you so Tatiana could have her fresh start with that mountain of muscle she's fallen in love with."

"A couple of pathetic suckers." At one time, the admission might have engendered dismay, even panic, but he'd turned a corner. It was impossible to spend the night wrapped in Lili's arms, surrounded by people he loved, and not *understand*, maybe for the first time, the dream Dallas O'Kane was selling.

Survival was important, necessary, but there were things beyond it. Even things more important, as perverse as that seemed. Every one of Dallas's people knew it, lived it. Breathed it. They were part of something bigger than themselves, a family that would live or die by their collective strength.

It was so much more massive than anything Eladio had taught him. They'd looked out for each other, of course—he and Gia and Ace—but there was always a line, a separation he couldn't quite put into words. They protected each other, but they never *lived* for one another. And when the time had come, they'd gone their separate ways.

He took a deep breath. "Eladio was so focused on teaching us how to be self-reliant that he never taught us how to trust."

"It would have been reckless," Gia said softly. "Where he was sending us, trust could have gotten us killed."

"I know," he told her quickly. "But sometimes I feel like a soldier who's won a war. It's time to go home, and I don't even know what that means."

"Mmm. I used to worry about Ace, about how much he let those women inside. We were never that reckless." She swept in silence for several long moments, nudging the sparkling shards of glass into a neat pile. "But now he has a pretty boy who wants to be corrupted and a pretty girl who wants to kneel at his feet and smile. I'm violently jealous."

"Meanwhile, Ace feels guilty for leaving us behind."

"Idiot," she said, but she was smiling. "You're not the only one Dallas O'Kane has courted, darling. I never blamed him for giving in any more than you did. And I wouldn't blame you, either."

She thought he was being seduced by a pretty face. If she knew the truth, she wouldn't just blame him, she'd kick his ass. "Don't worry, I'm not thinking of joining up because of Lili," he hedged.

"But you want to go home to her."

"Yeah." Admitting it no longer felt optional—though, considering the hellish mess he was standing in, maybe it should have. A better man would have taken the opportunity to reflect on the danger of his life, and then taken steps to make damn sure Lili was protected from it.

But Lili was an O'Kane now, or soon would be, and O'Kanes didn't shy away from danger. They confronted it.

Gia set aside the broom and crossed the room. She was tall in her designer heels, almost tall enough to look him straight in the eye. Her strong fingers framed his face as she studied his expression, and she smiled softly. "Nothing in this world would make me as happy as having a reason to be violently jealous of you, too."

Despite his relationship with Ace, he'd always been closer to Gia. They were more alike, closer in age and experience, everything. She was his sister, as good as blood, and he'd have given anything to be able to say the same to her.

But Gia's happiness was a tricky thing, less tied up in other people and more about what she was willing to let herself feel. So he smiled back, kissed the top of her head, and nodded. "I'm working on it."

"Good." She stepped back and laid her hand on the bucket. "So, are you going to quit? Or are we going to take all of their fucking money?"

We. "Quitting is for people who've never been hungry."

Her smile turned a little sad. "Poor Eladio. He tried so hard to raise us to be properly ruthless. Sometimes I wonder just how disappointed in me he'd be."

"I think he'd be proud," Jared told her gently. "Gia, he didn't teach us what he did because he *wanted* us to be hard. It was just...all he knew."

"I know." She rested her forehead against his cheek. "Now we have to live better lives for him."

Jared tipped her chin up. "What do you think Eladio

would do? Send cheeky grand opening invitations to all the Council members?"

She grinned. "Or everyone *but* them. The only thing worse than being invited to a den of sin is not being invited."

"You were right. I *do* need you."

"I know, darling." She patted his cheek and broke away. "Let's get this cleaned up and show Eden why you don't fuck with sector brats."

"Because they'll punch you in the balls?" Even as he murmured the dry words, he knew what she really meant. You didn't fuck with sector brats because they were used to being knocked down, and they'd always get back up.

Which was exactly what Jared was going to do.

scarlet

J ADE HAD THE softest skin, the kind you could lose
yourself in. And not just in the usual places, like the
small of her back or the spot where her thigh met the lus-
cious curve of her ass, either. *Everywhere*.

All of those milk baths and warm oil massages, no
doubt. Sometimes, when Scarlet was high on pleasure and
surrounded by the scent of coconut oil, she was pretty
damn sure that the only good thing to ever come out of
Sector Two was Jade's skin.

Jade was braiding her hair now, the strands shining
with that oil. She smiled at Scarlet as she tied off the end.
"You look like you're thinking hard."

"Hardly thinking." She rolled her head back on the
pillow and reached out. "Come back."

"In a moment." She wiped her hands and reached for
another jar from her vanity.

"You don't need it, Jade."

"It isn't about need." Jade twisted the cap off and lifted it, inhaling and then sighing. "My mother taught me this recipe."

Scarlet dragged the sheet up to her chest as she rolled over and grabbed her cigarettes from Jade's neatly organized bedside table. "What is it?"

"Lotion. Tatiana makes fancier ones, but..." She shrugged and smoothed the white cream across her cheeks in slow circles. "I used to teach the girls this—have a ritual. Sometimes the familiar is the only soothing thing you have."

"Like my music." Scarlet snapped her lighter shut and dropped it on the bed beside her. "It was the one thing that kept me from going nuts."

Jade met her gaze in the mirror, her small, knowing smile back. "I think everyone appreciates your music."

"Yeah? Sounds like you're the one thinking hard."

"Are we going to pretend Mad hasn't been watching you since the concert?"

Her tone was teasing, light, but there was a question beneath the words. Scarlet shrugged. "Saint Adrian likes pretty things. My voice qualifies—at least when I'm singing."

"Come now, Scarlet. He's not *that* shallow." Jade rose, leaving her robe behind in the chair. She approached the bed naked and unselfconscious, her perfect brown skin unmarked except for the O'Kane cuffs around her delicate wrists. "And he doesn't like pretty things. He likes *fragile* things. Your voice certainly does not qualify."

Scarlet had noticed him, watching her. Riveted, really, staring at her like he'd never seen her before, and she was torn between being flattered and being irritated. For someone who prided himself on being sensitive and aware, he sure the hell hadn't noticed what was right in front of his face.

Or maybe he had, and he was shocked that a woman like Scarlet wasn't always about hard lines and razor-sharp edges. That she could be just as soft as Jade, only in different ways. Different places.

"Perhaps he considers himself a connoisseur of vocal talent." Scarlet wrapped one hand around the back of Jade's knee and stroked her thumb over her skin. "Why don't you say what you're really thinking?"

Jade tilted her head. "I'm thinking...that I know what a man looks like when he sees something he wants. And I know what he looks like when he sees something he needs."

Don't ask. Don't fucking ask— "Which one am I?"

"Which one do you want to be?"

Scarlet tugged sharply, dragging Jade down to the bed. Down to her. "I want to be right where I am."

Jade laughed, warm and soft. "I put that towel on my pillow for a reason," she protested, tugging away—but not very hard. "I'll get coconut oil all over you."

"You have no idea." Scarlet crushed out her cigarette and walked her fingers up the center of Jade's body, lingering between her breasts. "Out of curiosity, which one do *you* want to be?"

"I want..." She trailed off with a soft sigh, her eyes fluttering shut. She arched into Scarlet's touch, slow and languid. "I want everyone to be happy."

"Spoken like a true O'Kane."

"They have their appeal, don't they?"

"Certain members more than others."

Jade caught Scarlet's hand and opened her eyes. "He needs you, or someone like you. Someone strong. And he'll never see that in me."

Scarlet didn't give two happy shits what he needed. She knew what he wanted, though, and it wasn't her. Not by a long shot. "Do you love him?"

"Mad?" Her voice didn't waver. "No."

"Then what does it matter?"

"Because I'm not the only one in this bed."

Scarlet froze. "You think I have a thing for the crown prince of Sector One?"

Jade tightened her grip on Scarlet's hand. "It would be all right, you know. He *is* from Sector One. They don't look at love the same way other sectors do."

"Yeah? Well, I'm not from One." She pulled her hand free and dragged it through her hair. "Besides, last time I checked, Mad wasn't exactly sleeping alone."

"I'm sorry."

It was the perfect chance to step back, let it slide, but Scarlet had always been shit at that. So she pressed on. "Everyone wants a hero, right? But the thing about heroes is that they're just people. And the second you start thinking they can solve all your problems, you've already lost yourself."

Jade touched Scarlet's cheek, turning her face back. "Even heroes need saving sometimes."

She sounded so solemn that it was impossible to tell if she was still talking about Mad—or Scarlet herself. "I'm no hero, Jade."

"That's what a hero would say."

Scarlet reversed their positions, flipping Jade beneath her, heedless of her freshly oiled hair spreading out over the pillows. "I'm no hero," she said again, dropping her hands to Jade's waist. The delicate lines of her hipbones beckoned, and Scarlet traced them with her thumbs. "But I am *here*. Isn't that enough?"

Jade smiled. "It's everything."

Everything. It skated dangerously, viciously close to the line Scarlet knew she couldn't cross, the one where Jade called her a hero...and she started to believe her.

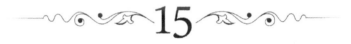

15

T HE SCRAPE OF the key in the lock jerked Lili out of restless nightmares.

Fighting disorientation, she pushed herself upright as the door opened. Jared's couch was comfortable, but the living room seemed ominous like this, cast in eerie shadows thanks to the light from Eden's walls spilling through the wide windows. The dreams had already slipped through her fingers, leaving behind vague feelings of anxiety and dread that had everything to do with the source of that light.

Jared had been due back from the city hours ago. Dinner lay cold and untouched on the table, the candles she'd lit in a fit of whimsy burned to lumpy stubs. Wax spilled over the holders, pooling on the tablecloth in splotches of bright red that reminded her of blood.

She shook away the thought and rose, because Jared

233

was stepping through the door now, alive and whole, and her nightmares were just that. Not premonitions, not a warning, but the product of too much wine and too much worry.

"Lili." He dropped his keys on the table beside the door, frowning. "What are you doing here?"

That provoked a pang in her chest. "It's Wednesday. We were supposed to have dinner?"

He winced. "Fuck, I'm sorry. I've been covered over this week, arranging things for the opening. I didn't even think."

She'd sat in silent vigil over a hundred cold dinners in her life, usually with relief at her husband's absence. Disappointment was a new sensation, and it felt utterly, ridiculously selfish.

Jared looked exhausted. Worn and stiff, and clearly braced for a confrontation. So she swallowed her hurt and circled the table. "Have you eaten at all today?"

"I grabbed something from the market before I headed into the city this morning." He paused, then shook his head. "No, that was yesterday."

Which might very well mean he'd slept at the bar the previous night. Guilt joined the uncomfortable tangle in her gut, and she hid it by easing his coat from his shoulders and pushing him gently toward the table. "Sit. Most of this will reheat just fine."

He turned instead, caught her hand, and dragged it to his face. "I missed you."

She believed him. His cheek was warm beneath her fingers. His eyes were dark but hotter now, as if bits of Eden were sliding away.

And she was still acting like a Sector Five housewife. Training, maybe, or habit. Muscle memory. It was so *easy* to fall back into the patterns she'd learned out of self-defense. She'd been foolish to think pleasure could wipe away her past in a few short weeks.

She forced herself to take a deep breath as she stroked his cheek. "I missed you, too. But you still need to eat." He took a step, nudging her back toward the couch. "I don't want to."

"Jared..." Her instincts had evolved. She could read his intent, the slow shift in mood that her own body echoed.

His hand trailed up her arm, leaving goose bumps in its wake. "Would you rather have dinner?"

Dinner was safer. That was a performance she could give—*had* given—stoned out of her mind. Reheat the food. Refill the drinks. Ask polite, bland questions about his day, each carefully composed to allow answers without substance. Because the last thing she'd want to risk was knowing too much.

They were both so *good* at playing the game. But when he touched her, when they touched each other—that was the only time she was sure she wasn't playing at all.

Safe was an illusion, anyway. "No. I'm not hungry."

"Not hungry?" He bent his head, his lips barely brushing her ear. "Not even a little?"

"Not for dinner."

"For what?"

She tilted her head back. "You. Being hungry for me."

He slid his hand up to rest across the vulnerable expanse of her throat. "I've been dreaming about you, how hot it is to watch you come. How it's even hotter when you let go."

Little bits of Sector Five were slipping away from her, all right. Every time her body stirred, it was new and amazing and just for him. "I know you have to hold back in Eden. Don't hold back with me."

He went rigid, his muscles tensing beneath his tailored shirt. "Are you certain, Lili?"

"Give and take," she reminded him softly. "It's your turn to take."

The dam broke. He hauled her to his chest and crushed her lips beneath his. There was a desperation in his touch, as if every bit of that hard-won control had splintered and might shatter at any moment.

She dug her hands into his hair and let her nails prick his scalp—rough, because it was the best way she knew to say *yes*.

He backed her against the counter, the sharp edge biting into her lower back. Then Jared lifted her and held her there, half on and half off the countertop, his eyes blazing. "Say it. You have to say it, love."

She fought for breath. "I want you. Now. However you need me."

He nodded, his chest heaving. He dropped her to the smooth surface, and his hands skipped down to the hem of her dress and began to slowly gather it.

Fast. No careful seduction this time, but she didn't *need* to be seduced. As much as she loved his relentless, teasing touches, they seemed tame compared to the impact of his obvious arousal. His hands were shaking this time, as if he was the one feeling too much.

Needing too much.

She reached for him, stroked her fingers up his arms. "Do you want me to keep saying it?"

"Can you?" he rasped as his fingers slid under the lace of her panties. He drew them down her legs until they caught on her shoe, and he left them there to dangle from one ankle. "Not for long."

"I want you." Her voice wavered, so she edged her knees apart and *showed* him.

He worked his belt open, then his pants. He was ready, his dick hard and hot as he braced her with one hand across her ass. But he didn't push into her, just kept moving, rocking, every roll of his hips grinding against her clit and making her wetter.

She clung to his shoulders and let her head fall back.

beyond innocence

"I—I want—" He twisted his hips, and she gasped as heat flashed through her. "Oh *God.*"

He sucked in a breath, raw and rough. "That's it." His shaft was wet now, slick with her arousal as his movements slowed but turned harder. More focused.

Perfect.

She dug her nails into his shoulders, hating the fabric that stopped her from touching his skin but loving it, too. This was a different kind of obscene—desperate and rushed, clothing shoved aside, grinding against her in the kitchen, of all places. The next time she cooked for him, she wouldn't be able to think of anything but this feeling.

Maybe if they did this in every room, she'd never be able to slip back into old habits again.

Release was rushing toward her already. She moaned again, moaned his *name*, and tried to pull him closer.

But he was a rock, immovable. "Come for me first," he whispered, soft, seductive words with a sharp sting of command that shivered through her. "Come for me, and I'll fuck you."

That shiver didn't scare her anymore. She understood what it meant—and what it didn't. She understood the sweetness of trust and the strength it took to offer it. Teetering on the edge, she forced her head up and met his eyes. "Because I'm yours."

"Damn right." He caught her chin. "Now, Lili."

As if she had any choice. The friction was too exquisite, and he knew it. Her breath seized as she hung for an endless moment, held there by his gaze.

Then she fell.

She came fast, hard. She came shuddering, writhing in his grip and clutching at his shirt until it tore open, and she had the frantic, hysterical thought that she'd have to take up mending because she couldn't stop tearing his clothes from his body. And then that thought was gone, too, swept away in a rush of joy.

237

kit rocha

Jared's groan echoed in her ears as he slid both hands under her ass. "Don't stop," he ordered, a mere heartbeat before he thrust into her. Hard. *Deep.* Her body was still tight, still clenching, but he was slick and so was she, and she wanted him so much. She wrapped her legs around his hips and clung to him, panting for breath as discomfort fought lingering pleasure—and lost. "More."

She didn't have to ask again. He pulled back and drove into her, harder this time, and she had to grab the counter to brace herself. Every deep thrust hit that spot that hollowed her out, twisting her into tighter and tighter knots.

Her head fell back, bumping into the cupboards be-hind her. Jared wrapped his hand around the back of her head, protecting it from the wood as he pounded into her mercilessly, never slowing or hesitating for an instant.

The physical pleasure was maddening, but that wasn't the part that stripped her bare. It was the naked need on his face, the shredded control, the *sounds*—her breathless moans and his low grunts, both of them re-duced to base instinct.

No masks. No games. When she came again, she screamed—not a sweet whimper or a breathless moan, but a hoarse cry as jagged and out of control as she felt. The release of tension was almost violent, her entire body clenching tight.

Jared hauled her to him, all the way on the edge of the counter, so that the only thing holding her up was him—his body against hers, his hands on her head and then her mouth, silencing her cries. He flexed his hips, growling when she gripped his cock even more tightly. "Again," he ordered.

She shivered when he flexed his hips again. The angle was so different, stroking new places, and his fingers across her lips muffled her moan. Tingles prickled over her

beyond innocence

as she stared up into his eyes, his dark, demanding eyes. This was Jared, naked. This was his basest desire. Not to coax pleasure from her, but to demand it. Not from anyone else.

From her.

"Fuck," he groaned. "The way you look at me..."

She must be as naked as he was. Her vulnerability. Her trust. The growing awareness that they had careened past *friends* long ago, and were headed for something too big to wrap her pleasure-addled wits around.

And she was addled. Her body was primed now, the stretch of his cock pure pleasure and the grinding pressure on her clit too much to resist. Release didn't crash into her this time. It snuck over her, little pulses that grew brighter and brighter, until she was groaning against his hand and shaking.

Jared breathed her name, his voice as tight and trembling as the rest of her world. He drove deep, as deep as he could go, then arched as he shuddered through the force of his orgasm.

Her fingers ached from gripping the counter. She forced them open and wrapped her arms around Jared. He dropped his hand from her mouth, lifted her from the counter, and began carrying her toward his bedroom.

How he could walk at all was a mystery. Her limbs were liquid, all her previous tension melted away. She stroked her fingers over the back of his neck as a sleepy smile curved her lips. "I ripped your shirt again."

"I don't care." He grinned as he set her down beside the bed and stripped her dress over her head. "You can go in my closet and tear them *all* up. But later."

Or she could mend them. It might be nice to put more of the skills she'd learned out of obligation to use for a better cause. Her final rude gesture to her old life, in true O'Kane spirit. "I imagine the ripping is only fun when you're wearing them."

"Touché." He knelt at her feet and began unbuckling her heeled sandals. "I *am* sorry, you know. About dinner."

"I know." She slipped her fingers into his hair and smoothed the strands back into place. "You're working so hard to get the bar ready. I don't want to add more stress."

"You're not," he assured her.

"How close are you to being finished?"

"To having things settled for opening night? Not close enough." He rose, kicked off his shoes, and stripped off his socks and pants.

"Is there anything I can do to help?" She smiled a little ruefully. "I know more than I want to about hosting parties for Eden's elite."

He shook his head as he pulled the covers back. "I've got it under control. Hop in."

She obeyed, because he looked like he needed sleep far more than anything else. "You open next week still, right?"

"That's the plan." Jared settled into his pillow with a sigh and drew her close to his side, but he didn't elaborate. And, as loose as her limbs felt, his were stiff again.

Tense muscles. Short answers. A lifetime of wary attention to the moods of the men around her had taught her one course of action when presented with Jared's body language: agreeable silence.

She turned into him and stroked his chest lightly, drawing absent patterns until his breathing lengthened and the tension in his muscles slowly relaxed. He slipped into sleep, and Lili watched him until she was sure he wouldn't stir.

Then she climbed from the bed.

The candles still burned in the dining room. She blew them out and winced at the mess the wax had left all over the tablecloth. She spent a few absent minutes trying to scrape up the red splatters with a butter knife, but the stains would be hopeless without an iron and some paper towels.

beyond innocence

She let it go and gathered the plates instead. Putting away the food and washing the dishes was hypnotic. Her body went through the motions without input from her mind, which was skittering in too many directions.

Jared was exhausted. The stress of the grand opening would weigh on him, no matter how carefully he'd planned it. That stiffness in him hadn't been distance, just the natural result of having too much on his mind and too little time.

A perfectly reasonable explanation. And it felt hollow.

Even after she settled back into bed, Lili couldn't quiet her mind. Not with slow, steady breaths, not by pressing into Jared's side.

She could feel the distance. It was slight, subtle, locking into place despite their moment of total openness. He wanted her—she was sure of that. She'd offered herself, and he'd taken. Without thought, without hesitation, without—

Her body stiffened, and she realized what had been different. Not just his eagerness. Not just their total abandon. Jared had been so lost in her, he hadn't stopped to get a condom. And she'd been so lost in him, she hadn't remembered that she might need one.

Might. It was the slimmest possibility. She'd taken the fertility drugs months ago, and so briefly they might not have had time to take effect to begin with. But even that slim possibility made her stomach churn.

Not that she could tell him. Such a faint chance wasn't worth the stress it would add to his shoulders. She'd talk to the O'Kanes' doctor instead. Reassure herself. Rebuild her walls.

Jared didn't need a trembling Sector Five housewife who cracked under a missed dinner and a few short words. He needed someone like Lex—a partner who could be strong in her own right, who dealt with her own problems and always had his back.

kit rocha

He needed an O'Kane. And she could become one.

242

16

LIEUTENANT MALHOTRA HAD obviously not cleared his new no-more-bribes policy with the rest of Eden's Council.

Jared slid a fat envelope across Smith Peterson's desk and schooled his features to keep from wrinkling his nose at the sheer greed that lit the other man's eyes. "It's all there."

Peterson held up a hand, his other sliding quickly over the large inset tablet on his desk. A strange hum filled the room, and Peterson shrugged. "Can't be too careful, can we?"

A program to jam surveillance equipment, then. "I'm not wearing a wire."

"Of course not." Derision dripped from the words.

Jared bit the inside of his cheek to hold back a smile.

No, he wasn't wearing a wire—but he had something better, something that Dallas's resident hacker, Noah, had pieced together. The tiny box hidden inside his silver cigarette lighter case was designed, as best as Jared could understand, to gather data being transmitted over Eden's ubiquitous wireless signals. All it needed was close range and enough time to complete the transfer.

Jared could keep Peterson talking. Hell, it might be able to scrape all his data before the man could finish lovingly counting Jared's money.

Which was what he was doing now. "In light of recent...unpleasantness, a less agreeable man might require an additional donation to the security fund."

"Unpleasantness?" Oh, he'd make the bastard say it.

"So much activity. Things breaking. Things being repaired. It's hard to turn a blind eye."

Especially hard, Jared assumed, when you were the one responsible. "It could have been worse. I do regret the loss of my rug, though. It was an antique."

"A pity." Peterson finished counting the bills and tucked them back into the envelope. "I could arrange for additional security, but it doesn't come free."

"Nothing ever does." Jesus Christ, this place was exhausting. He could barely fathom why Lili wanted to hear about his day when his day consisted of sitting across desks from smarmy assholes like Smith Peterson, smiling and playing nice instead of cracking their skulls.

And she *did* want to. The guilt rose again, choking and thick. She wanted to be part of his life, for him to share things with her, all the normal things you did when you were falling in love with someone.

It wasn't her fault that all he had to share were horror stories.

"It's your choice," Peterson said with an oily smile. "You may want to decide before your big night, though."

beyond innocence

These Council bastards were nothing if not predictable. Jared pulled the second envelope he'd prepared from
his inner jacket pocket and slid it across the desk. "I believe in being prepared, sir."
It was amusing, watching the man's greed war with
his spite. Should he taunt Jared with the threat of destroy-
ing his opening night, or take all that beautiful money?
The money won. In Eden, the money always won. Peterson picked up the envelope and thumbed through it.
"The Council appreciates your dedication to improving our
city's security."
"Anything I can do to make it a better place." Includ-
ing burning it to the fucking ground.
"Yes, well." Peterson cleared his throat. "In the future,
visiting my office won't be necessary. Someone will check
up on you weekly."
"I see. How should I prepare for this guest?"
"With the usual donation. Unless you have a guilty
conscience about something...?"
Jared stared at him.
Peterson stared back, something far uglier than greed
lurking behind his bland expression. "If you want to do
business in Eden, an association with an unscrupulous
reprobate like Alexander Santana can only hurt you. Especially when it's common knowledge that he's Dallas
O'Kane's creature."
Rage surged, burning through Jared's veins like fire.
A quick glance at his reflection in the window behind Peterson revealed no change in his expression, but what lay
in his heart was pure murder. "Ace is a friend," he said,
marveling at his miraculously bland tone. "He's also retired."
"From one sort of criminal endeavor, perhaps. But a
man who wants to succeed in the city can't afford too many
connections to the sectors."
"You'll have your money, Peterson." Jared rose and

buttoned his suit jacket. "And since I won't even ask you to scrounge around for it in Alexander Santana's pants, I presume it will suffice."

Peterson's face froze. "Money buys tolerance. You'll never have enough to erase what you are."

"Have a good day, Councilman." He turned and headed for the door without waiting for a response. He had to, because everything in the room had started to look like a weapon—the phone on the desk, the vases and artwork lining the shelves on the far wall, even the chair he'd abandoned.

With just a few simple words, Smith Peterson had gone from necessary, irritating evil to being high on Jared's list of motherfuckers who needed to die.

The O'Kanes' doctor was a drug addict.

Perhaps *addict* wasn't the right word. As rough around the edges as Dylan Jordan appeared, Lili didn't imagine he was a man who had to make do with drugs that caused physical dependency. But she knew all too well that there was more than one way to *need* the quiet comfort of oblivion.

If Lili's eyes had been half as haunted as Doc's, it was a miracle anyone had ever had any hope for her.

"I wouldn't worry about it," he was saying. "The medications that restore fertility are short-acting. After three months, they're not even in your bloodstream anymore."

Lili couldn't quite help her relieved sigh. "I hoped you'd say that."

He held up a hand. "Some people are more sensitive to the drugs than others. There's a *slight* chance you could still get pregnant, but only if your partner was taking the meds, too."

A thought so preposterous, she couldn't even bring herself to worry. Jared had been neatly carving potential responsibilities from his life for months now. He'd barely allowed himself to risk a friend. Paying the exorbitant expense of fertility drugs just to risk a *child?*

"No," she said quietly. "That's not a concern."

"Then you should be fine." He hesitated, then laid his arm on her shoulder. "How is everything else?"

She couldn't tell if the question was from a doctor to a patient, or from one connoisseur of pharmaceutical dabbling to another. "Better. It was overwhelming at first, feeling things. But it's better now."

"Good. Lex was worried."

Even a few weeks ago, Lili might have argued that Lex was incapable of so soft and vulnerable an emotion as worry. But learning to see nuance had meant coming to see those around her more clearly.

Lex wasn't hard because there was no softness in her. Lex was hard because she was strong enough to be cold without losing her inner warmth. Noelle couldn't have done the same without losing the sweetness that made her who she was.

Lex could. And she did, so other people wouldn't have to. "If Lex asks, tell her I've never been better. It's the truth."

A hint of a smile curved his lips. It lent his face a startling attractiveness, transforming it from forbiddingly handsome to something warmer. "Take care of yourself, Miss Fleming."

"You do the same, Dr. Jordan."

Lili left the office Doc used while he was on the compound, relief humming quietly beneath her skin. Relief for herself and for Jared, and for his mission and what it meant for the O'Kanes.

But not as much relief as she'd expected.

Not that she *wanted* a child. Maybe someday, in some

hazy, less dangerous future, she could imagine the appeal. But the fear gripping her hadn't been the wild terror of helplessness this time, but wholly practical.

It wasn't a good time to be pregnant. But if it had happened—if it *did* happen—it wouldn't be the end of her life. Because she was not her mother. Jared would never be her father.

And the O'Kanes wouldn't abandon her to suffer through the ordeal alone.

She traced her fingertip over her wrist as she stepped out into the sunny courtyard, remembering Rachel's words. Membership was hers for the asking, because Dallas O'Kane paid his debts.

As if the thought had conjured her, Rachel stepped out of the warehouse a dozen yards ahead of Lili, a clipboard in one hand. The sound of metal grating against metal filled the air as the huge loading doors opened, quickly drowned by the rumble of trucks pulling in to the lot.

Lili hurried her pace, stopping by Rachel's side as men began to stream from the warehouse, loaded down with wooden cases branded with the O'Kanes' logo. "That's a lot of liquor."

"This?" Rachel blew her bangs out of her face. "This is your boyfriend, waiting until the last minute to stock his bar. Not that I blame him, I guess. Not under the circumstances."

Worry immediately kindled in Lili's gut. "Did something happen? I haven't seen him in a few days."

"No. Shit, no," Rachel said quickly. "I'm talking about his place getting busted up."

Lili tried to school her expression, but it was difficult. Her guard wasn't up, and the pain slashing through her was a new sort of hurt, the kind she wasn't used to managing.

She'd never trusted someone enough to feel betrayed before.

Rachel glanced at her, then did a double take. "He didn't tell you, huh? He was probably right not to. I mean, it's not a big deal."

"It's not?"

"It happens. Anytime you're trying to do something that doesn't fit with Eden's image, they try to knock you down." Rachel slid an arm around her shoulders. "They trashed his bar, but no one was there. No one got hurt. And Jared probably didn't want you to worry, that's all."

Except he'd worried. Alone. The nights he'd spent at the bar made a different, chilling sort of sense now, as did the late hours. Redoing all of his work, protecting it from further harm—and having to face coming home to her and putting on a good front.

"I'm going to worry either way," she said, leaning into Rachel's support. "I want to help him."

"You want to help him?" She took a step forward, pulling Lili along with her. "Come on. Let's grab a box."

Just like that, Rachel dragged her into the warehouse and shoved a heavy crate into her arms. No one looked at her like she was too fragile or too delicate to pitch in. But she had been, not so long ago—and maybe that was why no one had asked.

Maybe that was why *Jared* never asked. More than anyone, Jared understood how thin her protections were. Jared understood how easy it would be for her to view requests for help as conditions put on her continued safety. She'd been looking for the strings attached to every kindness from the moment she arrived here, starting with his.

Of course Jared wouldn't burden her with stories of the political backstabbing she'd escaped in Sector Five. Of course he wouldn't ask for her help.

She had to offer it. And as soon as these trucks were on their way back to Eden, she'd figure out how—and how much.

No one in Sector Four wanted a trophy wife. But a

man playing politics in Eden might need one.

17

I N SPITE OF his nonstop work, Jared had a hundred
things left to do before opening night. Some things on
his list were big and some were small, but they all needed
doing.

What *he* needed was a friendly face.

He knocked on Lili's door and tried to manage the
wave of relief that washed over him when she greeted him
with warm eyes and a ready smile. "Jared. I didn't expect
to see you until after your opening."

"I wanted to—" He closed the door behind him and
leaned against it. "No, I *needed* to see you."

"I'm here." She caught his hands and stepped back,
tugging him along with her. "Come and sit down. I actually have something to drink in here. Something Nessa
gave me."

Her hands were warm in his, and he wanted them on

him—anywhere. Everywhere. "She must be fond of you."
Lili laughed. "Free range of the kitchens makes it easy
to bribe people. Everyone has something their parents or
grandparents used to make. Finding the spices for Viet-
namese recipes wasn't easy, but Zan helped. Which got
him a bottle of the good liquor, too."

She was finding her place, carving out a spot in the
O'Kanes' hearts as surely as she had his, and Jared was
glad. It made the distance bearable as he geared up to
properly launch his mission in Eden.

He might be alone, but she wouldn't be, and that was
what mattered.

Lili nudged him toward the edge of the bed and retreated to her vanity. "It's not what I imagined, you know.
I thought I'd have to work all the time to put three meals
a day on the table, but most of the O'Kanes are used to
feeding themselves. And when someone wants something
special, they offer to trade."

"That's what most people in the sectors do. What
they're used to."

"Being paid for my work is novel." She smiled again
and waved a hand at the top of her vanity, which was clut-
tered with tiny tins and bottles. "I might have gone
overboard with Tatiana's generosity."

"You're happy," he murmured.

"I was already happy." She returned with a glass of a
honey-colored liquor and offered it to him. "I've been
happy since you helped me see what was going on right in
front of me. You gave my new life context."

He'd only told her that what she needed was there,
and that she could have it. Everything after had been entirely Lili's doing. So he lifted his glass. "To new
beginnings."

"New beginnings," she echoed. But instead of fetching
a glass for herself, she picked up a shirt. *His* shirt, the one
he'd been wearing the night of their dinner with Ace, Cruz,

and Rachel. The shirt she'd ripped from his body.

It was pristine now, expertly mended, the missing buttons replaced and the shirt itself as crisply pressed as if he'd had it done in Eden. "I don't know if this is really your favorite shirt, but if it is... I wanted you to have it. Maybe you can wear it tomorrow."

He took it from her and ran his thumb over the starched collar. "You didn't have to do this."

"I know." She settled next to him on the bed, slipped her arm around his waist, and laid her cheek on his shoulder. "I need you to believe that. I know what I have to do, and what I don't. I understand, finally."

He couldn't stop looking at the white cloth, perfect, inviolate. As if it had never been ripped. As if that moment had never happened, had been erased from the fabric of time as well as the literal fabric of his damn shirt.

He understood, too. Lili had meant to mend his shirt as a helpful gesture, a way to show she cared, but it resonated on another level. Slowly, piece by piece, he'd been separating himself from Sector Four. It had started as a half-measure, a matter of practicality, but what if that wasn't enough? What if the best thing was to simply let go?

He didn't know if he could.

Her arm tightened around him. "Jared?"

A thousand things flitted through his head, and not a single one sounded reasonable, rational. "I'm tired, Lili. That's all."

"I know." She rubbed her cheek against his shoulder. "Let me help you. Not because I have to, but because I *want* to."

The words made as much sense as the ones tripping over his tongue. "What?"

"Rachel told me about what happened. I helped her load up the liquor this morning, and she told me you waited until the last minute because someone had wrecked your bar."

Fuck. "That's… I don't like to bring that shit back here with me." Eden, always Eden, clinging to him like dirt and grime he couldn't wash away.

Her fingertips skimmed up his back to rest between his shoulder blades, where muscles knotted from tension ached. "But you do, even when you don't speak of it. I'm strong enough to help you carry this weight."

"It's not about being strong, Lili." He set his glass on the nearest surface—the edge of her piano—and rose. "I don't *want* to talk about it. It doesn't help. So when I leave there, I just want to put it behind me instead of letting it drag me down."

"That's not what I meant." She rose, too, wreathed in a sort of confidence he'd never seen in her before. "This is what I spent my life training to do. I know how to put these men at ease—"

"No." The word ripped free of him before his brain caught up to it, an instinctive reaction to the purpose radiating off of her.

She talked right over him. "—and I know how to make them talk, Jared. I could do it in my sleep. I did it on *drugs*. Let me do it for a good cause. I can help you."

On his worst days, Jared felt like the city was a great, yawning mouth ready to snap shut, not on his body—that much, he knew as fact—but on his soul. Nothing had ever been more horrible than the thought that he might lose himself to it, forget all the reasons he was fighting in the first place.

Nothing…until now.

"I don't need you to convince me," he told her, firm words through numb lips. "No, Lili. You could ask a thousand times—a *million*—and it would always be no."

Her hands fisted. "Because you don't think I can do it?"

He thought of Peterson, of his ugly comments and

even uglier eyes. "Because no one can. If you don't understand that already, you have no business there, Lili. None."

She went still, and her eyes turned cool. "I understand what powerful men do when you cross them."

"It's not the same as your husband thinking your family was a threat to be eliminated." His throat wanted to close on the harsh words, but he forced himself to keep going. "Your mother could have rallied support behind her—maybe not in Five, but in the other sectors. She could have taken control from Beckett in a heartbeat. In Eden, you don't have to be a threat. They'll kill you if they don't like the *idea* of you."

"I know." She didn't tremble. She didn't flinch. "If what you stand to gain wasn't worth the risk, you wouldn't be there. Why can't I make the same choice?"

"Because I won't let you." The truth, stark and damning, but he'd rather have Lili out here, safely hating his guts in Sector Four, than anywhere near the fucking vultures in the city. "Sorry, love, but there it is."

After a tense moment, she nodded stiffly and turned. Every movement was carefully precise as she poured herself a drink and took a sip. "You're wrong, you know. My mother never could have rallied support. She was no threat, and everyone knew it. She was broken." She eyed him over the edge of her glass. "She was obedient."

But not Lili. Fire burned in her eyes, and Jared loved her for it even as it scared the hell out of him. "There are plenty of ways to spread your wings here."

"I know," she said again, and this time there was pain in her words. In her *eyes*. "I can't say you didn't warn me. But I thought we'd grown past friends. I thought—" She shook her head. "It doesn't matter. Maybe I'm still naïve after all."

"I'm sorry." Not for his actions or words, but for the necessity of them. There was nothing he wouldn't risk to keep Lili safe—his happiness, his heart. His life. "What do you want from me?" She finished her drink and met his gaze. "Or, more to the point, what will you allow me to give you?"

"Does it matter?" he asked softly.

Her lips curved in a tiny, sad smile. "You're the one drawing the lines. I'd give you everything. That doesn't obligate you to take it."

She wanted proclamations—or maybe even finality. "I can't do this right now."

Wordlessly, she retrieved his empty glass, refilled it, and offered it to him. It was mindless, automatic, as if she'd reverted to habit. Shut down.

He grasped her chin and tilted her face up to his. "Lili."

"I'm sorry. I shouldn't have bothered you when you're under so much stress."

It chilled him to his core—not just the words, but the flat, careful tone. "Lili, *stop.*"

"I can't." Her eyes glistened, and she blinked rapidly. When that didn't banish the tears, she fought his grip, trying to twist her face away. "You can't deal with my feelings right now. So I can hide them or I can lose you."

You could never lose me. Hollow reassurance, considering the harsh reality of their situation, and he couldn't bring himself to say it. Instead, he released her. "Tomorrow night, after the opening," he whispered. "Wait for me?"

She rubbed at her eyes, as if she could wipe away the evidence of her melancholy. But when she looked back up at him, her cheeks were smudged with eyeliner and tears glistened on her lashes. "Will you let me make you breakfast? And actually eat it?"

"Anything you want, love." But his chest ached, and the knot between his shoulders had twisted tighter, because there was nothing left to say. No right or wrong, only

beyond innocence

two people in pain, and no way to fix it.

18

T HE GRAND OPENING was an unqualified success. Jared had stopped trying to count the number of people who showed up—plenty he recognized, but many he didn't, as well. Influential people, ones who had always remained outside his circle of acquaintance because their tastes ran more to drinking and gambling than whoring.

And the *politicians.* Men from the Council, who were careful to pretend they'd only answered their invitations out of civic duty, to make sure nothing untoward was going on in his illegal underground bar. Men who aspired to the Council, but who were biding their time in lower positions, waiting for their turns to come.

In and out the door, men and women, old and young, rich and richer. Jared smiled, shook their hands, suggested the perfect drinks. He even made a few introductions. The consummate host.

All the while, he was ticking them off in his head, sorting them, making lists. Which ones carried secrets close to their chests. Which ones carried other people's secrets, like burdens they couldn't wait to lay down. Who could be persuaded, and who could be bought.

Outside, he was smiling. Inside, he was deadly, cold, as efficient as the data skimmer Noah had created.

The last stragglers stumbled out the door, and one of the servers shut it hastily behind them, leaning against it for good measure. "Thank God. If they'd stayed much longer, they'd have been wanting breakfast cocktails."

A quick glance at his watch confirmed that the sun would be rising soon, if it hadn't already peeked over the vast horizon far outside the city. "Dianna, you did a wonderful job tonight. Thank you."

The brunette grinned at him. "Don't thank me. Just tell me I get to keep some of the credits I have stuffed in my bra."

"They're yours. You earned them."

Her grin widened as she pushed away from the door. "No taking that back after you see how much I made. These Eden bastards will swoon over a bare ankle and *imagining* my tits."

Of course they would. Add to it the heady adrenaline rush of doing something forbidden, something dangerous, and Jared was surprised they'd been as well-behaved as they had—something that might not last.

More security. Another mental note to add to the list. "Make sure you lock up," he advised. "If you need me, I'm stepping out back for a minute."

"I'll be here." She eyed the sticky tables and the piles of glasses. "Until noon."

"I'll come back and help," he assured her, already reaching inside his jacket for his cigarettes.

The door screeched as he pushed it open and stepped out into the alley. The air was chilly, the deep shadows

dulled by the eerie gray predawn light. Jared lit his cigarette, leaned against the rough brick, and rubbed the back
of his wrist over his forehead.

He had an hour, two at the most, to figure out how to
fix things with Lili.

Except there wasn't any fixing it, was there? He'd
thought he was doing the right thing by telling her the
truth about his job, but he'd failed to make sure she understood what it meant. He'd failed, period. Everything
after that was on him.

And knowing it changed nothing. It was selfish to ask
her to wait at home in Sector Four while he waded through
the slime in the city, and even more selfish to lock her out
emotionally in a strange mirror image of the marriage
she'd fled. He would never hurt her physically or purposefully, but he understood now that it didn't matter. Every
terse answer, every sidestepped question, would pierce
her in ways Logan Beckett could never have dreamed of.

Which left Jared shit out of options.

He took a long drag on his cigarette and froze when
the back of his neck prickled. Something was different,
off—

"I'm sorry." That was it, just the two words—and a
hiss of air followed by a sharp pain in his neck.

Lieutenant Malhotra. Recognition swept over Jared
along with an unpleasant numbness that left him slump-
ing against the wall. His mind fuzzed, heavy, like fog
sweeping out over the reservoir.

The last time the man had dragged him away from his
bar, it had been to Council headquarters. His likely destination now—

Except this time, Jared was pretty fucking sure he
wasn't going through the front door.

By dawn, Lili had given up any pretense of calm se‑
renity and was waiting for Jared on the roof of the
barracks building. She could see the entire compound from
here, as well as the roads leading to it. The dawn was
chilly but bearable as she huddled in her fur coat, one of
the few possessions she'd brought with her out of Five.
The waiting, however, was agony.

Eden's walls gleamed even before the first light
spilled over the mountains in the east. The electricity they
consumed simply to light their city could have powered the
sectors for a decade. That was what Eden did—greedily
devour everything as whim struck. Power. Resources.
Lives.

The sectors were dark by comparison. Lights flared
here and there—little spots of brightness where people
burned whatever they could put their hands on to fight off
the cold and the dark. Most had burned low by the time
light crept through the streets. One block at a time, chas‑
ing the shadows back, and Lili watched it creep toward the
outer edge of the compound.

One more street.

One more street, and she'd go to Dallas and Lex. One
more street, and she'd admit something was wrong.

Her eyes hurt from squinting. But still she stared at
the main street as if she could make Jared materialize by
stubborn force of will.

Instead workers begin to appear, trudging toward the
marketplace or meeting on corners. Men first, then
women, then teenagers ducking between them, and it
wasn't just dawn. It was *day*.

And Jared hadn't come home.

Numbness wrapped around her as she headed for the
door. Just a thin layer over terror, but familiar and com‑
forting. She knew how to fear and still function. A legacy
of her father and husband that she found useful as she

listened to her heels echo on the concrete steps. All the way down to the first floor, into the section of the building reserved for the king and queen.

She tried the office first, and her last shred of hope died when Lex opened the door fully dressed, somber, and silently stepped aside to let her in.

Lili clutched her coat around her to fight off a sudden shiver as she edged past Lex. "You've heard something."

"Gia sent a runner," she confirmed softly. "Jared was closing up the bar this morning, and he just...vanished. Staff didn't hear or see anything."

Lili turned away, but there was no comfort in the rest of the room. Only Dallas O'Kane himself, hard and tired, sitting at his desk looking like Lili was the last person he wanted to be laying eyes on right now.

Her gut knew what that look meant. Her heart needed for her gut to be wrong. "What are you going to do?"

Dallas clenched his jaw and said nothing.

Lex touched her shoulder lightly, and Lili barely felt it through the thick fur and icy numbness. "If the military police picked him up, that means Council involvement—" She broke off and cleared her throat. "It's too risky, Lili. I'm sorry."

She refused to look away from Dallas. "He's *yours*," she whispered roughly. "I know he is. I know what he's risking. For you."

"For all of us," Dallas corrected. "You think I don't want to go in there after him, girl? If it was just my skin, or my men, I'd risk it. But if the Council decides I crossed the line, they'll blow this whole fucking sector off the map. Jared knew that. And he made me promise."

Her lips were numb now, too. And no amount of huddling in her coat would help, because the cold was coming from inside. "What promise?"

"That I wouldn't risk all those lives for a chance to save his."

Lex pried her fingers open and pressed a glass into them. "We have to wait it out. They've picked him up for questioning before. It might be as simple as that."

Another thing he'd never told her. Her hand was oddly steady as she lifted the glass to her lips, but she could barely taste the liquor. "How long did they keep him that time?"

Dallas stared at her in silence, his gaze so intense she had the sudden queasy feeling that he could see beneath her skin. She'd never felt stripped so bare by a simple look—or felt so demandingly judged.

Whatever he saw made him rise and cross to a safe against the far wall. The keypad beeped as he typed in a lengthy code, followed by a soft *click*. He returned with a file stuffed with scrawled notes. Not Jared's elegant handwriting, but something tight and barely legible.

He shuffled through them, came up with a printed sheet, and held it out to Lili. "Markovic picked him up last time. Left him cooling his heels for a while before asking him a lot of interesting questions."

She took the paper and blinked until she could focus on the words. And when she did, her stomach turned over again.

It sounded like Jared. She didn't even know how—it was just a report of a conversation, but the observations were witty and pointed, the occasional deft turn of phrase both formal and wryly self-aware.

The picture it painted was an odd one, for a councilman. A man of earnest intentions, one who wanted to do good. Not just within the walls of Eden, but for everyone who stood in the city's shadow. Jared's impression hadn't been that of a man searching for a link to the O'Kanes in order to condemn, but of one hoping for a link in order to...

Something. That was the question at the end of the page. Markovic's endgame. His motives seemed pure, but what he hoped to accomplish remained a mystery. Jared had indicated a willingness to nurture that contact and deduce exactly what Markovic's plans might involve—and whether an alliance with Dallas was truly his goal.

"Markovic suspects Jared's connection to the O'Kanes," Lex said. "If he does, you can bet the others do, too. An O'Kane rushing in to save him would only confirm it."

She might be made of ice again, but the eye for nuance that Jared had helped her develop still lingered. She didn't think she was imagining the slight inflection in Lex's words, or the tightly leashed impatience in Dallas's eyes.

An *O'Kane* rushing in to save him would only confirm it.

"If Jared *is* in trouble, Markovic could get damn near any fucking thing he wants from me in exchange for stepping in." Dallas tugged the paper from her hand and returned it to the file. "You know that."

No one knew better. In exchange for her public performance of pain, Dallas had given her safety, a chance at family, and hope for a future she never could have dreamed possible. Dallas O'Kane paid his debts.

Someone needed to tell Nikolas Markovic that. Someone who knew it, firsthand.

Someone who wasn't an O'Kane.

Dallas and Lex would never ask. If they had to ask, she wouldn't be strong enough for it. If they had to ask, she might do it out of obligation or fear or the belief that her future in Sector Four depended on her risking her life.

If they had to ask, Jared would never, ever forgive them.

That coldness inside didn't feel like her enemy anymore, and now she knew it had never been only the drugs. She could be steel when she had to be, as hard as Lex, as ruthless as Dallas. The courage to shoot a guard and walk across two sectors in the middle of the night was part of her, just like the protective fury gathering beneath her icy calm.

She'd never had a chance to save her family. She wasn't going to sit quietly in her room and wait for news that it was too late to save Jared, too.

Turning, she met Lex's eyes. "How would you get into Eden, if you had to?"

"I'd call in a favor," she answered quietly. "From someone who loves Jared as much as I do."

Gia. It had to be. Not just because Ace was an O'Kane, but because Gia was the one with the connections and the power and the money.

And the secrets.

Lili set down her glass, reached for Lex's hand, and tried to come up with the right words. Something that could convey the depth of Lili's gratitude. For the truth. For a chance. For seeing something in Lili that even Jared hadn't—someone who had the right to fight for the people she loved.

Nothing came. Words weren't enough. So she squeezed Lex's fingers and kept it simple. "Thank you."

"Save it, honey." Lex gently brushed Lili's hair back from her cheek. "You might feel differently once you get inside those walls."

"I'm not afraid of Eden," she replied.

It was the raw truth. She'd survived growing up with her father's unpredictable rages. She'd endured marriage as a child bride, and had come to maturity pouring drinks and planning meals for the people who made Eden the gilded cesspool it had become.

She wasn't the desert or the flowers. She wasn't ice or steel. She was a goddamn diamond, formed under terrible pressure, as hard and unforgiving as the rock Logan had put on her finger.

And she'd cut the fuck out of anyone who didn't get out of her way.

19

I UNDERSTAND WHAT *powerful men do when you cross them.*

Lili's words rang in Jared's brain as another blow snapped his head to the left, and the taste of blood filled his mouth.

He flexed his hands, and the plastic zip-tie cuffs dug into his wrists. The drugs were wearing off, but the MPs hadn't waited to start the beating. Clearly, whoever had ordered it—*come, Jared, don't be obtuse, you know it was Peterson*—didn't care about information so much as making him bleed.

Another blow, and his nose gave a sickening crack. "Not so pretty now, are you?"

"Still prettier than you," Jared drawled, as if none of it could touch him. Hurt him.

That earned him a growl and a fist in the belly. "I can

fix that."

Oh, they could smash him up good, fuck up his face in ways even Bren Donnelly would be jealous of once they were finished. The thought—combined with his lingering high—dragged a laugh out of him.

"Crazy motherfucker," the guard snarled, but fear lurked beneath the words. Fear that Jared wouldn't be cowed. Fear that only made the blows fall faster and harder, and Christ only knew how much damage they were doing that had nothing to do with his pretty face.

"Enough," snapped a familiar voice, and the beating stopped abruptly. When Jared forced his swollen eyes open, he wasn't surprised to see Ashwin standing just inside the door, his arms crossed over his chest, his expression utterly blank.

The guard who'd been hitting him looked queasy. "I was just—"

"I can see what you were doing." Ashwin's gaze slid methodically over Jared, cataloguing his injuries. "If your enthusiasm results in a delay in questioning, the counselor will hold you personally responsible."

Counselor. The word was enough to make a man's blood run cold.

The door opened, and a short woman in a white coat wheeled in a cart loaded with vials and machines. Behind her was a slender, unremarkable man in a dark uniform, vaguely similar to the ones the military police wore. But instead of rank and insignia, his bore only a small, ringed star on the collar.

He stopped in front of Jared's chair and studied him. "Can he talk?"

"I'm not sure." Ashwin's gaze drilled into Jared's, with no hint of the apology he'd uttered in the alleyway. Just even, unemotional assessment. "The guards were overzealous."

Jared seized the opportunity to mumble something

unintelligible, but the counselor grabbed his chin, forced his mouth open, and frowned down at him. Then he backhanded him across the cheek, hard enough for stars to explode behind Jared's eyelids. "Lies will get you hurt, Mr. Capello. I'm sure we'd all like to avoid that." He paused. "Do you know why you're here?"

Jared's mouth had filled with blood by now, and he spat it on the floor, perversely pleased when it splashed on the man's shoes. "Because Mr. Peterson sends his regards?"

The counselor straightened with a sigh and nodded to the woman with the cart. "May as well get set up."

She nodded, then reached for a vial and unwrapped a huge, wicked-looking syringe.

It wasn't fear thumping through Jared's veins, closing his throat a little more with every breath. It was *anger*, sheer rage that these motherfuckers in the city would claim civility, *superiority*, when they were no more righteous than the lowest sector thug. Dallas O'Kane would beat a man for information. Apparently, when push came to shove, so would the sparkling leaders in Eden. The only difference was in who would own up to it.

The man with the star on his collar began to roll up his sleeves. "You're here because you're a known associate of Declan O'Kane. You're suspected of being a member of his criminal organization, and of engaging in espionage activities within the city."

His pulse throbbed in his ears, but Jared kept his mouth shut.

"Most innocent people would defend themselves of these charges."

"Charges?" Jared asked softly. "That implies some form of legal process, doesn't it? Not a bunch of fists in a basement room and a cart full of torture devices."

The man laughed—melodic, genuinely amused—and Jared steeled himself against a wince. He did it again as the woman in the lab coat jabbed a needle into his neck. The world swam in dizzy waves as the edges of Jared's vision went dark and then bright, brighter than the sun in the desert. He blinked, squinted, tried to recoil, but the light was *in* him, turning the world into some distant, drifting thing he could barely touch.

The counselor knelt in front of him. "The cart, Mr. Capello, is full of medical supplies. Things to keep you alive during our session. *I* am the torture device. What do you think about that?"

Jared's lips moved, as detached from the rest of him as the pulsing light that had settled behind his eyes. "I think you can fuck right off."

"Yes, good." The man smiled. "What is your occupation, Mr. Capello?"

"I'm a whore." The answer flowed from him without thought, so easily that the injection could only have been a drug to loosen his tongue. He tried to care, but all he could do was keep talking. "*Was* a whore, I mean. A damn good one. Ask Peterson's wife."

One of the guards snickered, and Ashwin silenced him with a sharp look.

"But you've retired." Counselor Whoever tipped Jared's head back, refocusing his gaze on his face. "And now you have your illegal establishment. Is it a front?"

"It's a bar. People drink, they have a good time." *They spill their secrets.* He almost said it, but bit his tongue instead. The pain helped center him. Remind him that this man, this utterly *normal*-looking man with the flat eyes was waiting for him to reveal the wrong fucking thing.

"Are you one of O'Kane's men?"

Whatever the hell they'd shot him up with, it made him want to speak truth, stark and bold. So he did, just in his own way. "I'm not good enough for that."

"Did O'Kane send you here?"

Jared shook his head.

beyond innocence

"Words, Mr. Capello."

His face was swelling, making it hard to speak. "No." The man's lips pressed into a thin, hard line. "Does he have other agents in the city? Tell me the truth."

Real honesty was made up of a million facts and feelings, filtered through everything from morality and society to kindness and disregard. Love and hate. That made the truth a complicated thing. A tool that you could still use to lie.

Jared had been doing it for decades. He could lie the way most people breathed, lie with his voice and his eyes and his whole damn body. With his soul.

He did it now. "Dallas hasn't sent anyone into Eden."

It wasn't the answer the man with the star wanted. Jared could see it in his eyes, a tiny flash of anger, just as he straightened. He circled the chair, and the next thing Jared felt was a hard, nauseating kick to his left forearm.

Bone snapped, and unbelievable agony washed away everything else in a blinding rush. Jared gritted his teeth, gasped for air, but he was drowning, drowning in pain so inescapable it threatened to swallow the world.

He was still just trying to breathe when the man spoke, as flat and unaffected as ever. "Heal the arm so I can break it again."

271

20

G IA WAS BEAUTIFUL, deadly, and as viciously pro-tective as any O'Kane.

Under different circumstances, Lili might have found herself a little dazed by the woman who lifted a phone, made a single call, and procured them an armored car with a silent driver and ID tags that got them through the gates without being stopped.

With Jared's life on the line, she was coolly approving. Gia got things done. And the short drive through Eden had made it starkly clear that if Lili couldn't strike a deal with Nikolas Markovic that secured Jared's safety, Gia would be calling in far less harmless favors from far more dangerous men.

"Only after I get you back to Dallas, sweetling." Gia held Lili's chin, her hand steady as she touched up Lili's makeup with surprising deftness, considering they were in the back of a moving car. "Jared may never speak to me again as it is. If I have to choose one person to save, I'll choose you. So don't make me choose."

Her tone invited no argument, so Lili didn't bother. Convincing Gia to let her take this risk to begin with had been victory enough. Reminding her of that fact might get Lili shuffled back to the sectors and locked in a closet while Gia risked her own life by blackmailing her way through the Council—an outcome Jared was equally unlikely to care for.

So Lili distracted her. "What do you know about Markovic?"

"Not much." Gia smudged the eyeliner with the edge of her finger. "He doesn't seem to sin, which is a pity and a waste, as I've heard he's young enough to be plenty virile. Do you know who Cerys is?"

"The leader of Sector Two?"

"Mmm. She specializes in whores who are also spies." Gia's lips compressed. "I've heard she's made no less than three attempts at him, and with girls from Rose House. She wouldn't keep trying if she wasn't sure she knew what he wanted."

"I don't understand. Rose House?"

"Yes. Sweet girls. Very biddable, very submissive." Gia released Lili's chin and stroked her cheek. "You've got fire in your eyes and steel in your spine. Do you remember how to bend?"

She'd never forget. But it wasn't her life now, a claustrophobic role keeping her small and stretching into forever. It was an act, a mask she could slip on when necessary and leave behind when work was done. "I know how to appeal to men like him."

"Good girl." Gia stroked her cheek again as the car eased to a stop, then smoothed a strand of her hair back into place. "I shouldn't go in with you. I'm recognizable. Some might say memorable."

beyond innocence

How could she be anything else? She was bold and vivid, a personality so strong she *shone*. Lili, on the other hand, knew how to vanish into her surroundings. "It's all right. I can do this."

"I know you can."

Lili clung to that vote of confidence when she stepped from the car. The sidewalk was pristine, but that wasn't the part that stole her breath. Some of the buildings in Sector Five were considered tall for the sectors—five or six stories, with a few that might climb to ten or higher. Intellectually, she'd always known the buildings in Eden must be massive to be visible above the walls from so far away.

But knowing was different from seeing. She understood the term *skyscraper* now, because the Council was headquartered in a building that seemed to climb up into the clouds, with floor after floor of glass windows reflecting the sunlight. She couldn't even see the top without tilting her head back, which she refused to do. Staring open-mouthed was hardly conducive with blending into the background.

Clenching her fur coat, she stiffened her spine and mounted the endless stone steps. Men in suits and women in coats as elaborate as her own jostled by, a sea of humanity coming and going and living casually amidst dizzying glamour, as if oblivious to the stark, brutal lives that ended too soon, just because someone had been born on the wrong side of a wall.

Lex was right. You couldn't come inside and not have it change you. But instead of yearning or heartbreak, Lili's shock crystallized into purpose.

These bastards had everything. They weren't allowed to take Jared, too.

Purpose helped her keep her expression calm and deferential as she inquired after her destination. Purpose helped her hide her discomfort at being directed into a tiny

275

metal box that proved to be something she'd heard about only in pre-Flare stories—an elevator, which whisked her upwards so quickly it left her stomach behind somewhere on the second floor.

Purpose let her gather the memory of a hundred supplications around her like armor as she waited in an antechamber for Nikolas Markovic to agree to see her. Purpose, and the memory of Jared's face the last time she'd seen him—so hurt, so lost, so sure Lili would toss him aside, because he wasn't worth fighting for.

She'd fight for him. She'd crawl for him. Whichever one it took.

"Miss Fleming?" The man's voice held a curiosity too benign to be recognition. Maybe there were a dozen Flemings in this city, or a hundred, or maybe the idea that the daughter of a murdered sector leader would be sitting primly outside his office was too absurd for consideration.

But Lili recognized him. From years ago—the very first year of her marriage, in fact, when she'd been fifteen and more likely to be hidden away, out of sight of the more important visitors from Eden. She'd had to prove her capabilities first, her knack for invisibility and her commitment to silence.

She'd seen dozens of almost important men from Eden in that first year. Most were a blur. Markovic was only memorable because of the tight disapproval in his eyes when she'd been presented to him. A terrified girl married to a cruel man—undoubtedly just one of a thousand unpleasant things he'd faced on his climb to power. It was no wonder he didn't remember her. He was the one who was unique.

He gave a damn. Maybe enough of one to make this work.

Rising, Lili kept Gia's words in mind and kept her gaze low and her voice soft. "Please, sir. If you could spare a few minutes. It's important."

beyond innocence

Wordlessly, he held open his office door and gestured her inside. The room was neatly furnished, tasteful but understated. Money spent, but not wasted. The most amazing part was the view from the window. Now she knew how high up she was—and how far she had to fall.

Warning prickled over the back of her neck, some instinct that made her turn as the door clicked shut behind her.

The friendly curiosity and polite lack of recognition were gone. Nikolas Markovic stared at her with the sort of suspicion she imagined had kept him alive in these lofty but vicious political circles.

"So." He folded his arms over his chest, an aggressive stance that emphasized his size—and the fact that he was blocking the only way out of the room. "Mac Fleming's daughter has come to Eden. Or are you here as Logan Beckett's widow?"

Because those had always been her options, the definitions of her existence—daughter to a horrible man, wife to a worse one. That cloak of sweet obedience she'd wrapped herself in no longer felt like armor. It was smothering her, choking her. And it was a lie.

So she set aside her false submission and met Markovic's eyes squarely. Honestly. There was mistrust there, sharp enough to cut. Perversely, it soothed her. His dislike for her father and husband made him more trustworthy.

His dislike for her? That was the part she'd have to change. "I'm here as proof."

He raised one eyebrow, not *quite* mocking but close. "Of?"

"How Dallas O'Kane repays favors."

His face clouded over, and he turned abruptly, already reaching for the door. "If he thinks he can buy me with a woman—"

She knew what she had to do. Knew in her gut, even if it was contrary to everything Gia had told her, because

277

Gia only knew how to seduce the corrupt. The only thing that could touch Markovic was the truth he wanted to hear—that he wasn't alone in his fight for a better world.

Striding back to his side, she slapped her hand against the door, as if she had the strength in her body to stop him if he tried to open it. "I'm not a daughter or a widow or a *bribe.* I'm a person. And if you can't speak to me like one, then you're no better than my dead father *or* my dead husband."

Markovic flinched. Actually *flinched,* and stepped back with a look in his eyes she recognized well enough. He was thinking about those words—*daughter* and *wife*— and imagining her as a person forced to endure their reality.

His pity was hardly welcome, but it was useful.

"You're right," he said finally, inclining his head. "My apologies."

Satisfied, she dropped her hand as her brain did battle with her gut. The smart thing was to take this slowly, to talk circles around the point until she found the right approach.

Her gut told her to press her advantage. He was off balance. He was a man who prided himself on being Good and Just, and he'd been caught being anything but. He felt bad, and he wanted to prove himself.

And every heartbeat was a moment Jared could be suffering.

Lili listened to her gut. "Jared went missing from behind his bar just before dawn."

She watched for a reaction, and wasn't surprised when he didn't give her one. She knew from his previous smiles that he could hide his true feelings. From his words now, she learned that he was clever. "And Dallas O'Kane repays favors."

"Yes," she agreed simply. "When my husband broke faith with Dallas O'Kane, I stood before the other sector leaders and told them the truth of who Logan Beckett was. In return, the O'Kanes took me in."

"And that's why you think you're proof." Markovic shook his head. "Not to sound dismissive, but to a man with O'Kane's resources, feeding and housing one girl is hardly an act of supreme generosity."

"It's more generosity than thousands of girls growing up in the sectors will ever see." She could feel every heartbeat in her clenched fist, but she forced her voice to chilly calm. "I was a burden. I was numb with grief and loaded up with drugs. They could have left me like that, but they didn't just feed and house me. They got me clean and helped me build a life."

"Forgive me, Miss Fleming, but that sounds like a fairy tale."

The words were so familiar, she couldn't help it. She felt her lips curve, even more when he looked perplexed at her smile. "I know. But they're not too good to be true, Mr. Markovic. They have plenty of vices you'd find appalling. But a man in your position could do worse than having Dallas O'Kane owe him a favor."

Markovic huffed. "A man in my position could die for having Dallas O'Kane owe him a favor."

True enough. And whatever else the man standing before her was, he wasn't suicidally reckless. Which was why he needed an offer too tempting to refuse. Not just a favor and the promise of an alliance beyond the walls, but a triumph that could secure his position in the heart of Eden.

He needed a victory—and Lili hoped someday, Jared would forgive her for giving him one. "Not if you're their new hero."

21

MINUTES HAD BLED into hours, until time no longer existed. All that was left was agony, and Jared clung to his suffering to keep from slipping into blackness.

Ashwin's voice came for the first time in hours, or *days*, still even and bland. "At a certain point, pain overrides the efficacy of even our best drugs. A man who needs the agony to stop will accept any truth that grants him relief."

"He isn't screaming yet." The counselor. "Stabilize him for the next round."

The woman's face swam into view, and cool hands touched Jared's cheeks and forehead. Not an angel—the thought bubbled up along with something suspiciously like a laugh—but a demon, despite the regret dulling her eyes.

—you wind up in a little room in Eden where there are no windows and no cameras—

He'd seen that haunted look before. When Dylan had warned him about the city's methods of torture, Jared had assumed that he'd been on the receiving end of it.

—you'll wish all they'd done was set you on fire—

Splintered bones, sliced skin. Blows and kicks hard enough to rupture organs. Dylan hadn't suffered through them, he'd suffered *along* with them, repairing the damage so that more could be inflicted.

"No wonder he hates himself," Jared mumbled, though only half the words came out sounding like words at all.

"Counselor." Ashwin's voice was sharper this time. "You're taking risks with a potentially valuable asset. Until we've assessed the depth and breadth of his strategic knowledge of the sectors, I would request you show restraint."

"And I would suggest you back off, Malhotra. I have my orders."

"If you feel confident the orders will hold up under internal investigation."

"Don't threaten me." The man lowered his voice. "Peterson doesn't care what he knows or doesn't know. He wants this guy gone. If you have a problem with that, take it up with him."

Well, no wonder it had been such a piss-poor interrogation. It wasn't about information or suspicion at all, just vindictive payback. The thought cheered Jared up—when he was dead, no one else would be at risk, and Peterson would go on with his life, satisfied with his retribution.

A perfect ending—with a few exceptions.

Dallas and Lex would feel guilty, as if they'd sent him to this fate after all, because they'd never know it had been set into motion years ago. Ace would be crushed, but he had Cruz and Rachel to get him through it. Poor Gia would have to go it alone, as always.

And Lili—

Pain twisted in his chest, breathtaking in its intensity, worse than any of the boots or blades sinking into his skin. The way they'd left things would hurt, maybe someday even more than his loss. Grief was something you could work through, but regret lived forever, tormenting you with everything you might have done differently.

"I'm sorry." He had to say it out loud, put it out into the world, one way or another.

"For what?" Ashwin again. He captured Jared's gaze and held it, an intensity in his dark eyes that hadn't been there before. "Choose your final words carefully. I can't offer mercy, but you still have a chance at peace."

So many layers of meaning. For a heartbeat, it felt like more than an admonition to a dying man. It felt heavy, like a message.

Or a chance to send one.

There was only one thing that mattered now. "I love you," Jared whispered. "It's not your fault."

The doctor caught her breath. "He's delirious. There's nothing more I can do."

"Fine." Metal brushed leather, followed by the unmistakable click of a gun safety being thumbed off. "Anyone who'd like to step out—"

"Anyone who doesn't want to face charges of treason should absolutely step out." Nikolas Markovic stepped through the door, flanked by burly, silent soldiers with the same nondescript, insignia-free uniforms Ashwin wore.

Special Tasks soldiers. And they had their weapons trained on the counselor, who looked nothing if not confused. "I'm here on Council orders. This man is a suspected sector spy."

"No, this man is a confirmed spy." Markovic stepped forward, looming over the counselor. "*My* spy. And your idiocy has almost cost us the single most precious weapon we have against sector corruption."

Jared had to give it to the man—he recovered quickly. "My mistake. I should have confirmed my orders." He held up under interrogation, if that's any consolation."

"I would expect nothing less." Markovic glanced at the doctor. "Take her to a holding cell. Lieutenant Malhotra will debrief her once we've handled this situation."

Turning pale, the doctor scurried for the door, and one of the soldiers followed her out into the hallway as Markovic turned back to the counselor. "I trust you understand the delicacy of this, and how swiftly the Council will move to contain it. This man is within weeks of full infiltration into O'Kane's organization. If anything were to interrupt his progress..."

"I understand, sir. No more interference."

"Perhaps this isn't a complete loss. Lieutenant?" Markovic nodded toward Jared, and Ashwin stepped forward and drew a switchblade. In another moment, Jared's wrists were free. "Mr. Capello, while I apologize for this unpleasantness, I trust you have the wits to use it to your advantage. A car is waiting to return you to the sectors. Once there, perhaps your injuries will allow you to gain O'Kane's trust. Full membership would make you an invaluable Council asset."

Whatever game he was playing, Jared wasn't about to question it. He climbed to his feet, surprised and grateful that his legs would still hold him. "Don't worry, Markovic. I can make anything look good."

Markovic smiled easily at him. "I have every confidence. Lieutenant, the car is waiting for him in the east alley. Discretion is of the utmost importance."

Ashwin wrapped a firm hand around Jared's arm and guided him out the door. Quickly, silently. And by the time they turned the third brightly lit corner, away from the interrogation room, Jared worked up the nerve to say it. "I don't understand."

"What don't you understand?"

"Dallas wasn't supposed to come for me. That was the deal."

Ashwin hurried his steps, forcing Jared to move as fast as his legs could carry him. "Sometimes deals change. Like your deal with Markovic."

He had one now, whether he liked it or not. "What will he want?"

"I don't know." Ashwin shoved open the exit, revealing an alley wreathed in shadows. "Get the hell out of this city, and you might live long enough to find out."

A car with tinted windows sat idling a few feet away—exactly the kind of car Gia used when she needed to travel inside the city walls.

Jared's heart wrenched, and he dragged open the back door, already growling as he climbed in. "Giovanna, what the fuck—" He cut off as he found himself face-to-face with Lili.

"Close the door," she said hoarsely, her hands already sliding over his stained shirt. "Oh God, Gia, he's covered in blood."

Gia rapped sharply on the tinted glass dividing them from the driver, and the car rolled forward before Jared managed to shut his door. "He walked here under his own steam, darling, and has enough energy to chide me. I think he'll be all right."

Jared stared at Lili. He was going to kill Dallas—stone fucking dead. "He wasn't supposed to send anyone," he choked out. "And he sent *you?*"

"No one sent me." She caught his chin in gentle fingers, her thumb the softest glide along his jaw. "They never would have asked, but they didn't have to. You were mine to save, not theirs."

"So you went to Markovic?"

"I went to Markovic," she agreed. "I convinced him Dallas O'Kane repays his debts, and I told him how to save you. If you want to be furious with someone, be furious with me, because I took away your choice. Now you have to become an O'Kane. A public one."

He was furious, all right—furious and relieved, grateful and mad as hell that she would risk this, risk *anything*, for him. He'd been ready. He'd made his peace with his fate, only to have that peace snatched out from under him in a confusing whirlwind of subterfuge and secret deals.

It was too much to process. Even trying left him dizzy, lightheaded, so Jared did the only thing he could do. The manly thing.

He passed the fuck out.

22

REGENERATION TECHNOLOGY WAS one of Eden's true miracles.

The moment Jared slumped into Lili's arms, Gia had pulled out a tablet and sent a message to the O'Kanes. By the time the car pulled into the O'Kane compound, someone had already been dispatched for the doctor.

Lili's composure, which had survived Eden, negotiating with a councilman, and waiting outside a torture compound to see how much of Jared was left to save, nearly shattered when Dallas tried to peel her away to discuss her meeting with Markovic while the regen tech worked.

Lex's swift intervention had bought her a respite. Gia's strong arm around her waist while they waited held her together.

The O'Kanes rallied. They always did. Within hours,

Jared was tucked into Lili's bed, asleep and breathing easily. Lili listened dully to the list of complications to watch for, promised Dallas a full report first thing in the morning, and closed the door on the world.

And then she watched him breathe until she believed he wasn't going to slip away.

Regeneration technology *was* miraculous. But the worse the damage was, the worse the scarring it left behind. Jared's perfect body was a latticework of pain, some marks white and barely visible, some pink, some red and angry.

Each an accusation. If she had trusted herself sooner. Moved faster. Spoken with more conviction. She hadn't believed in her own power, so she hadn't used it in time to spare him this abuse.

She wouldn't make that mistake again.

As much as she wanted to curl around him, she couldn't crawl into bed with him. She'd been too selfish to let him sleep under anyone else's care, but the fury in his eyes before he'd passed out haunted her. She didn't have the right to hold him. Not yet. Maybe not ever.

Lili sat at her piano instead. She stroked her fingers over the keys and remembered the way he'd smiled at her on the day he'd given it to her, as if being the one to introduce her to the possibilities of a better world had truly pleased him.

"Lili?"

His voice was hoarse and broke on her name, but Lili didn't care. She spun on the seat, her heart kicking violently when she saw his eyes open. The clock beside her bed, illuminated by the soft glow of a candle, told her hours had passed since they'd tucked him beneath the sheets.

Time was an odd thing, bending and twisting—unsurprising, when she hadn't slept in nearly two days. Her own voice was as rough as his. "Jared. Are you all right?"

"I'm fine." He struggled into a sitting position. "My

head hurts."

Lili hurried to his side and indulged herself by settling another pillow behind his back. "Dallas called a regen tech. She said that's natural, and that you'll be tired and hungry for a few days."

He tipped his head back and closed his eyes. "What a fucking mess."

She reached for his shoulder and froze, her fingers hovering over his skin. "I'm sorry. I did what I had to, Jared. I couldn't live with knowing you'd died while I sat at home, waiting."

"But I'm supposed to live with knowing you put yourself in danger, in *Eden*, for me?"

"Yes." She let her hand fall to her side. "Because you ask the same of me."

"I wasn't in Eden for you." He turned his head. "I was there for myself."

Pain was seeping through the ice, and she'd been wrong to think she understood the reality of it. A life of pain without joy was a life blissfully ignorant of everything you were missing. She could never reclaim that innocence.

This broken heart was going to hurt so very, very much. "Help me understand," she whispered.

It took him a long time to answer. "Twenty-two years. That's how long I was in the business. Don't do the math on it unless you want to puke." He glanced at her, but only for a split second. "Twenty-two years, and I never, *ever* thought about trying to bring that place down. Not once. I just smiled, did my job, and got paid."

She didn't know what to say, because words couldn't make the ugly truth of it any better. "We survive however we can," she murmured, hating how shallow it sounded. How patronizing.

"Sure, maybe. That was what Ace did, you know—survived long enough to get the hell out. If I'd done that, I

kit rocha

think I'd give myself a pass. But I didn't just survive, Lili.
I thrived. I got rich." He finally turned to her, his eyes
alight with intensity. "Did you know Lex is a thief?"
She shook her head.
"Not so much anymore, but at one point she was damn
prolific." Jared leaned closer. "You know what she did with
the goods and money she stole?"
"No," she whispered, though she could guess just from
the tortured look in his eyes. Something noble, heroic.
Something that made Jared feel less than worthy.
"She gave it all away. To people who needed it."
Lili could have told him that Lex was hardly a saint.
The O'Kanes did good things, but they indulged themselves without guilt or shame. Lex could give away every
credit she stole because Dallas O'Kane had so many already, and his people spent them recklessly in pursuit of
passion and pleasure.
But this wasn't about Lex, not really. It wasn't even
about Lili, a realization that threatened to shatter her
bruised heart, because it would have been so much easier
to come to terms with knowing Jared hated her.
She didn't know if she could survive knowing he sometimes hated himself.
Moving slowly, she settled on the edge of the bed and
cupped his cheek. "You took a risk no one else could, and
now you have a chance no one else has—to be a bridge between Dallas and Markovic."
The first hint of a smile curved his lips. "You did well,
Lili. You were smart."
"I was, a little." She touched his lower lip. "But I
cheated. I remembered overhearing my father, gloating to
Logan about how he'd put a man right under Dallas's
nose."
"Noah?"
"Mm-hmm." Her father had been so proud of himself,
too egotistical to imagine a world where he'd been fooled.

"My first night here, I went to Dallas and told him there was a spy. And he just smiled and said, 'So Noah had everyone convinced, did he?'"

Jared clutched his side and winced through a laugh. "Double agent, huh? I guess that's something he and I have in common now."

She let herself touch his shoulder this time. Softly, ghosting her fingertips along his arm until she could twine her fingers with his. "It works for a reason. None of them understand loyalty the way Dallas does. None of them believe another person could be worth dying for."

He fell silent, and his hand tightened around hers. "Would you do it again?"

She wet her lips. "Every night, if you'd let me."

His eyes shuttered, and he pulled away. "I was afraid you'd say that."

Lili grabbed his hand again, clinging to it too tightly. "I'm not asking for an answer tonight. You need to think about what you want to do, and whether *you* want to go back. No one would blame you for wanting to just disappear."

"Of course I'm going back," he told her. "But nothing's changed, Lili. I can't be there *and* be worrying about you and what you'd risk if something happened to me. I can't do it."

As if he could stop her from risking herself for him. It was the culmination of all those steps down the path he'd guided her along, the one toward claiming her own strength.

"So bring me with you," she said, trying to smile to soften the steel in her words. "I'll keep anything from happening to you."

"It's not a joke to me, Lili."

"No." She released his hand and rose, because if she kept touching him, she'd buckle under his pain. "If I thought you just didn't believe in me, I could deal with that. I could try to prove myself. Because I can do this, Jared. I *know* I can."

"So do I." He moved slowly, swinging his legs over the side of the bed until his feet rested on the floor. "It's never been a question of what you can handle, love."

"Then let me love you." Her voice wavered, tears dangerously close. "Let me be your partner, that's all I want. To be yours, and to have you be mine."

"I'll always be yours." The way he said it, it was more than a promise. It was fact, pure and simple.

And it still sounded like *goodbye*. "Jared..."

"Just—" He held up a hand. "Leave me alone with it for a while, Lili. Let me try to think of a way it won't kill me to have you there. For you to—" His voice broke.

Her heart was *bleeding*. It had to be, for the pain in her chest to be so acute. She choked it down and walked back to the bed, pressing gentle hands to his shoulders. "Lie down," she whispered. "You need rest. I'll go, just...take care of yourself. Promise me."

"Yeah." He rolled to his side and faced the wall.

On the worst night of her life, Lili had killed a man and walked through the slums of two sectors with his blood splattered on her nightgown.

The short walk to Ace's room seemed longer.

He answered on her second knock, took one look at her face, and went ashen. "Is Jared—?"

"In my room," she cut him off, barely recognizing her own chilly, remote voice. Everything was remote. "He needs someone. Someone who isn't me."

"Hey." Rachel edged in front of him and wrapped her arm around Lili's shoulders. "Come on. We'll make you some tea, okay?"

Ace stepped aside, and Lili gave in and let Rachel guide her deeper into the room. Her eyes burned, and she couldn't tell if it was the exhaustion crashing down on her or the inevitable tears.

beyond innocence

The room blurred, and she stumbled. Rachel caught her, and Lili turned blindly into her friend's strength as the last of her protections crumbled. "It's hopeless. We're killing each other."

"No, you're not," Rachel soothed. "You're figuring some things out, that's all. Like a puzzle, right? Sometimes you have to turn the pieces different ways before they fit."

She shook her head, because she didn't want to give voice to the words on the tip of her tongue. *And sometimes they're from two different puzzles.*

The one thing Jared wanted was the only thing it hurt her to give. And she could try, she *would* try, but that was the curse of a lover who could read your pleasure and your pain. He'd know how much it was killing her to stay behind.

And he'd hate himself more for it.

The tears broke free, hot on her cheeks, silent even as her shoulders shook with her sobs. Distantly, she heard murmured voices, the door whispering shut, and she knew Ace had left to watch over Jared.

She tried to stop crying. She tried to pull herself together, to be cold and hard again, but pain was like pleasure. Now that she'd started feeling it, she couldn't stop. It bubbled up and up until it boiled over, a lifetime of hurts she had never let herself feel, a string of losses that had seemed inevitable until she'd woken up in a world where everything you loved wasn't doomed to die.

Lili cried for Jared's pain. She cried for the things he'd endured in Eden, for the things he'd endured for twenty-two years, getting rich while his heart bled. She cried for her family, whose deaths she'd avenged without letting herself feel, because the helplessness of the loss had been too great.

Her tired mother, who had never been warm because warmth might have given Lili a false sense of hope. She'd

prepared her as best she could for the only life she knew—
a hellish one. Her older siblings, already growing wary
with the world. Her younger siblings, who barely remembered laughter because it had been five years since Lili
had been there to share it with them.

The baby, who'd never had a chance.

She cried until she was empty, until she was hollowed
out inside, too tired to sob even as the tears slipped over
her cheeks. Then she buried her face in Rachel's lap and
let the woman's soothing murmurs and comforting
touches coax her into the only sort of relief left to her—
numb, exhausted sleep.

23

A FTER GETTING THE shit beaten out of you by Eden's finest, even ink on the delicate skin of your inner wrists was a piece of cake.

Jared watched the last of the lines take shape, the O'Kane logo centered on an elaborate shield, like the crest of some adventuring medieval knight. Crossed swords completed the design on his inner arms, connected to the shield by twisting vines bearing flowers just shy of bloom. It was beautiful work—but then, Ace's ink always was.

"There we go." Ace sat back and admired his work, a pleased smile curving his lips. "Perfect. How could it not be?"

"The artist at work." Jared turned his arm, admiring the shiny black lines. "Thank you."

"I've been wanting to do these for years." Ace rolled his stool to a cart and rattled around in a drawer until he came up with a tube of med-gel. "I tweaked the design a little, though. Now that you're a big badass hero."

"I thought badass heroes rode in on white steeds to save the day."

"Surviving even one hour with one of Eden's counselors qualifies," Cruz said from the door. "Surviving five is damn near unheard of, outside of Special Tasks recruits."

It was so quintessentially *Eden* that Jared rolled his eyes. "Why am I not surprised to learn they put their own men through systematic beatings?"

Cruz shrugged. "It's easier when you know they won't kill you at the end. Of course, *they* know that, so they get a lot meaner."

"Fine, you're both badasses," Ace grumbled as he smoothed the gel over Jared's wrists. "Panties fall off when you enter a room. Virgins swoon."

"Don't worry, Santana," Jared said dryly. "You're still the king of disintegrating lingerie."

"He doesn't care," Cruz said, curling a hand around the back of Ace's neck. "He prefers taking it off with his own two hands. Or his teeth."

"See?" Ace grinned. "He gets me."

Ace was doing his best to keep the mood light, but the unmistakable sympathy in Cruz's gaze was impossible to ignore. Jared looked away as Cruz leaned down to kiss the top of Ace's head. "I need a few minutes with him. Work stuff."

"Sure." Ace rose and leveled a finger at Jared. "Don't mess up my masterpiece, or I'll kick your ass."

"Yes, sir." Jared picked up the roll of gauze and began to loosely wrap his wrists.

When Ace was gone, Cruz pulled something silver from his pocket and held it out. It was Jared's lighter, the one with Noah's data device secreted inside. He'd left it in his jacket back at Council headquarters, but it was no big mystery how Cruz had obtained it.

beyond innocence

He took the lighter and ran his fingers over the delicate raised filigree. "How long have you known Lieutenant Malhotra?"

"I can't remember *not* knowing him." Cruz claimed the stool Ace had abandoned and took over wrapping Jared's wrists. "There are different classes of soldiers on the Base. I'm the kind prepared from birth to be the perfect weapon. I was elite. Ashwin Malhotra is the kind they started preparing *before* birth. He was...more than elite."

"So he's your contact in the city." So many things about it made sense—especially Cruz's certainty that he could handle any trouble Jared ran into within Eden's walls. "He was very careful with me. But he wasn't about to intervene to save my life."

"Soldiers like Ashwin don't get distracted by emotion. They have missions, and a sense of honor tied to their understanding of the mission. Ashwin won't save your life out of affection for me. I don't even know if he can feel affection."

The thought was enough to make a man's blood chill. But Jared was too focused on what Cruz hadn't said to linger over Ashwin's capacity for love. "And if saving someone *was* the mission?"

"You can't change his endgame. But if he thinks you could be useful to his goals..." Cruz trailed off and met Jared's eyes. "He respects you now, Jared. That doesn't mean he'll save someone for you, but it might mean he'd save someone for you—for a price."

"What sort of price?"

"A favor." Cruz smoothed the end of the gauze into place, his gaze fixed on his fingers, his eyes shadowed. "He's the reason Ace is alive. Someday, Ashwin will need something, and I'll have to hope it doesn't break me to repay. But I'd do it again."

He didn't have to ask if it was worth it. The fact that Cruz and Rachel were still laughing, smiling, *breathing—*

that was all the proof anyone could ever need. Cruz had traded his favor for Ace's life. Jared would gladly trade his for a promise. But first, he had to *know.* "And this is part of his honor system, delivering for these favors?"

"Yes, but you need to understand what you're asking. Ashwin can be painfully literal." Cruz's lips tilted up, not quite a smile. "You can ask him to keep Lili safe if something goes wrong, whatever the cost, and that's what he'll do. *Whatever the cost.* Whether or not she fights him, whether or not it means leaving you to die. Even if he has to cut down enemies *and* friends on his way out of the city."

"I can be pretty goddamn literal, too." Knowing there would be someone there to protect Lili if things went south meant the difference between being terrified of her being in the city and welcoming her help. And, if worse came to worst, that was all Jared cared about—nothing else, no *one* else, not even himself. "You know him. What would he want from me?"

"The same thing everyone wants. Information." Cruz took a deep breath and glanced around Ace's studio, as if making certain they were alone. "I have a gut feeling. Bren, Dallas, and Lex are the only ones who know. But if Ashwin asks questions, pay attention to what he's asking. It may tell us if my gut is right or not."

It raised the hair on the back of Jared's neck. "You think he's planning something."

"I think the Base may not be under Eden's control anymore." Cruz rose. "And since soldiers like Ashwin seem to be putting their support behind men like Nikolas Markovic, I think the days of corrupt politicians running Eden into the ground may be numbered."

"Then I'll tell him any damn thing he wants to know." Hell, he'd do that for free.

"Good." This time Cruz's smile was unmistakable. "You may not be in as much danger as you think, you

beyond innocence

know. Apparently Markovic is clever under pressure. He called a meeting of the full Council before you'd even cleared the city, presented his triumph, and gave Peterson credit for figuring out a way to lend you the last bit of necessary credibility to infiltrate Dallas's inner circle."

Which meant Peterson's star was now tied to Jared's, and pursuing his vendetta would hurt him. "Clever, indeed."

"He and Dallas will have to meet someday. I hope I'm there to see it."

"Let's hope we all are." Jared flexed his wrists, focusing on the slight ache of his freshly inked skin instead of the more profound ache in his chest. "Ace or Rachel—would you trust Ashwin with *their* lives in Eden?"

Cruz hesitated for only a moment before nodding. "Maybe even before I'd trust myself, because I'd be distracted. Ashwin doesn't get distracted."

"I see. Thank you, Lorenzo." He held up the lighter. "For everything."

He nodded and laid a hand on Jared's shoulder. "Heal up, Jared. Now that you're openly an O'Kane, I'll be kicking your ass twice as often."

Something told him Cruz had already made the same offer to Lili. "You sure the sexual tension won't kill us?"

Yes, Cruz still blushed. But he didn't back down anymore. "I guess finding out is part of the fun."

"If Rachel and Ace don't mind." *And Lili*, he added silently.

If she would still have him, and that was one giant fucking *if*. The apologies he had to deliver—and the concessions he was prepared to make—might not be enough. It didn't make him wrong, not any more than her wanting to stand beside him in Eden was wrong. It simply *was*, and that was the hardest part of it all.

In fairy tales, there were always ogres or evil queens or circumstances to be overcome. But in real life, you could

give everything you had, everything you were, for someone, and still fall short.

He closed his eyes—and wished like hell for the fairy
tale.

It had seemed like such a good idea at the time, but
now that his plan was underway, odds were good Lili
might murder him.

He leaned against the wall in the empty spot where
her piano had stood, slinky silk draped over one arm, and
ticked down the minutes. Lex had said her kitchen shift
ended at three, which meant she should be arriving—

The doorknob clicked, and he straightened.

Lili froze in the doorway, her gaze sliding over him.
He had dressed deliberately, *carefully*, straight down to
the slightly open shirt and the carefully polished shoes—
and Lili looked flatteringly stunned.

She recovered quickly and frowned. "My piano..."

"I had it moved," he told her. "Don't worry, love. It's
still yours."

She closed the door and came toward him—tentative,
skittish, but there was hope in her eyes and her slow
smile. "Well, that's a relief." She nodded to his wrists. "You
got your cuffs already?"

"I did." He unclasped one cufflink and pulled back his
sleeve to show her. "Ace fancies me some sort of knight in
shining armor."

Lili traced her fingers along the edge of the shield.
"Ace sees people more clearly than they like to be seen,
sometimes."

"Usually." Jared flicked his cuff down and sighed. "I
happen to think my armor of late has been tarnished."

She swallowed hard and looked away. "I was tired. I

shouldn't have pressed things when you were hurt and I hadn't slept in two days."

If they got caught up in second-guessing and recriminations, they'd never make it out of her room. So Jared shook his head and held out the fabric draped over his arm. "Vintage silk. Bias cut. Trix said it would look like a dream on you."

She studied his outfit again before reaching out to take the dress. "It's beautiful. Do you want me to...?"

"Mmm. Put it on, Miss Fleming."

His voice could still bring color to her cheeks. She turned and laid the dress on the bed and, with her back still to him, began to undress.

Her shoes first, and then her shirt. Her wrists bore new ink as well, the O'Kane logo framed by intricate, lacy fractals. She eased down the zipper on her skirt and glanced back at him as the fabric slipped to the floor.

The look in her eyes could bring a man to his knees. He *had* to touch her, so he stepped closer, close enough to lay his hands on her hips and stroke his thumbs over the top edge of her panties. "These, too."

"Help me," she whispered.

Jared twisted his hands in the delicate fabric, but only long enough to hear her breath catch. Then he eased his grip and guided the lace down, off her hips and ass. "Better?"

She laughed softly and covered his hands with her own, sliding them both down. The panties joined her skirt, and she stepped out of the discarded clothing and lifted the dress.

It slid over her like water, settling into place as if it had been made to steal his breath. She stepped back into her heels and turned back to him. "It's perfect."

"Yes, it is." He retrieved her coat and held it up and open for her. "If you'll do me the honor of accompanying me tonight?"

She stared at him forever with those big eyes, still wary. But she slipped her arms into the coat and wrapped it tightly around her body. "Always."

He had a car waiting—one of Dallas's finds, though after all the hours Bren and Finn and now Hawk had put into it, it could safely be called a recreation. A Corvette from the early years, all sleek round lines and whitewall tires, in a color Hawk had glowingly called Venetian Red. Jared held the door for Lili, then climbed behind the leather-wrapped wheel.

Lili ran her fingers over the lovingly restored dashboard. "This is incredible. Nessa told me Hawk fixes up cars, but *fixes up* doesn't quite do this justice."

"Dallas is very happy to have him in the garage."

He fell silent, and stayed that way for the drive to the gates. His bar code was still intact, surrounded and framed by his new ink, and he'd prepared a bribe to hand over for Lili's entrance into the city.

But when the guard at the checkpoint waved his scanner over Jared's bar code, his brow furrowed. Then his eyes widened, and he took a hasty step back. "Sorry, sir." He raised his voice to the other guards. "Clear!"

Well. Nikolas Markovic certainly was a useful man to know.

The streets were nearly empty at the edge of the city, in the darker, rougher spaces that the city leaders liked to pretend didn't exist. Jared pulled to a stop outside his building and shut off the car. "This is it."

Lili twisted her hands together in her lap. "Your bar?"

"Come inside and see."

Her hand was shaking when he helped her out of the car. By the time he unlocked the grate and the door and flipped on the lights, so were his.

He'd had her piano placed along the wall near the bar, beneath one of the newly replaced chandeliers. Light sparkled off the crystal and danced across the surface of the

beyond innocence

wood, and Jared held his breath.

"Oh..." It was barely a word, more of a sigh. She crossed to touch the keys, her face alight with wonder. "You said it's still mine."

The expression on her face hurt to see. "It is. And if you want to play when we're not here, we still have the baby grand at home."

She didn't respond. Instead she moved to the bar, running her hand along its surface before moving to one of the tables. Her lips quirked up, her smile growing as she peeked behind the bar and examined one of the booths. "You did all of this in a few weeks?"

It was just money. Enough of it could buy damn near anything, and he told her so. "I could have found another piano to bring here instead of taking yours. I need you to understand why I didn't."

She turned, and the carefully constrained hope in her eyes hurt even more. "You said we."

"I did." He took off his jacket and draped it over one of the barstools. "I haven't changed my mind, Lili. I still can't bear the thought of you here in the city, in danger. But there is a way you can be looked after, so if danger comes for us, then you'll be safe."

She dug her teeth into her lower lip, as if holding back her immediate response. After a moment, she tilted her head. "Cruz knows someone, doesn't he? He didn't quite say it..."

"Yes. Someone who can protect you if my cover's blown, or if the Council decides I'm a bigger liability than asset." His hands wouldn't stop shaking, so he shoved them into his pockets. "I need that assurance, love. I always will. I need to know that, no matter what else happens, you won't be hurt because of me."

She took a step closer, a different kind of skittish now. Big-eyed and shy and staring at him the way she had the first night he'd kissed her. Overwhelmed and nervous but

303

willing to trust. "But I'd still be here, in Eden. Playing dangerous games with terrible people. Can you handle that?"

He wouldn't like it, but she'd been right before. He'd been asking her to deal with the same thing since the moment he'd first kissed her. "It won't be easy," he admitted, "but you'll have me. We'll have each other."

"I'd like that." She took another step. "We'll both have to learn how to let someone else protect us."

"Which might be the hardest prospect of all." He took a deep breath and released it, forging ahead. "But I want you, Lili, more than anything else. I want you so much it's killing me."

One more step, and she was close enough to touch him. But she didn't. "Do you want me enough to let me love you?"

That was the real question, wasn't it? The only one that mattered. "Yes." He reached out and grazed one blonde curl with his knuckles. "If you'll have me, Lili Fleming."

"I'm already yours." She lifted her hand to his, twining their fingers together. It pushed their wrists together as well, fresh ink bright on their skin, and Lili smiled. "And you're mine. Dallas will have to endeavor not to be *too* jealous."

"Jealous?" Jared wrapped his other arm around her, drawing her up against him, almost off her feet. "Noelle and Jasper. Bren and Six. Ace, Rachel, and Cruz. I think Dallas knows how this goes by now."

"Good." Her lips were so close, her breath warm and teasing. "Because I can be dangerous when it comes to you."

He couldn't kiss her—not yet—or he'd never stop. "You need a cover story. Can you pretend to hate Dallas and the rest of the O'Kanes while also pretending to hide it?"

beyond innocence

"I'm sure people would believe it." She smiled against his mouth. "Finn killed my father *and* my husband, and Dallas rewarded him for it. They don't have to know I want to buy him a present for it, too."

He framed her face with his hands and brushed his lips over hers. "If it *ever* gets to be too much—"

"Then we'll talk about it." She wrapped her arms around his neck, pressing even closer. "Neither of us can do this alone. But together we can do anything."

He did lift her then, relief and desire mixing until they were one incandescent emotion that lit him from the inside out. Holding her to his chest, he crossed the room until he could set her down on the closed lid of her piano.

She laughed and broke their kiss, her hands busy with the buttons on his shirt. "Are you trying to make sure I can never concentrate again? I already can't go into your kitchen without thinking about what you did to me on the counter."

"I have plenty of other places to ruin forever." He tugged her dress up, careful not to snag or stretch the silk. From now on, whenever she wore it, he would remember this moment. "The car outside, for instance?"

"Is there even *room*?"

"No, but I—" His words melted into a groan as she pressed her open mouth to his chest and bit him. "I wouldn't let it stop me."

He felt her smile against his skin. "Where else?"

"Your bedroom. The kitchens back at the compound." He grasped her hair and pulled her head up until her eyes met his. "The next O'Kane party."

Her breath caught. Her eyes went impossibly wide. "With everyone watching?"

"Everyone." The silk cleared her hips, and he gripped her ass. "You remember what they're like—skin and sex. And the sounds?"

She whimpered and tugged at his belt, trying to pull

305

him closer. "Remind me. Make me make sounds."

He tugged her hands away from his belt and placed them on the piano, then moved the piano stool and sat. "You sure about that?" he asked, looking up at her from between her parted thighs.

She stared down at him, disheveled, gorgeous—and not at all nervous. "Yes."

Jared guided her legs over his shoulders and grasped her hips, pulling her just far enough off the solid wood surface to leave her balanced precariously—and completely open to his mouth.

She was wet already, and he tasted her slowly, gliding his tongue until he reached spots that made her gasp, tremble. He lingered over those, drawing out even more desperate reactions—a jerk, a moan—until she sank one hand into his hair, fingers tangling tight.

"Oh, *God*—"

"Slow," he whispered against her skin. "Is that what you want?"

She shook her head restlessly, thighs trembling. "I want to feel you."

He turned his head and bit her thigh.

"*Jared.*" She pulled his hair again, a little more command in her grip. "Don't tease. I need you."

"That's it, love." He rose, dragging her hand slowly down from his hair, across his chest and stomach, to his belt. "Take what you want."

And she did, with no fumbling, no shy hesitation. She coaxed open his belt and his pants, and then her hands were on him, slender, clever fingers curling to stroke him to insanity and beyond. Her thumb swiped across the head of his cock, gathering the bit of wetness there, and her eyes found his as she lifted her hand and licked the taste of him away.

"Whatever you want." He wrapped her legs around his hips and rubbed his cock teasingly against her wet flesh.

"Whenever you want it. Anything."

"Just be Jared." She arched, pulling him closer. "I love him. I love *you*."

He knew it, *felt* it, the same way he felt his blood rushing through his veins or her breath falling on the hollow of his throat. Real, like the clasp of her pussy as he drove deep, and the sting of her nails on his ass.

In his heart, pumping through him along with his blood.

Jared sank his teeth into her lower lip. "I love you, too."

dallas

LILI WAS GOING to drink them *all* under the table—
and laugh while doing it.

If someone had told him a year ago that he'd be watching Mac Fleming's daughter knock back her twelfth
initiation shot with a steady hand and a smug grin, he
would have assumed the crazy bastard had knocked back
an impressive number of shots of his own. But there she
was, goddamn *glowing* as she made the circle of hugs and
kisses—though fewer of the latter, with Jared following
close on her heels. The legend of his run-in with Eden's
torture chambers grew with every retelling, affording him
a respectful awe previously reserved for Dallas himself.

Dallas didn't begrudge him that. Fuck, Dallas couldn't
begrudge the man anything right now.

A comforting hand slid around his waist, and Dallas

knew he'd been scowling again. He modified his expression—and then denied it. "I wasn't brooding."

"Liar." Lex tipped her head against his shoulders and laughed. "But you're very good at it, so."

Lili had reached Ace, who smacked a kiss to her lips in complete disregard of Jared's possessive gaze before spinning her into Rachel's laughing embrace. Lili might be steady on her feet, but she still looked...soft. Vulnerable. *Young.*

And he'd let her stroll into Eden to face down a fucking councilman. "How the fuck did this not go sideways on us?"

"We got lucky, that's how." Lex circled him, switching their positions so that he was the one cradling her. "In more ways than one."

Losing Jared would have broken something between Dallas and Ace. Maybe not Ace's loyalty, but his *trust*, his faith that Dallas would only risk his men's lives when there was no other choice—and his belief that Dallas would never leave one of them behind.

Jared had made him promise. But Dallas had let him. And when the worst happened... "I sent that girl into Eden like a lost little lamb into a pack of wolves."

"No," Lex said firmly. "You sent a woman who's spent her life surrounded by wolves, who knows how they operate and why, into a pack of wolves. There's a big fucking difference, honey."

A sop to his conscience. It only worked at all because it was Lex, and Lex had never allowed him to tell himself comforting lies to justify using people. "She's still just a damn girl."

"Don't be so cranky." She patted his arm. "It *was* a risk. But if you think the mighty word of Dallas O'Kane could have stopped her from trying to save Jared..."

Ouch. Soft words, but his ego was stinging. It always

did when things had spun out of his grasp, which was an-other thing Lex had chided him over. The days of kicking back and trusting events to follow the course he'd laid out were over. Which meant letting go and trusting the people around him to pick up the slack. The *people*. Not just the men.

He watched Lili take her thirteenth and fourteenth shots—with a screwed-up face this time, even though she should be well past the point of tasting anything she drank. She'd come to them broken and haunted, and he'd passed her off to Lex and put her from his mind.

But damn near *everyone* came to the O'Kanes broken and haunted. "I'm being an asshole again, aren't I?"

"A little bit, yeah."

Dallas tightened his arms around her and rested his chin on her head. "You gonna stab me?"

"Not yet, Declan." She wiggled her ass against him and turned to look up at him. "But don't lose hope. The night is still young."

He grinned at her and slid his hands down to her hips. Too much wiggling and he'd say fuck the responsible-leader shit and scandalize everyone by leaving early. "Maybe all this change is starting to make me feel old. Life was easier when the only question was what I could get away with."

"Life was easier because the dilemmas were simple—stay alive, make enough product, hold off territory takeo-vers." She winked at him. "Now? It's all philosophical. Instead of *what can I do* it's *what should I do*."

And that was the damn problem. The larger the scope became, the easier it was to slip into viewing it as a game. To view people as tools and bloodshed as acceptable loss. He loved the thrill of competition. The heady rush of vic-tory, of conquering. To play the game, to keep them all safe, he needed to be ruthless. But winning wouldn't mean a damn thing if he turned into the bastards he'd been fighting.

Over Lex's head, he saw his people. Their people. In the earliest days, it had been a brotherhood, their women brought into the circle of protection because men worked better when they weren't distracted. But Lex had kicked through that door. She'd knocked it off its hinges and trampled over every assumption he'd ever made, challenged him with every breath.

It was easy to make an exception for Lex, who would leave you bleeding up one side and down the other if you didn't. It was even easy to watch Six take a man apart in the cage and admit, however grudgingly at first, that she was a soldier in his army.

But he had a bigger army now. And if he was going to win this game without turning into as big a monster as Mac Fleming, he had to cultivate more than one kind of battlefield—and more than one kind of strength.

He looked down into Lex's eyes again and found her staring up at him with that knowing look, like she could read every thought spinning through his head. He slipped his fingers into her hair—soft, because there'd be time for rough later—and smiled. "Okay, Alexa," he said softly. "You win."

"Whatever do you mean?"

"Oh, you know. Just that little argument we've been having since the day you demanded ink." He caught one of her wrists and rubbed his thumb over her cuff. The first time he'd marked her, and even then it had made him crazy, having something on her skin that was *his.* "I concede the fucking point."

"That the women belong here as much as the men?" She arched an eyebrow. "Can you even say it?"

"Having the right to be here was never the question, darling." He matched her expression. "Well, not recently. But it's a lot harder to admit you have the right to fight and bleed alongside us."

Lex caught his hand. "It's our home, too. Our dream." She glanced over her shoulder. "Look at them. Everyone here would die for that dream. To protect it."

He obeyed, feeling a tightness in his throat that he didn't want to acknowledge. Mia, with her skill for brutal efficiency. Noelle's instinctive understanding of the technology that Dallas could barely make work. Rachel's similar knack for machinery. Scarlet's dangerous charisma and Jade's quieter but no less deadly skill for manipulation. Trix, Tatiana, and Emma, who might not share Six's passion for violence, but were all capable of tearing a man up in a fight.

Letting them risk themselves would hurt him. Not letting them try was hurting *them*. "You're gonna have to help me see what they can do. Kick my ass when I hold them back."

"And when you push them too far." She rested her hand on his face, warm and soothing. "I've got your back, honey. That's what a queen does for her king."

epilogue

E DEN WAS EVERYTHING Lili had always dreamed it would be. Bright, gleaming, glamorous...and full of liars who weren't very good at telling lies.

It was an excellent night for business.

Her current target was the wife of one of Eden's endless bureaucrats, notable only because he'd been responsible for managing the requisition orders for Sector Five for as long as Lili could remember. And, for as long as Lili could remember, Sarah Jensen had accompanied her husband to business dinners and made a sport of finding creative ways to insult Lili's mother.

Some things, it seemed, never changed. "You look so much like her, darling. Except that she always seemed so *tired.*"

Lili channeled her irritation into big, sad eyes. "Losing her was a shock, of course."

kit rocha

"Of course," Mrs. Jensen echoed. "And then your father? You poor thing."

Her expression was all perfect sympathy, but her eyes held barely concealed excitement. The truth about what had happened in Sector Five was still clouded in confused gossip and conflicting stories. A firsthand account of the gruesome tragedy would make Mrs. Jensen the star of every dinner party she attended for the next month.

Lili was happy to give her one—in exchange for a story of her own.

She rested her hand on the woman's wrist and concentrated all of that pain into her eyes. "You don't know what it means to see a familiar face from home. I had to leave everything behind. If someone who hated my father had taken control..." She trailed off, knowing no horror she could conjure would be as terrible as whatever salacious story was brewing behind the heinous woman's eyes.

"You could have been killed," she breathed, the excitement in her stare bleeding into her voice. "Murdered, like your mother."

Lili tightened her fingers around her glass and reminded herself that a gracious hostess wouldn't fantasize about smashing it against a table and grinding the broken edges into a guest, even if that guest was getting hot and bothered imagining Lili's death. The self-defense lessons with Six and Bren were most likely responsible—Six had described just such a maneuver in loving detail while Bren nodded his agreement.

A nice thought as a last resort, but Lili had to use different weapons. "Until a leader is announced, I won't know if I'll ever be able to go back."

Sarah Jensen looked around, her gaze darting from side to side as she leaned closer. "Pharmaceutical orders were going through a committee made up of most of your father's highest ranking men. Until recently."

Lili made her eyes wide, awed. That was what this

316

woman had always wanted—to feel superior, because her position in Eden was barely high enough to grant her access to the elite circles. "Oh, Mrs. Jensen. Please, if you know something..."

"Just a rumor. But the requisitions have been coming back with the same signature on them for weeks now."

Slow, Lili. Slow. She clutched the woman's wrist and closed her eyes. "That night was so terrifying. Men screaming, gunfire. I hid in a closet. I didn't know who I could trust. But I saw one man..." All lies, but she managed to make her voice tremble.

Mrs. Jensen made a soft noise of agreement. "Ryder."

She should have known. Ryder had always been quietly competent and more than a little intimidating—but he'd been new, too. She couldn't remember having seen him until a few years into her marriage, showing up as Logan's bodyguard when Eden officials ventured into the sectors.

Apparently his quiet competence had resulted in a big promotion.

Mrs. Jensen was watching her with undisguised anticipation, so Lili shuddered dramatically and gave the woman what she wanted—a highly fanciful, impossible-to-verify story about the treacherous betrayal of Mac Fleming, laced with just enough protesting-too-much assurance that Lili appreciated Dallas O'Kane's generosity.

Then she excused herself and headed for the bar.

Jared was leaning against it, so exquisite her heart skipped a beat. She loved watching him do his job in a way she couldn't have imagined. Because when the two of them worked a room together, it *was* a game. Dangerous, of course, and involving a level of corruption that could and often did turn her stomach.

But a game. One he played so, so skillfully.

She caught his eye as she passed him, just for a moment, and that was all it took to send a silent message.

She continued down the hallway, past the open doors where high-stakes card games were in full swing, and men might lose a mill worker's yearly salary in one hand. The storage closet at the end was surprisingly roomy. Shelves lined three walls, stuffed with spare glasses and napkins, more expensive garnishes for the top-shelf liquor, extra decks of cards and poker chips, everything they might need to woo and seduce men and women into being loose with their money and their secrets.

The fourth wall was stacked high with crates branded with Dallas's logo. They seemed to vanish as fast as Rachel's family could bring them in, but tonight there were enough for Lili to perch on the front row and slip off her shoes.

She was still rubbing the ache out of her left foot when Jared slipped in.

He took over, lifting her foot to work his thumbs over the arch. "Did she know?"

"She had a name. Ryder."

"Mmm." Jared's hands drifted higher, up to her lower calf. "Are you all right?"

No doubt he could feel the tension in her body. Just like she'd felt the tension in him the night a former client had arrived and spent her evening trying to negotiate him out of retirement. True to the promise they'd made all those weeks ago, she didn't lie. "Not really. I need a bit before I go back out, or I'll use one of those moves Six taught me on her."

"I wouldn't cry." The corner of his mouth quirked up. "Might get us in some trouble, though."

Lili closed her eyes and let the warm press of his fingers soothe away the knots caused by stress and rage. "She used to come to dinners and say the cruelest things to my mother. She couldn't sharpen her claws on anyone in Eden because her husband's a glorified clerk, but sector wives aren't allowed to show offense."

beyond innocence

"She'll get what she deserves," he whispered. "I've never really believed that—I've never seen it in action, you know? But I believe it now."

They'd *put* it in action, using the endless opportunities they were given to whisper the right words into the right ears. Noelle's father had turned out to be a surprisingly useful tool, for all that he abhorred their existence and their necessity. The only thing he hated more was corruption for its own sake, and a note to him, passed via Markovic, had brought several vile people to justice.

But there was more than one way to take his words, and Lili didn't want to waste her stolen moments in the mud. She wanted to remember why it was worth wading through it. "You better believe it. Because you deserve me."

Jared leaned over her—and smiled. "How long can we lock ourselves in here before *scandalous* tips over into *unacceptable*?"

"We're O'Kanes," she reminded him, teasing her foot up his side. "Anything short of *unacceptable* would be a scandal. We'd lose business, for sure."

He wrapped his hand around the front of her throat before sliding it into her hair. "Then we should take our time. And be very, very loud."

The last time he'd convinced her to be very, very loud had been up against the door, his hand pinning hers above her head, her cheek pressed to the wood. He'd thrust so deep like that, but it had been his clever fingers on her clit that had her sobbing, and then begging, and then fighting and failing to muffle screams against her own arm.

The time before that had been against the door, too, only then it had been her back and shoulders braced against the wood while he wrapped her legs over his shoulders and spent a leisurely eternity making her come on his tongue.

It was always transcendent, always pleasurable

319

enough to leave her legs weak and mind blessedly clear. But the tension in her tonight wasn't the usual stress of the job, but something deeply personal and still too raw— the reminder of how recently she'd been helpless.

Tonight, she didn't want to be helpless. Not even with Jared. Tonight, she wanted to do what he'd been coaxing her to do all along.

Take what she wanted.

She slipped her hands up to his shoulders and pushed, guiding him back. "Stand up."

He obeyed, his eyes gleaming. "I like it when you get bossy."

"I know." The leather of his belt was smooth. He'd teased her with the idea of it before, of feeling it around her wrists while he took her. It intrigued her, just like it intrigued her to imagine doing the same to him.

Everything intrigued her, it turned out, when it involved Jared.

For now, she only had one goal. And she was getting practiced at reaching it, which was a blessing. Tearing his clothes when they had to go back out onto the floor was slightly more scandal than either of them needed. So she was careful until she had his cock in her hands, smooth, velvety-soft skin over hot, hard flesh.

He groaned and grabbed the back of her head. "I said slow, didn't I? I'm an idiot."

"So very slow." She knew it didn't matter, though. Once she fell to her knees, Jared didn't care if she swallowed as much of him as she could or took half the night teasing him. He'd let her do anything she wanted to him, and love it because it delighted her.

It was enough power to make her dizzy. She stroked him again, her fingertips feather-soft, and savored the way his hands flexed on her head. Not tugging, not yet, but she could fix that.

Just enough light filtered under the door for her to

meet his eyes as she parted her lips and traced the tip of her tongue up his cock.

He let her have that moment—that endless, beautiful moment—and then turned it into something better with a low growl that melted into her name.

She smiled, giddy with the joy of putting so much desperation into him so quickly. "If you're in a hurry, you know what inspires me."

He flashed another filthy grin. "Go on and suck my cock, love. Nice and deep. I want to feel you moaning around me."

An order, but not really, because he was giving her what she'd demanded. The dirty words she was learning to love, because each one sounded like shards of repression and innocence grinding into dust. She rewarded him by wrapping her lips around him and sliding down until her mouth met her hand.

"Just like that." His thumb brushed her cheek, and his hands were trembling.

So she moaned for him.

His breathing hitched. "Again."

This time it *was* an order. Lili pulled back and ran her thumb across the crown. "Now *you're* being bossy. Is that what you want, Jared?"

"Yes." With another soft growl, he touched her lips, then pushed his fingers between them to slick over her tongue. "I don't want to wait, not tonight. Make me come."

This. This was her secret thrill. Not his commands, but the desire it took before he'd issue them. Nothing was more fragile, more precious, than the moment Jared trusted her so much that he stopped trying to be her fantasy.

Instead, she got to be his.

She sucked his fingers until he pulled them back, and didn't wait for another command. She closed her lips around him, taking him as deep as she could, and used every trick she'd learned to reduce him to naked want.

The trembling turned to shudders, and Jared chanted her name, slow and soft, then louder as he grew harder in her mouth. She could have pulled away. Could have dragged him down and climbed astride him, because she was wet enough to take him deep and aroused enough to follow close behind him.

But she didn't. Because Jared was wrapped in his own fantasy, and she was making it come true.

His hands were rough now. His hips jerked, and she moaned her approval. When he came, it was with a shout. He banged his head on the door hard enough to rattle the jars and bottles on the shelves, and his fingers tightened in her hair, pulling to the point of pain.

But only for a moment. Even lost in release, Jared was too careful with her. He loosened his grip, and she distracted him with soft touches and tugged on his hips until he slid down the door to join her.

On the floor. Of their supply closet. The next time Gia felt like throwing money at them, Lili was going to invest in fixing up one of spare rooms with a nice, comfortable bed.

Slowly, his breathing evened, returned to normal. "Now *that* was properly scandalous."

Lili settled back against him and decided the floor wasn't so bad, not when she had the warmth of Jared's body behind her and his arms around her. "And here I thought I was behaving. Not like the last time I got on my knees."

"And ruin this dress?" He plucked at the fabric with a breathless chuckle. "Never."

No, the last time she'd pulled back at the last moment, just to see how wild his eyes got—a feat better performed naked than in silk that cost more than one of those crates of liquor. "Don't lie. You'd just buy me a new one. And it would be worth it, if it made us happy."

beyond innocence

"Always, love." He tipped her head back and met her eyes. "The rest of the night is easy. We just have to make it through. Then we can go home."

Home. They had so many now. An apartment in the city, for when they needed to engage in more clandestine meetings. Her room on the O'Kane compound, for when they needed the security that only came with having their backs guarded by family.

And, in between, Jared's apartment. The midpoint between their dual lives. The place where they could be Jared and Lili, naked of masks, free of games. The place where he'd kissed her awake, taught her to feel—the place where she'd taught him how to be loved.

But even that wasn't home, not really. She turned her cheek to his chest and closed her eyes. His heart was still pounding strongly, and every beat was life. Not just his, but hers.

Even the cold floor of a supply closet could be home, if he was there with her. "I already am."

ABOUT KIT

Kit Rocha is the pseudonym for co-writing team Donna Herren and Bree Bridges. After penning dozens of paranormal novels, novellas and stories as Moira Rogers, they branched out into gritty, sexy dystopian romance.

The Beyond series has appeared on the New York Times and USA Today bestseller lists, and was honored with a 2013 RT Reviewer's Choice award.

ACKNOWLEDGMENTS
& THANKS

The list of people without whom these books would not exist is massive, and it grows every day. Our editor, Sasha Knight. Our proofreader, Sharon Muha. And the lady who keeps all our facts and timelines straight, Lillie Applegarth. We owe you guys.

We give special thanks to Jay and Tracy, who watch over the bar when we're out, roaming the city. And to our friends at the AIC, who keep us sane and always hold our earrings.

Last, but never least, to all the O'Kanes out there. Whether you've been marked for a while or are new to Sector Four, thank you for buying, reading, sharing and celebrating. When the apocalypse comes, you know drinks are on the house.

OUR BOOKS

Beyond Shame

Beyond Control

Beyond Pain

Beyond Temptation
(novella — first published in the MARKED anthology)

Beyond Jealousy

Beyond Solitude
(novella — first published in ALPHAS AFTER DARK)

Beyond Addiction

Beyond Possession
(novella)

Beyond Innocence

Beyond Ruin
(coming later in 2015)

Made in the USA
Columbia, SC
15 October 2024

44388894R00183